ABOUT THE AUTHOR

". . . . a knowledge and a power beyond the scope of any other contemporary American writer.

". . . . shows the same slow-burning intensity, the buffalolike stubbornness, and the uncompromising honesty. . . ."

The New Yorker

Few writers today can equal the powerful realism of James T. Farrell. In this collection of short stories the author vividly portrays the struggle for life, love and happiness in the teeming back streets of Chicago and New York as well as some scenes from Paris. Often earthy, often violent, they reflect a warmth and friendliness that shows the writer's mastery of humans and human events.

As the New York Herald Tribune said of him, "James T. Farrell has always been a highly controversial novelist in the controversial tradition of American naturalism."

Other Books by

JAMES T. FARRELL

Boarding House Blues
Young Lonigan
The Young Manhood of Studs Lonigan
Judgment Day
No Star is Lost
A World I Never Made
Father and Son
Bernard Carr
An American Dream Girl
French Girls Are Vicious
Saturday Night
When Boyhood Dreams Come True
A Dangerous Woman
My Days of Anger
The Face of Time

JAMES T. FARRELL
is recognized throughout the world as one of America's foremost
novelists and short story writers. Born on the South Side of Chicago,
he is best known for his STUDS LONIGAN trilogy and his four
magnificent novels about Danny O'Neill—A WORLD I NEVER
MADE, NO STAR IS LOST, FATHER AND SON, and MY
DAYS OF ANGER. Danny O'Neill also appears in BOARDING
HOUSE BLUES.

SIDE STREET

AND OTHER STORIES

by JAMES T. FARRELL

PAPERBACK LIBRARY, Inc.
New York

Acknowledgements:

SIDE STREET was (c) and first appeared in *Manhunt* magazine, September, 1955.

THE STUFF DREAMS ARE MADE OF was (c) and first appeared in *Audience* magazine, December, 1958.

GEORGE LONG was (c) and first appeared in *Audit* magazine, Winter-Spring Edition, 1961.

THE OLD FLAME was (c) and first appeared in *Manhunt* magazine, May, 1954.

TICKLE 'EM IN THE RIBS was (c) and first appeared in *Bluebook For Men,* June, 1961.

PUBLISHER'S NOTE

The remaining stories in this volume have
never appeared in print before. The entire
collection has never appeared in book form.

PAPERBACK LIBRARY ORIGINAL
First Printing: September, 1961

SIDE STREET

This might be the most terrible day in his life, Tommy Brandon knew. He wished none of this had ever come about.

He drifted back and forth along the quiet side street, a very slender, very blond young man with a round face and dull blue eyes. Each time he passed the red-brick building in the middle of the block he glanced at it briefly, and then moved on. Behind the green curtains on the first floor lay mystery and terror. Adeline was in there, and God only knew what was happening to her. How long would he have to wait? What would happen to him?

Well, at least I haven't been a son of a bitch, he thought. At least I'm doing the decent thing by her. I'm being fair. I don't love her any more, but I'm not running away.

He walked along, oblivious to the buildings, the people passing him, the young children on the sidewalk, the passing automobiles. The sun was not too warm. It spread a promise of autumn over the brick and asphalt of the treeless East Side street in New York City.

In the popular songs of love, he reflected, love was something wonderful that was related to the one and only girl, to moonlight and roses, to the change of seasons, to beauty, to hopes of happiness. But that wasn't the way it really was. Not at all. Love was risk and danger. The girl took the risk, and you pitied her. And you pitied yourself, too, because the girl wasn't the only one who suffered. Love was so different from the songs and the movies and the stories about love.

He thought of the nights with Adeline, and as always
he remembered the toilet bowl. Her apartment consisted of
only one small room and the bathroom, and the bathroom
had no door. He thought about how it had been with
her, once the newness of her body was gone. When he
walked on the street with her, he compared her with other
girls. He couldn't help making the comparisons, and
almost always he found himself pitying Adeline and wanting the other girls.

He knew all Adeline's little secrets of dress and make
up. He knew how she hunted for bargains in order to
look pretty. He knew how she had to save money to buy
new dresses. But the new dresses didn't help very much.
It was funny, but her body never seemed quite the same
from one time to the next. Sometimes her thighs seemed
too big; sometimes her buttocks were too large; sometimes
she seemed too thick-waisted. And now this body of hers
was causing him so much trouble, so much worry.

He turned at the corner and started back again. A pretty
girl came out of a building, reading a letter. Her legs were
slim and beautiful, and he looked at her with painful
longing, wondering if anything like this had ever happened
to her. The girl passed him and he turned to look after
her, watching the proud, lithe swing of her hips. Then he
remembered that women were formed the way they were
because they had to bear babies, and he walked on.

He glanced at the red-brick house, then looked quickly
away. Was Adeline afraid? he wondered. Did she blame
him? Had it happened yet? God, would she never come
out?

It was strange, the way he and Adeline had been so
sure nothing like this would happen to them. He broke out
in a sweat. Two men, passing, with briefcases in their
hands, looked at him, and he walked on, fearful that they
might be suspicious of him. He walked all the way to the
corner, paused in front of the theater for a moment, then
started back. Adeline and he had seen so many movies
together. There hadn't been much else to do. They couldn't
spend all their time sleeping together, and they couldn't
just walk the streets. They'd talked themselves out a long
time ago, and so they had gone to the movies. The pictures almost always ended happily. Love and a happy
ending. And there, behind those mysterious green curtains,

there was the happy ending. Pain and blood and fear and danger.

He walked on.

A jeep went by on the street, and then another. If he were a soldier, he reflected, he might become a hero. He might return with medals, have his picture in the paper, and find the road to fame. He wanted to be somebody. But how could he, with Adeline in the way? Adeline wanted something, too. He often felt that she was just as dissatisfied as he. He remembered the way she primped at the mirror, spending so much time on her face and hair. Didn't she want to be like the glamor girls? To live in exciting luxury and to have love and endless happiness like the women in the movies? He recalled the way she liked to take off her clothes for him, the way she would put on that one fine silk nightgown and walk up to him and let him take it off again. Just like she imagined the movie queens would do. Maybe Adeline was right. Maybe they did it just that way. But what did movie queens do about babies they didn't want?

A girl passed him, and he glanced back at her. Girls were so lovely to look at. But no matter how lovely she was, you always got tired of her and wanted a new one. Maybe he was a son of a bitch, after all, he mused. Thinking about other girls this was a hell of a thing to do while Adeline was in there going through so much pain and terror. God, if this waiting were only over!

He walked faster now, thinking about the money this had cost. He'd saved so long, putting a few dollars in the bank every week, and now it was all gone. Three hundred dollars for this—and if Adeline died, he could go to jail.

He was sweating again. She will die, he thought. She'll die, and then the police will come for me and throw me in a cell. He'd read about such things. They happened all the time. Suppose this place was raided? He watched an approaching automobile. Detectives could be in this car. The car passed the red-brick building. Tommy Brandon sighed and his shoulders sagged.

A girl came out of the building. She walked very stiffly, holding to another girl's arm for support. They walked slowly to the corner and got into a taxi.

That girl came through, he thought. She's in pain, and she can hardly walk, but she came through.

Adeline wouldn't feel like moving around for a few days, he knew. He'd have to take care of her, even if he had to lose a few days' work. But what would he do if she died on his hands?

He tried to think of something else.

A little boy passed, holding his mother's hand.

"Mommy!" the little boy said, "Mommy, why is the sun?"

"For God's sake," the mother said, "stop asking me questions before I go crazy."

"But *why,* mommy?" the little boy asked.

God, Tommy thought. Oh, God. If he and Adeline were married, and had children, they'd meet that. That, and diapers and wetting and being tied down and worries about money. This way was better—if only Adeline lived through it.

But if she died, it would be his fault. If he hadn't encouraged her, she wouldn't have consented to do this. He knew she had been waiting for him to suggest marriage. She hadn't thought of his side of it at all. All right, maybe he *was* a bastard. But what could he do? Had he no right to want to be free? To get somewhere? Could he help it if he didn't love her any more? Lots of guys in his position would have run away. It happened every day. It wasn't as if he *had* to stay.

Tommy gazed about him at the normal, minute by minute life of a quiet street in New York. None of these people knew the terrible drama that was going on right here in their midst. They didn't know Adeline might be dying behind those green curtains in that red-brick house. It didn't seem fair somehow that everyone else should look so happy, so unafraid. He envied them. They could go about their business, feeling safe and secure, with no worry on their minds, no fear of going to jail as an accomplice to a crime that was almost the same as murder.

God, he thought. Today might be the ruin of his life. Adeline might die, and then he would be blamed and his name and picture would be in the paper. He fantasied how it would be. He could see the expressions on people's faces as they read about him on the crowded subway trains. People would point him out on the street. He could hear them talking about him, condemning him, envying him the pleasure he'd had with Adeline. The fantasy had a morbid fascination. Here he was, walking up and down this street, and in just a short while he might be the central figure in a tragedy, a tragedy and a scandal.

What would he say? What would he tell the police? Why, he'd tell them he had loved her. He'd tell them how he had stood by her. He walked along, framing answers for the police and the district attorney. They would question him for hours, probably, while he sweated and lit one cigarette from the end of another and gave the same answers over and over again. Maybe they would come right out and accuse him of murder.

But maybe Adeline wouldn't die, after all. Lots of girls went through the same thing, didn't they? Thousands of them, every year. It was pretty bad, but they lived through it. A couple of days, and they were as well as ever.

He turned at the corner and started back. It didn't seem possible that everyone around him could be so calm and quiet and unworried. If these people had troubles at all, they were nothing like this. God, if he could only be one of them.

He lit a cigarette, then threw it away. How much longer must he wait? It couldn't be much longer. He couldn't bear it.

She lay in bed. The little apartment was disorderly. Clothes lay scattered about everywhere, and the small room was heavy with the scents of cosmetics and cigarettes. The furniture was old and the walls were sooty, and through the open doorway to the bathroom he could see the toilet bowl. The ugly toilet bowl seemed to dominate the whole place.

This is our love nest, Tommy thought. This is the outcome of our love.

There was nothing he could do now but sit. She had told him about the operation and then fallen asleep.

She awoke suddenly. Her eyes grew round, and for a moment he thought she was going to scream.

"What's the matter?" he asked anxiously.

She shook her head. "I dreamed I was dead."

He leaned over and put his arm around her.

"It was so awful," she said, sobbing.

God, he thought. Why doesn't she stop it?

He gave her a cigarette, and took one himself. She wiped her tears away and smiled weakly.

They looked at each other. There was nothing to say, nothing to do. Tommy got up, went to the small radio near the head of the bed, and turned it on. A crooner sang a love song.

Tommy smiled at her, and then he rose and went to the bathroom. He had postponed going as long as he could, but now he could wait no longer. Somehow it didn't seem right to use the ugly toilet at a time like this, when he knew that Adeline couldn't help seeing him, but it couldn't be helped.

Another love song began to murmur from the radio.

Tommy turned and, with an embarrassed blush on his face, came back and sat down beside the bed. They tried to smile at each other while the gurgling toilet drowned out the love song.

THE ECHO OF FAME

I

Chris Terrett had reluctantly agreed to participate in the weekend baseball clinic for kids. The appeals of Tom Nichols, young sports editor of the local newspaper, did not move Chris. Tom spoke of what a baseball clinic would mean to the kids with former and present day big leaguers acting as instructors. But Chris believed, or at least he thought he believed that he was sore at baseball.

After a brilliant career, Chris had been retired for fourteen years, because of a dead arm. Breaking into the American League at twenty, he had won twenty or more games during his first seven years, and had been recognized as one of the outstanding hurlers of his time. At thirty, he had checked off twenty-six wins with a fifth-place club, and he had looked forward to many good years, believing himself to be in his prime. But the next spring, he came down with pneumonia on the trip back from spring training in Florida. He did not get going until the end of May, and lost three hard luck games in a row by one run. Then he won four, and was out to notch his fifth straight when, after throwing a curve, he felt a sharp pain in his arm near the shoulder.

This was a moment he would never forget. While that pain had hurt and caused him to grimace, he had not been seriously disturbed at the time. Walking off the mound with a three-nothing lead, he had not believed that his time had come. The club trainer or doctors could fix him up. Other pitchers had had sore arms: he, himself, had. But as weeks went by, that moment became vivid in his mind. It had been in Chicago where he had never been popular

11

and boos had accompanied his short walk to the dugout.

"Terrett you bum, you're faking," a fan behind the
visitors' dugout had screeched. "What are you doing,
goin' to the races?"

In memory, this insult had rankled.

"I'll be all right. It's just a pain that shot through my
arm," he had told the manager.

"Fix it up, Doc—I've lost over a month already this
season," he had told the trainer while hot towels were being
put on his arm.

But Chris never regained his speed. He had thrown the
last of those hopping fast balls which troubled batters so
much. At first, he had hoped from day to day, and had
kept telling his teammates that he was going to be O.K.
very soon. Out of some need, he was impelled to keep re-
peating this vain hope and to blame his sore arm on the
attack of pneumonia that had laid him low for almost two
months.

But worry and bitterness became his lot. Chris had been
haughty and temperamental, the type of pitcher who might
tear up or wreck a clubhouse if he lost a tough game. A
pitcher with fine control, he often bolted and protested to
umpires when they called balls on him when he pitched for
the corners. To have his arm suddenly go dead had been
a humiliating experience. He had imagined other players
and the umpires taking delight in his misfortune, and he
would often become defensively surly. Although this was
something which had always gratified him, he realized more
fully how much the respect of other baseball players
meant to him. And suddenly before his time, this and his
whole way of life was endangered because of a dead
arm.

At seventeen, and immediately following his graduation
from high school in an Indiana small town, Chris had entered organized baseball. He could easily have gone to
college, but baseball had been his sole interest. He wanted
only to become a big-league star and his hero was Walter
Johnson. Although bright, he had been unable to show
any interest in his studies; he thought of baseball and felt
sorry for and looked down upon other boys because they
couldn't play as he could. Briefly, he was a star and enjoyed all of the glory of his fame. The time when his play-

ing days would end had seemed to be in a very distant future. To think of them was almost like thinking of one's own death. And then one day it had happened to him. For two years, he tried to pitch and hoped to make a comeback. But he was through. Several teams, including a first-place club, took him on but he was of virtually no use to them.

And so at the age of thirty-three, his best years were behind him. One year he had had a salary of twenty-two thousand five hundred dollars; two years later he had no salary. He found no job in baseball, but fortunately, with his savings, he had been able to go into partnership in a store selling sporting goods in Florida. He did not have to work hard, and his partner attended to most of the business details. Other than the money he had put into the business, his other main contribution had been the use of his name.

And so time had swept along. Chris hunted and fished, played bridge, drank beer at the local Elks club, and sometimes saw old-time ball players. Every year at the time for spring training, he was both eager and depressed. Memories of his own great days would flood back upon him. He would visit the ball parks and watch the players working out or playing exhibition games. Seeing young prospects, full of hustle and wanting to play ball and to make it, he would think of his own youth. It was gone and nothing in his life, following his retirement from the game, was as rewarding as the gratifications, satisfactions, pleasures and the spotlight he had known when he had been one of the best pitchers in the American League.

Often he was bitter and surly. He knew nothing well but baseball. The fact that his income was sufficient for him to live comfortably did not ease or soften his bitterness. From the age of twenty-one he had made good money. He resented those who seemed more educated than he, and was ill at ease in their presence. Frequently, he was bored, and would freeze up in company, to sit frowning and silent. When he read the sports pages of the newspapers, *Sporting News* or the baseball magazines, and would see other old timers mentioned, he would become resentful. Once his name had been regularly printed in the scores of big-league games: now, he rarely saw his name in print.

About two hundred kids from eight to sixteen showed up for the week-end clinic, and fifteen old-time and contemporary ball players were on hand to instruct them. Besides Chris, there were two other pitchers, Dexter Nunn, a twenty-game winner on Chris' old club, and Sam Arthur, a pitching coach on a big-league team. One of the old-timers was a Hall of Famer, and there were old-time stars, including four who had been big-league batting champions. One of the old-timers, a great fielder and batting champion in his day, became so enthusiastic that he hit flies out to the kids until his hands were blistered.

The kids were divided into groups according to age and positions and one of the ball players took a group over. Chris was assigned a squad of fifteen pitchers who were around fourteen years of age. He gave them a simple lecture about pitching and found to his surprise that he was articulate; he could talk and communicate. He illustrated how to throw curves, sliders, a knuckle ball and a screw ball, and told them how to take care of themselves and to keep their arms in condition.

"When I was in the big leagues," he explained, "I would begin to do a lot of walking every January. I'd do it on a golf course, but it wasn't only because I liked to play golf. I'd walk, I'd play eighteen holes a day. All of that walking was a way of getting my legs in shape. You got to take care of your legs as well as your arms if you want to pitch big-league baseball."

As he talked, he saw eager, interested faces that were full of respect. To these kids he wasn't a has-been: he was important, a man to be looked up to. There was surprise in this discovery, and there was even more surprise in his discovery of how these boys loved baseball. He saw this on their faces. He remembered himself as a kid going out to play, and the time when he was fifteen, and his father bought him his first pair of spiked shoes. Demonstrating how he had used to throw curves, he thought that one of these kids might make it, just as he had. But if one of these kids did, what would happen to him when he was washed up? Chris watched a red-headed kid throw: the boy had a good curve and looked as though he was going to be big and powerful.

It was a balmy Florida day, sunny but with a soothing wind. Scattered all over the ball park—it was one of the best in Florida and a big-league team used it for spring training—there were groups of kids. The air rang with shouts. The crack of bats on ball was heard regularly, and now and then, as Chris worked with his group, he heard the voice of another instructor praising or giving encouragement to a boy. His irritations and bitterness disappeared. He began to feel his own sweat and liked it.

I love this damn game, he told himself.

II

At lunch time all of the instructors gathered in a room next to the clubhouse which was under the stand behind home plate. A big bay window looked out on the playing field. Camp chairs were spread about and on a stand in one corner there was bread, cheese, cold meats, butter and mustard. There was also beer and cold soft drinks. The instructors helped themselves and stood or sat talking.

They were old and young, slender and in condition, and fat and paunchy. There was gray hair and bald heads. Representatives of four generations of big-league ball players were present, and the oldest was the venerable, seventy-two year old Tip Connell, who had pitched his first ball game back in the 1890's.

"Jesus Christ, I remember a game I pitched in Cincinnati, Ohio, and then we went to a beer garden. We had big steins. I don't know how many I put away," he was saying.

Nearby, Les Earl, the Hall of Famer, was eating a cheese sandwich and drinking a coke. He was telling a burly big-league pitcher how he took movies and used them in instructing hitters; he served as batting coach for a big-league organization.

"In my time," said a former National League batting champion, "we had none of that. But we still managed to hit the ball."

"I'll never forget the way Ty Cobb hit," said a big, burly, gray-haired former American League batting champion.

"I remember pitching a game in Louisville. I won it four-nothing. Then we went to a saloon of a friend of mine, Brick Burns," Tip Connell was saying with a voice full of nostalgia and enthusiasm. "Brick Burns is dead now. Well, did we drink beer that night."

"We owe something to these kids," said Larry Dorton. He was slender, youthful and clean cut. He looked more like a boy at the clinic than a ball player, but he had, one year, led the American League in batting. "We owe it to the kids. Look at what baseball is doing for us."

Hearing this, Chris went over to stand by Larry Dorton and Ed Harmon, a big-league outfielder. They were still in the game and he felt a burst of envy for them and their youth. He wanted to talk. What did baseball do for anyone? He knew that it was doing a lot for these players, and that it had done much for him: it had given him his chance and a different kind of life than he would have otherwise had. And through it, he had found fame, hadn't he? These thoughts which he knew to be true bothered him because they contradicted his bitter feelings. He wanted to unleash his bitterness but found himself tongue-tied.

"Did you get a good workout?" Larry asked Chris, smiling with youthful geniality.

"Oh yes—by the time this is over with, my ass will be dragging. I'm going to pitch an inning tomorrow in the old-timers' game and then my ass will drag. I threw a few balls out there. It was the first time I threw a ball in about a year."

"I took it a little easy—but, then, I always keep in trim in winter," Larry said.

"I always did. I was tellin' some of the kids in my group about condition. You know, that's one thing kids don't know much about. I had to learn it myself—but maybe if a few of us can give them a few tips it will help them along."

"I never saw so much enthusiasm," Larry said.

"Yes," Ed Harmon said meaningfully.

"It brings back to you what you really feel about baseball, and how lucky a guy I am to be in it," Larry Dorton said. "I just felt proud to be a big leaguer when I was out there. It made me decide I'll try all the harder to live up to being a big leaguer."

Chris listened with interest, nodding his head several times in agreement. He had had thoughts like these when he'd been in the big leagues, but he'd scarcely ever dared admit them to himself.

"And it's a privilege to meet all of you old timers. We have here men I admired all of my life but never met before."

"Yes—over there is Bob Shafter—they tell me that he was one hell of a ball player in his day," Chris said, nodding in the direction of a lean, well-built, swarthy and rugged-looking man whose temples were but slightly touched with gray.

"You wouldn't think he's sixty either, would you?"

The three of them nodded.

"And Les Earl looks good," Larry Dorton said.

"Man, there was a hitter. I pitched to him once in an All-Star game. He was always loose and relaxed up there at the plate," Chris said. "I threw him my curve and it was breaking sharp that day, too." Chris made a face. "He met it and sent it out to right on a line."

"He sprayed his hits to any field, didn't he?" Ed Harmon asked.

Nodding, Chris looked through the window at the ball park. Kids were running about, and some were playing catch or pepper games. And all about others sat waiting. Just a word, a tip, a nod from himself or one of the others here and how happy these kids would be! Hell, he would have been the same when he was a kid. But then when he'd gotten his chance, he had been different. Hell, he'd been just about as fresh as any busher whoever went up to the big leagues. But he hadn't thought of himself as a busher. From the moment he'd first put his uniform on he'd known that he was a big leaguer.

One of the first times he'd pitched in an exhibition game during that first spring training, he'd thrown three innings, holding the Boston Braves hitless, and he'd hit a double down the third-base line. What was the use of wishing it back now? You were only young once.

It was already February and in a few weeks, the teams would be down here. This ball park would be full of big leaguers and kids wanting to make it. After he had made it, he'd taken everything for granted. He'd set his own pace in training, paying no attention to the rookies, but he always knew how they'd watch him. Sometimes, he'd tell himself:

—That busher wishes he was Chris Terrett.

Now he wished that he were any busher coming down to Florida this year for his first big-league tryout.

"No," said Larry Dorton, "I don't like night baseball, but it's here to stay."

"It came just at the end of my time," Chris said, turning away from the window.

"It probably does shorten many careers," Larry went on. "What's worst about it is the irregularity of your life. One day you eat at three. The next you have your big meal after the game. It might be O.K. if it were all day or all night, but when you mix the games up, a night, then another game the next afternoon, that's what gets you."

"Well, gentlemen, can we go on now with the afternoon session?" asked the sports writer, Tom Nichols.

A Sunday crowd of several thousand had gathered in the stands at the ball park. A series of three-inning games was played by the various groups of boys who had come out for the clinic. The ball-player instructors had picked the teams and managed them, and then, the clinic was to be closed with an old-timers' game. Only one of the instructors appeared in uniform, Patty McCann, who now served as a big-league coach. He had had a long career in the game as pitcher, outfielder, manager and coach, and while never a great ball player, he had been steady and reliable. The other instructors, both the old timers and contemporary players, appeared in khaki pants. Most of them no longer had uniforms or else these were put away and unavailable. Chris would like to have come in a uniform, but he no longer owned one. He still had a pair of spiked shoes and an old glove and he had brought these along with him in an affectionate nostalgic mood.

Before the old-timers' game, there was batting practice, and Otto Dresser, quondam batting practice pitcher and big-league coach, served up the pitches. Kids from the clinic shagged the balls. The town people in the stands clapped for each of the players as they took their licks. Just to hit a ball once more transported the old timers back to the best years of their lives. There was nothing else any of them could do or had ever been able to do as well as they could play ball. They had lived briefly again in memory, and in the boys they had instructed. In varying degrees, the years of retirement had been dull, punctuated with memories, and with ever-recurring fits of nostalgia. All of them had known gray days, slow days, days and months and years of sinking away from the glare of the major league spotlight into the shadows of anonymity. Some were fat, and a few were too old to perform in the three-inning exhibition game. Others were already stiff from their exertions with the kids. They knew that this exhibition game would leave them with tired limbs and muscles and that they could not run and throw as they once did. The pathos which the spectators saw in their movements upon the diamond was felt by them, also.

Chris, who had been a good hitting pitcher, stepped up to the plate. Dresser, experienced in serving up batting practice balls, pitched letter high. Chris put wood on two pitches and the ball sailed to the left field fence.

"We ought to sign you up, Chris," a fat old timer and a scout called to him.

Chris grinned, dropped his bat and walked over to the bench.

"Want to catch a few, Dutch?"

"All right, if you don't make me bend. You know I knew my number was up when I'd bend down and couldn't get up," joked Dutch Lewton, an old-time catcher.

Chris lobbed pitches to Lewton. His arm was tight and with each throw he feared a pain. But then he didn't have to let go. It didn't matter what happened when he went out there on the mound and threw for an inning. It was sad that it didn't matter because once it meant everything to him and he would fret, worry and tear his heart out to pitch a winning ball game. His arm was stiff. He wished that he hadn't agreed to play in this damned game. Christ, the way he could once throw! It hurt his pride to have fans and also the kids see him go out there and lob the ball up like a has-been. He caught the grass-stained ball which Dutch had just tossed back to him and gazed at it thoughtfully. It was merely a ball, a baseball. But that little round baseball, it caused all kinds of trouble, heartache and feelings of failure. He had almost wrecked dressing rooms because a ball like this had not been caught or else it had been hit too far.

"Are you ready, Chris?" Tom Nichols called to him.

"As ready as I'll ever be again."

"Which league do I belong to?" Chris asked Tom Nichols.

"The American League, naturally," answered the newspaper man.

"But I lost two-three games in the National League. I won one, too—the last game I ever pitched."

"Chris," called Fritz Gettel, a one-time American League batting champ, "Chris, why didn't you pitch in our league the way you did in the other league."

"If I did, I wouldn't have lasted as long in it. Not with fellows like you blasting me."

"We don't have enough ball players to go around. I'll have to use some of our high school kids," Tom Nichols said.

"Tell them not to show us up," said Otto Mann, who had been a great third baseman back before the 1920's.

"I'm glad, Mann, that you and Shafter are as old as you are," Chris joked. "I'd hate to have to pitch to you guys if you weren't. That is if all I hear about you is true."

"Oh, I could be gotten out." But Bob Shafter was a great hitter. And a fielder, too.

Tom Nichols called out the lineups, and as the American Leaguers, a combination of retired players, present day ones and high school kids took the field, there was a cheer. Nichols went to the public address system behind the screen in back of home plate, and Chris, head down, walked slowly to the mound.

The crowd was laughing at the antics of old Brick Burns. A baseball clown, Brick was to be the umpire. He had his cap on sidewise and looking dead-pan at Chris, his lips moved as though in talk. Suddenly, he made an expressive gesture with his left hand indicating that he was throwing Chris out of the ball game. The crowd laughed more. Chris grinned. Good old Brick Burns. Brick fumbled in his pocket, brought out a small rubber ball, and threw it to Chris. There was more laughter and also cheers from the stands. Chris tossed the rubber ball to the catcher, and got some laughs. Then Brick tossed him a new ball, and he warmed up, thinking how he'd get a kick out of setting the National Leaguers down one-two-three. It didn't matter. He'd lost his stuff a long time ago, and why should he kid himself and think like a goof?

Seven batters faced Chris, and three runs were scored. He sweated profusely, and wanted to get off the hill.

"I'm tired." Chris said, dropping his glove on the ground and sitting down on the bench when the inning was ended.

"Not in condition, huh, Chris?" asked Fritz Gettel.

"No—I'm in pretty good condition—hunting and golf keeps me in pretty good shape. But still it tired me out, out there throwing."

"You kept them from hitting to my field, Chris. Good pitching," Fritz joked.

The American Leaguers scored four runs. Chris hit a double between left and center field, but was left stranded on second base.

He played at short stop, and had no chances, and he didn't get another chance at bat. As soon as the two-inning game ended, he drove home.

Chris arrived early for the banquet. Now that the clinic was finished, he found himself glad that he had participated in it. He was more moved about baseball than he had been in years. But he was struggling with himself for feeling this way. He looked back on his baseball career with the idea that there had been something undone, unachieved. He did not believe that he had been as successful, as great a pitcher, as he might have been. Sometimes, he thought of old games and played them over in his mind, but almost invariably these were ones in which he had been the losing pitcher. He thought of different pitches he might have made to save ball games. He never pitched a World Series, and this he still regretted. All too frequently, his baseball career seemed to him to have been one of missed opportunities. Yet why should he feel this way? Hadn't he been one of the best pitchers in his day? No one was a superman.

Chris' wife was recovering from a virus infection and did not go with him to the banquet. It was being held at an inn at the edge of town where the old-time ball players often went. Fritz Gettel was at the bar with an elderly local judge whom Chris knew slightly. Fritz invited him to have a drink, and asked:

"How do you feel, Chris?"

"Pretty good. I was tired out there while throwing."

"Man, how we change. I remember when you loved nothing better than to be throwing." Fritz turned to his friends. "I was in the league when Chris came up."

"I knew you were. The first game I lost was because of you. Remember? You hit a ball out of the park in the tenth inning and beat me two to one." ·

"Yes," Fritz laughed. "And I never hit another home run off you. I was lucky."

The girl behind the bar served Chris his drink.

"Thank you, sweetheart," he said, noticing her for the first time; she wasn't bad, at all. A blond and he liked blondes. But then, why had he married a brunette? Why had he done most of the things in his life that he had done?

"You know I'd heard of Shafter and Mann for years—but this was the first time I ever met 'em," Chris said.

"They've been comin' down here to Florida for years," Fritz said. "Shafter—he's a shrewd one. He's the only ball player I know who really held out—he stayed out for a whole year because they wouldn't give him what he wanted."

"I guess he could afford it. We couldn't. I stormed about salary, but I always signed—what else was I going to do, Fritz?"

"We came too soon, Chris. Now they're workin' out a pension system for old ball players. It's different. Everything about the game is different now."

Chris nodded. In his day, he'd often met old-timers and sometimes he'd felt a little sorry for them. But he hadn't really understood a damned thing about how it felt to be an old-timer.

Patty McCann joined them but when Fritz asked him if he would drink, he refused.

"Say, Patty, how's that kid of yours coming along?" Fritz asked.

"Tom—he's gone back to school. He's taking an engineering course."

"I thought he wanted to be a ball player?" Chris asked.

"He does—but he also wants an education."

"Isn't he wasting his time—his best years?" asked Chris bitterly.

"The way I look at it is that an education doesn't do

anyone any harm. I'm glad Tommy made the decision."

"The way the game is today, he's throwing away the good years—and with night baseball, a player doesn't last as long as he once did."

"Maybe that's so and maybe it isn't, Chris—I don't know. But things are different from what they were when I started. I'm lucky I was able to stay in the game. I had no trade or no education—what would I do if I wasn't in the game?"

"Come on, Patty—you're well fixed," Fritz said. "Don't give us that line."

"I have no complaints. The game's been good to me. But suppose my boy should sacrifice his education and then, he doesn't make the grade? What's he going to do then? Or if he should get hurt and his career is cut short?"

Chris knew that Patty was talking sense, but he resisted accepting it.

"He's losing time. The years he loses in college can make all the difference in the world," Chris said, angrily.

"I'm not sure about that. He can get in some ball playing in college. Plenty of kids these days wait until they graduate from college."

"I was in the big leagues winning twenty or more games a season and starting to make good dough at the age those kids are studying."

"But pitchers like you don't come along often, Chris. I wish we had a couple for next season," Patty remarked. "If we did, we'd win the pennant in a walk, and the World's Championship."

"All I say is if a kid's gonna play ball, the sooner he starts the better off he'll be," Chris said stubbornly.

About seventy-five people attended the banquet and a chicken dinner was served. Chris sat at a table with Fritz, Bob Shafter, Otto Mann, Les Earl and his wife and a few others.

"Maybe the game's changed," Otto said in the midst of conversation about the modern game. "But a real good ball player in any time—that's what he is, real good. He could play now or in my time and make it. Bob here would be a star today just as good as he was in our day."

"He looks as if he could go out right now and still play in the majors," Chris commented.

"I try to take it easy—coming here for my winters every year and getting in a lot of hunting and fishing," Bob said

"I'd give my arm to have seen men like you play in your prime," Chris said. Then he grinned and added, "It isn't much to give now. A dead arm wouldn't get much in a trade."

"We're all in the same boat, Chris," Otto said. "Our legs, our arms are old. But it was a wonderful experience while it lasted. I wouldn't have missed it for anything."

"I think that's the sentiment of every one of us," Patty remarked. "I dare say it's the sentiment of ninety-nine out of a hundred old ball players."

"Yeh," Chris exclaimed.

And he wouldn't have. But even now, it was sometimes hard to realize that it was all over. You knew it couldn't happen again and yet, you sometimes almost had the feeling that you'd wake up one morning and find yourself back in uniform and going strong. It was a strange feeling. And then, you dreamed you were still in the big leagues. Whenever he had any of these dreams, he woke up in the morning glum and all out of sorts with himself and the world.

"No," Les Earl was saying, "I haven't had a drink in months. But when I was playing, I'd get kind of tense if I didn't. I'd leave a bottle in the clubhouse when we played a double-header and in between games I'd have one. If I didn't, I'd be tense and tight."

"It didn't affect your batting eye," Otto Mann said.

"I remember the first time I played against you," Bob Shafter said. "You lined a hit out to me in center field the first time up at bat." He turned to Otto Mann and joked: "I think Les cut short my playing days by wearing out my legs chasing the balls he hit. Wherever I played him was wrong, the wrong spot."

They continued talking about baseball and reminiscing through the meal. Chris' bitterness and anger faded from his mind. He thought how there should be more affairs like this, more get togethers of old-timers. Of course, down here in Florida, he did see some of them and he hadn't completely lost touch with the game, but that was not enough. Getting together like this gave you a warm feeling. For a few hours, it seemed as if time had been turned around and was going backward instead of forward. You were back in the baseball world and the game once again seemed to be part of you, and you a part of it.

Since his retirement, he'd often thought of his playing days, not only of the games, but of the scenes on trains, in hotels, and in the dressing room before and after a game. He hadn't understood then of how really important the fellowship of the game was, the jokes, the pranks, the rhubarbs and the talk. He missed this talk and the fellowship of baseball. Yes, it was great. The clinic had made him see how great it was.

Tom Nichols rose, rapped a spoon on a glass and announced that he had only a few words to speak.

"I just want to say a few words. Most of all I want to thank all of you ball players of today and the old-timers for your help and cooperation. You made the baseball clinic a success, and an inspiration to the kids of this town. Because of you, each weekend, we had a bigger turn-out, and also, we got national publicity for the clinic. It was a big success, and everybody did a darned good job.

"The kids loved it. They loved and respected you. And that's most important of all. We ran this clinic for them, and it was so successful that next year we're going to have a bigger clinic. Of course we hope that all of you will be back.

"Again thank you. That's all I had to say."

There was clapping. Chris clapped loudly. He was proud. He had contributed to making the clinic a success.

Tom Nichols rose again.

"We didn't plan on long speeches, but I would welcome anything that one of you baseball men have to say."

No one volunteered to speak, as Tom Nichols stood for a moment waiting. Chris watched him with a choke in his throat. Suddenly, and without having reflected, he was on his feet.

"Chris Terrett wants to say a few words. Take it away, Chris," Tom Nichols said, sitting down.

"All I want to say is that there ought to be more affairs, events like this one, more of such events. When I was a kid, I heard of men like Bob Shafter and Otto Mann, heard and knew what great ball players they were, but I never met 'em until we all got together at this clinic. We ball players and old-time ball players don't get together enough, don't talk enough. So all I say is let's have more affairs like this one."

Chris sat down and while he heard some hand-clapping, he wondered if he should have spoken. He had been carried away by himself. But he'd meant it, and now everyone at his table was congratulating him.

Tom Nichols again thanked everyone and said that the banquet was over.

The guests filed out, passing a few remarks. Chris knew that everyone felt warm, friendly, pleased with the whole affair. He did.

After handshakes and good-byes, he found his car and drove off. Suddenly he was lonely. At the end of a season, he had used to feel this way when he would go off by himself. But this was different, he felt great. There was a warm glow inside him. Next year, he'd be back in there with the kids and loving it.

AN OLD SWEETHEART

I

"Tom, you're getting fat," Martha said, after sweeping into Tom Garrett's office.

He smiled self-consciously, masking his hurt. He wasn't really getting fat. He was merely plump. He would never get fat, but now and then he did have some anxiety about his weight. And he hoped she wouldn't mention his graying hair.

When Martha had phoned him that she was in New York, he had been glad to hear her voice after so many years. All morning, he had been nervous and expectant. It was best that he and Martha hadn't married. He didn't regret this. But sometimes he did regret that he had never been able to have her. No man passes forty without such regrets. No man, he often reasoned to himself, reaches the forties without knowing that there are many things in life he could have had but didn't, many pleasures that were missed, many mistakes made. And he was sometimes inclined to think that it was perhaps because he had never had Martha that he felt such tender and nostalgic emotions for those days when they had gone together.

Now, she was seated before him, still handsome, but more nervous than ever. He could remember how nervous a girl she used to be, how she would not want to sit in a theatre, or stay long in one place, or talk at length on one subject. Tall and slender and dark-haired, she still showed almost no signs of age. She looked chic.

"Yes, Tom, you're fatter. It must be your success."

"I'm not any great shakes, Martha," he said with a weak smile.

"But Tom, you're an influential literary editor and critic,

27

aren't you? Why if I were a lady author, I would be court-ing you. There's nothing I wouldn't do to get rave reviews from you. Don't the reviews you print sell books?"

"Sometimes, I don't think anything sells books."

"See, I am still a provincial, a Midwestern girl aspiring to culture with a capital C. I'm not a sophisticated New Yorker. I'll bet I must bore you, coming here with all my provincialism."

"You ought to know I'm glad to see you."

"And I'm not interrupting you in your labors, setting the course of American Literature, in capital letters? But that's not so witty, is it? Maybe I'm not as witty as I used to be. You used to think I was a very witty girl, didn't you?"

She cast a haughty glance around the office, and said, tossing off her words:

"My, you do have an elegant place. You must get a good salary to go with the office."

"I don't earn as much as you might imagine," he said.

Tom now wished that she hadn't come. He didn't know what to say to her, and she made him uneasy. He had no strong convictions about his work. He felt the need to make too many compromises. It was necessary for reasons of policy and business to print favorable reviews of too many books he didn't actually admire. He knew that he was in a comfortable rut. Back in Chicago, it had all been different. He had dreamed of becoming a writer like Sherwood An-derson, and had vowed that he would never compromise. But those had been the illusions of his youth. He had learned since then that he lacked the ability to be a great writer and, seeing Martha, he felt a certain poignancy be-cause he had changed. He had abandoned the dreams of his youth, and yes, perhaps the ideals too.

"Well, Thomas," she then said, pronouncing his name ironically, "tell me all about yourself, just as you used to when you and I were lovers."

"There's not much to tell," Tom answered defensively.

There were things to tell, sorrows and troubles, and per-haps the reflections and conclusions of experience.

"Tom, you don't mean to say that you haven't broken at least a dozen hearts, and made love to beautiful women, and met all the scintillating authors of our time, especially the lady ones!"

"No, there's nothing like that to tell."

"You know I'm a well, and you know whatever you tell me will sink in the well. Tom, can't I be your confidant any more?"

He tried to hide his embarrassment behind a forced smile.

"No, Martha, I'm not romantic."

"You used to be so romantic. I thought you were. Or was it that I was wrong? Remember once we read Francis Thompson and there was a line about dreaming someone into loveliness? My memory for poetry is abominable. I don't read poetry any more. Poetry is for youth, except maybe T. S. Eliot or Pound. I always read them. Do you still read poetry?"

"When I have the time."

She watched him coyly:

"See, I knew it. You do still have a romantic heart."

He tapped a pencil on his desk. Then he took out his cigarette case and held it open before her. She took a cigarette. They lit up.

She smiled invitingly at him, and he was uncomfortable. Perhaps she wanted to. He asked himself why not? He might manage it here in the office. But that would be crazy.

"Don't you ever think of writing any more, Tom?"

"Oh, now and then I write a review. But I guess I've gotten lazy."

"Don't say that, Tom. It sounds so tragic."

He smiled at her, gently.

"Martha, what moved me at twenty doesn't move me now. In middle-age we don't see tragedy in the same way we did at twenty."

"Why you've grown positively philosophical."

"And you, what has been happening to you all these years?"

"Don't ask me, Tom; it's too dull to talk about. But aren't you going to take me to lunch?"

II

Tom and Martha had met in an English Lit course given by Professor Saxon at the University of Chicago. They had been drawn closer together because they both admired the conclusion to Walt Pater's *Studies in the Renaissance*. When Tom was a junior, Pater had seemed to express the essence of his own philosophy of life. He had wanted his life to be a succession of moments during which he would burn with a gem-like flame. And he had wanted the love of a girl with whom to share these precious moments. Martha, a rich girl, had impressed him as intelligent and independent. She had been to Paris, had gone to the Louvre, seen cathedrals, and had also been at an exhibition of Matisse. She spoke glibly of painting, music, cathedrals, and of the poetry of E. E. Cummings. He thought she was the most sophisticated girl he had ever met.

In the beginning, Tom regarded Martha as a girl with whom he could talk about the things he admired. He was from the North Side of Chicago, gentle and of a serious turn of mind. His parents had been decent middle class people; their home life had been rather quiet and easy, but unstimulating. His father had a good executive job with a coal company, and wanted Tom to follow in his footsteps. Tom had no use for business, and privately regarded his father as a Babbitt, although he did respect him. When Tom refused to work for the coal company, his father did not seriously oppose him. But he hoped that Tom would get those Bohemian ideas about art out of his system. He even reasoned that perhaps it was better for the boy to be interested in art, pictures and books than to drink and dissipate like the flaming youths of the time.

Rather shy, Tom had for months felt the need of someone to talk to, a beautiful and sympathetic girl. And Martha had seemed to him to be that girl. She was sharper than he was. She was definite in the expression of her opinions, in her likes and dislikes. And these traits had drawn Tom towards her. For he was not so definite. He was inclined to like most people, to make allowances for them and to be very tolerant. Often, when he looked at a picture, read a poem, or listened to music, he would not know what to say of it. He could not honestly make quick judgments. He was not even sure of his likes and dislikes. But Martha always knew her own mind. The first time they had sat together in the campus Coffee Shop, she had said:

"I'm not like other girls."

Tom was much impressed with this remark; he wanted to love a girl who was not like other girls.

"I'm not a clinging vine, and I'm not a club type, either." This had intrigued him.

A few days later they stood in front of Harper Library in the late afternoon, and Tom looked at her and became convinced that he loved her. He began to see her daily. They had dinner together often. They went to concerts, plays, to the Art Institute and to exhibitions of painting. Martha liked the moderns. Tom did, or at least he believed he did. He also liked many older masters, but Martha was usually intolerant of these. One day, they were talking about Michelangelo.

"Ah, he's fake," Martha had said.

Tom was disturbed.

"He's too heroic. Men aren't heroic. And women aren't pure and noble. I don't like any art that is fake, fake heroism, fake romance."

Tom still admired Michelangelo. But he didn't argue or try to persuade Martha. She was too aggressively confident of her opinions. Yet, these often disturbed him. He wished that she shared his admiration for the art of the past. But at the same time, he admired her for her definiteness and frankness. His mother had always agreed with his father. He knew that often, his mother thought differently, but she would never say so openly. This wasn't right. A woman should be an individual and intelligent. Martha was.

Tom associated her with Brancusi. Together, they saw some of Brancusi's work at an exhibition downtown, and Martha instantly said:

"Isn't it magnificent."

She spoke of the lines, the economy of the work. Tom wasn't able to say why he was so struck by the sculpture, but he was delighted to be in agreement with Martha. He began to think of her as his Brancusi girl.

Martha influenced him more than he did her. Tom admired the French painters of the nineteenth century, and he was especially fond of Courbet and Corot. Martha shrugged them off until he found himself no longer speaking of them. Sometimes, when he wanted to look at nineteenth century French paintings, he went alone to the Art Institute. But Martha did appreciate Cezanne as much as he. They could look at Cezanne's work together. Martha would speak of the lines and colors, the harmony and form.

But for Tom, it was more a mood of brooding melancholy which Cezanne evoked for him.

Martha judged people almost on sight. In particular, she was sharp and destructive about other girls. She especially detested what she called "the clinging vine type." Now and then, she would pointedly ask:

"Tom, you don't like the clinging vine type, do you?"

He would always answer that he didn't. But sometimes he would wonder if Martha were good for him.

After they had gone about together for a few months, he became very anxious, but wasn't sure why. He became afraid that she would disapprove of him. Sometimes she expressed disapproval humorously. Or she'd tell him:

"Tom, you're better than that. You're better than liking such a picture. You surprise me."

At times, he liked to study alone because Martha constantly interrupted him in the library in order to comment about books and people. They frequently kept up a running conversation. Besides interfering with his studying, she embarrassed him. She didn't seem to care that she annoyed others. He never tried to stop her. If he had, she might have disapproved of him. She would have jibed that he lacked a sense of humor, or else would have accused him of being secretly in training to become a Babbitt. One day in the library, another couple were whispering, much as he and Martha did. She became furious, and demanded that the other couple stop. Tom thought this very irrational, but refrained from saying so.

One day he met Sam Morgan, who had been in love with Martha when she was seventeen. Tall and handsome, Sam had been a fine high school athlete. He played basketball and baseball at the University, and was on the teams, but he was not outstanding. He was a genial, friendly type and more sensitive than most of the athletes on campus. He liked poetry.

"Sam used to be my beau."

"What happened?" Tom asked.

"God!" she exclaimed with ringing contempt.

The three of them sat together one afternoon in the Coffee Shop. Martha's manner towards Sam was possessive and derogatory, and Tom felt a little sorry for the guy. But Sam took it. It was obvious that Sam admired her, and Tom feared that he might still be in love with her.

"Did you lose another game?" she asked Sam.

"Yes. You didn't see our last game, did you?"

She looked at Sam as though he might have asked her if she had taken a trip to the moon.

"Sam, you know I have always loathed athletics. It's so boring. Muscles and he-men." She turned to Tom. "Sam is a he-man, an athlete. He was a star in high school. But he isn't doing so well now." She turned back to Sam. "Are you, Sammy?"

"No, I guess I'll never set the college basketball world on fire, nor will I become a Babe Ruth. But I get a kick out of it."

"Well, you're big enough to be an athlete," she said.

Tom wondered if Martha would one day treat him as she did Sam.

"Of all the dumb boobs," she said when Sam left.

"He didn't seem like a bad fellow. Of course, he'll never be an intellectual. . . ."

"An intellectual!" Martha paused to laugh ironically.

Tom suggested that they walk over towards Jackson Park, and they went slowly along Fifty-Seventh Street. It was a fine spring day.

"Sam's a boob. Privately, I always thought of him as my muscle-man. The way he mooned over me made me sick. God, he had the nerve to think that I would love him. I was only seventeen then, but even at seventeen I knew better than that." She laughed derisively. "And do you know, all the clinging vines at Park High were just wild, simply wild about him. But he only cared for me."

"Did you and he date?"

"Sometimes. But I wouldn't be seen often in public with him."

"Is there something the matter with Sam?"

"Didn't you meet him?"

Tom was taken aback.

"I used to let him come to see me on parlor dates. He'd swoon over me, and most of the time he didn't have the sense to put his arms around me and kiss me. He didn't have the courage to neck."

Tom thought that he wanted her. They were both modern and sophisticated. They went together. They shared tastes. Why shouldn't they? But he had up to this time not been able to bring himself to the point of really trying.

Again and again, he had resolved that he would. He had even proposed this walk in Jackson Park so that he could make headway. He hoped that they would spend the afternoon in the park, hugging and kissing and talking and walking. They would eat together. Then, maybe after dark they'd go back to the park. But he was very uncertain. He feared that this way of doing it for the first time might be crude and coarse. Wasn't she a very sensitive girl? He didn't want to seem unsensitive to her. But Christ, he wanted her!

Martha took his arm.

He was convinced that the time was ripe.

III

In the park that afternoon, everything was like poetry. The green park, the blue sky, the unruffled blue lake, the sense of quiet and ease, the spring air, the colors of the dresses of girls, playing children, strolling people, the strolling couples, the old men and women, a beautiful nurse wheeling a baby buggy, the park, the blue sky and the lake! Everything was poetry.

And they walked around. Now and then, he took her hand and she let him. They walked hand in hand.

"Isn't it a lovely day?" he exclaimed, squeezing her hand as they wandered across the grass.

"Yes," she said softly.

And a little later, she laughed, a low and very nervous laugh. This seemed curious to him. He wished that she had not laughed that way. He feared that she might be laughing at him because she might think that he was awkward.

They went to the wooded island, and sat on a bench. He put his arm around her.

"Don't."

"But Martha, why?"

"We don't need that between us."

"I love you, Martha."

Again, a nervous, rasping laugh. She turned her head away. He felt small, foolish, defeated. Now she might be contemptuous of him as she was of Sam.

They walked to the lake.

"We have magnificent times together, Tom," she said, squeezing his hand.

He felt better, and had new hope.

At dinner, they talked of books and pictures. Martha was spirited. Later, when he was saying goodbye to her on the porch of the big old wooden house where she lived, she unexpectedly flung her arms around him and kissed him feverishly. They clung to one another.

"Not now, dearest. The family's home. You are adorable," she said when he tried to caress her.

IV

Tom went with Martha for four years. But she never would have an affair with him. She was unpredictable. Often she responded to his kisses; but at unexpected moments, she became cold and aloof. She told him many times that they did not need *that* in their relationship. She described their love as intellectual. Once she said that intellectually they were closer to one another than any other human beings in the world.

After graduating from the University, Tom got a job as a copywriter in an advertising agency and wrote book reviews for Chicago newspapers. He also tried to write a novel. He still went with Martha, but found her very frustrating. They had become tied to one another, but she always refused him at the crucial moment. He visited a few brothels, and now and then had some pickup. Afterwards, he'd feel guilty and undignified. He wanted to tell Martha, but he was ashamed to.

On some nights, he left her in a mood of bitterness, and resolved to break with her. He couldn't. He was tied to her and he didn't know why.

Two years after graduation, he met Louise at a party.

V

Louise's light brown hair excited Tom. She was of medium height, sympathetic and maternal. She had gone to college, but was not what Tom considered an intellectual type. She read books, but her comments on them were always simple and direct, and she never pretended to like authors because they were popular or talked about. It was only after he had begun to know Louise that he was able to judge Martha more objectively. By contrast with Martha, Louise was simple and consistent. He was attracted by her simplicity, and felt very comfortable with her. In Louise's presence he was not apprehensive about making a mistake or uttering an opinion that was ordinary or commonplace.

During the first few months, when he saw Louise once or twice a week, he regarded her as less exciting than Martha. Louise's face was round and pretty, and he liked her cute little pug nose. She was blue-eyed. She smiled often and in a winning way. She dressed simply, and frequently wore sweaters which made her look even younger than she was. It wasn't easy for Tom to bring himself to believe that Martha wasn't a more fascinating girl. Martha spent much money on clothes; she was always dressed in a chic but sometimes a bit odd or extreme way. When she strode haughtily along a street, men turned to stare at her. Tom took pride in this. He didn't notice as many men staring after Louise. During these months, he was still more interested in Martha than in Louise.

Tom's love for Louise developed only slowly. He wanted to see her again and again without understanding why. Sometimes, he would feel rather ashamed. He didn't believe that he loved her. Yet, he would telephone her for a date even after he'd decided to let her just fade out of his life before their relationship became a serious one. He liked to see her especially when he was depressed. After a quarrel with Martha, his thoughts turned to Louise. With Martha he felt an inevitable sense of strain because of the tension in her personality. It was becoming more and more tiring to see her. It was relaxing to see Louise. Time passed easily with her, and after he kissed her goodnight, he walked away feeling content and good.

For over three years, Tom had assumed that one day he'd marry Martha, but he had seen this as a distant event. Martha never spoke of marriage. About six months after he'd met Louise, he got a raise and was in a position to marry and support a wife. He began to think of getting married. But now he wasn't sure that he wanted Martha. Louise was very much on his mind. One day he imagined himself proposing to Martha; the next day he would pic-

ture himself and Louise on their honeymoon. He was un-
decided and kept changing his mind. However, Martha had
a hold on his emotions. He speculated that possibly she
would change with marriage, and that her personality
would soften. One night at dinner, he attempted to steer
the conversation with Martha around to the idea of marriage. Martha curtly changed the subject. As time passed,
marriage and a choice between the two girls became a
pressing question in his mind. He fretted about it. He asked
himself if he weren't being unfair to Louise. He was certain
that she loved him. If he proposed, she would accept him.
But wasn't Martha his real love?

One autumn evening, Tom and Martha were finishing
dinner in Charles' Restaurant on Randolph Street. All evening Martha had been gay and lively. Her talk had been
very spirited. Suddenly, as he lifted his coffee cup, he decided that it must be now or never. He sensed that he must
do it. At that moment, he was profoundly convinced that
he had to have Martha. His happiness and his career de-
pended on her. He dreaded a refusal, but he blurted out:

"Martha, I want to marry you."

He waited, taut.

"Why Tom, how preposterous of you. Do you really
mean it?" she said, laughing incredulously.

"Yes, yes, I do."

"Tom, are you drunk? Did you have anything to drink
before we met tonight?"

"No," he said, feeling foolish.

"Wouldn't we be silly to get married?"

"Why?"

Martha shrugged her shoulders.

"Why should you want to marry me?"

"Because I love you."

"Oh, Tom, it's so old-fashioned to talk of love in 1928."

He reached across the table and squeezed her hand; he
was beginning to feel desperate.

She laughed in her unpleasantly nervous way.

"Martha," he said with feeling.

"What do you want to marry me for?"

Tom tried to tell her. Ignoring him, she said:

"I'm not worth marrying. I'd only make you unhappy. I
wasn't born to be married. I don't believe in it, even. I'm

not made for you. I'm made for myself, and I couldn'
sacrifice myself for anyone."

Tom knew that he had failed. For the rest of the evening
he was spiritless. But after saying goodnight to Martha
without kissing her, he suddenly knew that he was greatly
relieved.

VI

Martha's refusal hurt Tom, even though he knew that it
was best for both of them. After having gone with him for
years, she had rejected him. He felt inadequate and betrayed. Three days after her refusal, as he was walking
among the crowd on Wabash Avenue at the end of his
day's work, he suddenly stopped in his tracks and told himself, as though in a fog:

—She must have had contempt for me all these years.
But he should have known.

Tom walked on. He thought of Shakespeare's line:

*"Men have died from time to time, and worms have
eaten them, but not for love."*

This was true, profoundly so, but it didn't help his pride.
He climbed the elevated station steps at Randolph Street in
a state which bordered on despondency. He spent a lonely
night. He gave in to his own despair and brooded over his
loss. He acted as though it were the end of the world, and
in melancholy, quoted poetry to himself. He remembered
times when he and Martha had read Yeats, Keats and
Francis Thompson aloud. He had only dreamed her into
loveliness, and she wasn't worth it. She wasn't worth this
agony. But yet he persisted in it with a kind of perverse
sensuous enjoyment. It seemed unreal and childish. He was
acting like a boy. But he couldn't quite help himself.

In such a manner he passed almost three unhappy weeks.

Then, he phoned Louise and took her to dinner on the
near North Side. He was mostly silent. He wanted to tell
her about himself and Martha, but he didn't. She might be
wounded. And he would only be humiliating himself in her
eyes.

He watched her closely. She was lovely, beautiful to him.
And she was warm and understanding, a kind person. She

would be better for him than Martha, but if she, too, should turn him down, life wouldn't be bearable. His talk was formal. But he kept watching her and telling himself:

—She's lovely.

And to Louise, he seemed strange, different, unsure of himself. She sensed clearly that he had undergone some disturbing and possibly shattering experience. She was angered. She had begun to realize that she loved and wanted Tom. Marriage would be good for her, she knew. She wanted it. It would give her the opportunity to give the love, the attention, the kindness and the care that she needed to give to a man. Although she had a good job in an advertising office, she wanted a home and a family, not a career. Tom had grown upon her. He was really sweet, simple, kind and honest. She knew that she could be good to him. Seeing him so dispirited just hurt her. He deserved better. She guessed that Tom was this way because of Martha. She didn't like that woman. Martha was no good for a man like Tom. She was just no good.

While they were having coffee she suddenly decided that she didn't care if Martha had jilted Tom. She even hoped that this had happened. For then, he could be hers.

She smiled on Tom with love.

Tom saw Louise regularly. His mood lightened. He began to forget Martha, and was glad that he wasn't seeing her. She was merely an episode of his youth. Now, he told himself, he was growing up.

One early evening, Tom and Louise walked by Lake Michigan downtown. They sat in the grass, and gazed at the harbor, the lake, the yachts, the clean white sails, the Navy pier all enveloped in a golden haze of fading sunlight. And they looked behind them to stare at the Michigan Avenue skyline, magnificent and dreamy and like the towers of a fairyland. The scene was full of awe and strange beauty. They felt a common mood. The world was good, and they could share in its beauty. They knew that they were in love.

They were married within a month, and honeymooned in California. Then, they went to New York to live and found an apartment in Greenwich Village. Tom landed a job in an advertising agency which handled publishers' accounts. He began to review books for various of the New York literary reviews and newspapers. They were very happy. Tom was ambitious. He practically forgot Martha. He gave up his idea of writing novels, but did believe that he could become a critic. As a reviewer, he was painstaking, fair, honest and showed good judgment. He was liked by editors and publishers, and began to get important books to review. His name became better known. He saw that he had a literary future. And he had as happy a home life as a man could want.

Tom liked books. It was easy for him to praise many books which more demanding critics would have damned, or at least treated very critically. He wrote fluently. In two years, he had gained a New York reputation. Then, he was hired to work as an editor in a prosperous publishing house. From this he had gone to his job as literary editor. But once he became a literary editor, he wrote less frequently. He no longer relished writing, and he didn't have much time for it. He tried to be fair in the decisions he made about the books he gave out. His magazine was competent, and honestly edited.

The early bliss of love turned into quiet contentment. Tom and Louise had three children, two girls and a boy. They had had much worry over them. The oldest girl, at the age of seven, was stricken with infantile paralysis. Following her recovery, she had to be taken to a child psychiatrist. This was a heavy expense. There had been many other illnesses. But at the time when Martha looked Tom up, the illnesses and troubles of his family seemed to be behind him. The days were moving gently by for him and Louise. He fully accepted himself, his work and the life he led. He had no unfulfilled ambitions, no impossible desires. He was satisfied with what he was doing, and with the future in store for him. He was absorbed in his children, and in his home in Connecticut. But there was something wistful in his nature. At times, also, he sadly reflected that youth was gone.

VII

Tom took Martha to lunch in a crowded, dimly-lit restaurant. As she went along to a table in the rear, she seemed as stunning as ever, and for an instant his old pride in being seen with her came back. He remembered her sweeping into restaurants with him in the days of their youth. He nodded to several publishers and editors, hoping that she would notice this. He had not become the great writer he had dreamed of being, but after all, he wasn't a nobody.

The head waiter greeted him cordially. They ordered drinks. Their eyes met across the table. She was grinning. He smiled, shyly.

"Well, how do I look, Tom?"

"Really grand, Martha."

"And you're glad to see me?"

"Yes, I am."

"And your wife won't hit you with a rolling pin if you tell her you took me out to lunch?"

"Martha, after all . . . . this is a sophisticated world."

"I'll bet you've had quite an interesting love life, Tom," she teased.

Since he had married Louise, he had never touched another woman. This was a matter of pride and honor to him. Now and then, there had been the temptation and the desire, but his sense of loyalty was too strong.

Tom smiled at Martha, a little apologetically, and said:

"No, I live a quiet life. I suppose you'd call me bourgeois."

"Tom, how shocking!"

"I don't know that it is," he said very quickly.

"And do you have a garden?"

"Yes," he said, again with an apologetic smile.

"And a dog?"

"Yes, we have a police dog. I call him Jeff."

At this point the waiter arrived with their drinks. They tipped glasses. He hesitated for a moment before he could think of a toast.

"For *auld lang syne.*"

She grinned, and ironically repeated the toast.

Spilling some of her drink, she wiped her chin with her napkin.

"Tom, you don't resent me?"

"Why should I? We had good times together."

"Well, after all, I wouldn't go to bed with you."

Tom winced.

"That's years ago," he said, after a long pause.

"Tom, I have a confession to make."

"What?"

"I was a virgin."

He was surprised. He'd imagined that she had been more experienced sexually than he. But now, did all this matter?

"I was married since then, and I was also psycho-analyzed. Tom, you haven't been psycho-analyzed?"

"No."

"You should be. Everybody should be. Every woman has penis envy and every man wants to be a homosexual."

He didn't like such talk, and he didn't agree with it. In fact, he didn't even quite understand it.

"You've read Freud, haven't you?"

"Yes, a little," he answered, but he was really covering up: he had looked at some of Freud's work, and had picked up attitudes and notions about what Freud meant largely from conversations and from other books he'd read.

"I'm surprised you haven't been analyzed. Why I would have imagined that everybody in the social circles you travel in had been analyzed."

"I know many people who have gone to psychiatrists, but I know more who haven't."

"God, New York isn't as advanced as Chicago. Why every one of my friends has either been analyzed or is undergoing it now. I got analyzed and that's why I got divorced. But my husband wanted it because he was analyzed too, only I don't think he really completed his analysis. I did. Tom, do you know what I am?"

"What?"

"I'm a normal female."

He didn't know what to say. He pitied her a little.

VIII

Tom had been pleased with the way he had ordered luncheon. While he was not a gourmet, he did believe that he had developed some taste for good food, and he took pride in this. But Martha had paid little attention to that. She ate as though the food meant nothing special to her. He had, in fact, fished for a compliment about the meal, and the restaurant, but she hadn't bit. They had eaten for a while, talking most casually.

Tom felt queer. On and off through the years, he'd wondered what had happened to Martha, and he also hoped that she sometimes thought of him. Seeing her again was queer, strange, almost incredible. She had become a mere memory.

—The pathos of dead loves, he thought.

"Tom, I believe that I've changed more than you."

"I don't know how much I've changed. I guess that it's not easy to know if you've changed yourself or not," he answered.

"But of course, since I was analyzed, I should have changed more than you did."

"You're still handsome. You haven't changed that way. You look young and lovely, Martha."

"Oh, I wouldn't say that. But I don't care. What I learned by being analyzed is to accept myself. That's what I've learned."

"That's fine," he said politely.

He was thinking that if he had married her, he should have had a hell of a life. How lucky he was that she had rejected him. She was a rough deal. But that was all past. He was glad that it was, and yet, there was something poignant in leaving youth, in growing into middle age, in seeing an old sweetheart.

"Are you a good father?"

"I've tried to be. My kids like me, I guess. I hope they do. They act as if they might."

She laughed.

"If I should find the right man, I wouldn't mind having children. But where's the right man? That's the question, isn't it?" She continued, "An intelligent woman does not have an easy time of it in this world, Tom. How can most men interest an intelligent woman?"

He smiled, because he didn't know what to say. He remembered now how she had used to be so critical of most people, and how, at times, he had fallen in with this criticizing attitude. With Louise, he had never done this.

"Ninety-nine percent of the men in this world would bore me. And do you know what the cardinal sin is in life? It's to be bored. It's a sin to be bored, Tom."

"I guess I've changed, and maybe I'm stodgy," Tom said.

"Don't brag about it," she interrupted.

He raised his brows. Her remark hurt more than angered him. He accepted it as a judgment, and recognized that he must have become stodgy.

"Tom, I'm sorry. I didn't mean to hurt you," she said quickly and softly.

Her remark had stung him because of late he had been having doubts about himself. He had wanted to write. And now, didn't he make his living out of writers? This made him a little guilty at times.

"You still smile so charmingly. You must have something of the old Tom still left in you." She laughed peculiarly. "But to me, the old Tom is the young Tom. When you smiled a moment ago, you seemed very much the way you used to be when you were my beau."

"Well, thank you for that, Martha."

"Tom," she said earnestly.

He leaned forward, but the seriousness of her tone made him apprehensive.

"Tom, I treated you badly, but I suffered afterwards for it. I did. I couldn't look at myself. I couldn't excuse myself. I hope I didn't make you suffer too much by . . . by my bitchiness."

"You didn't," he said to allay any feeling of embarrassment she might be having.

Tom thought how easy it had been to get over his hurt and his disappointment. It hadn't hurt too much. It hadn't really damaged him. Martha, who had seemed so close, so important to him, was now really like a stranger. And he sensed in her an incurable unhappiness. She was still very nervous.

"I was afraid, Tom, and that's why I wouldn't let you."

He was too embarrassed to speak. He looked past her.

"Do you know what, Tom?"

"What?" he asked, still embarrassed.

"All of the time that you were my beau, I wanted to, and I wanted you to. I had some of my dreams analyzed later, and do you know what they meant? They meant that I wanted you to rape me."

Tom was flustered.

"You make me think of that play that Gertrude Lawrence was in, what was its name?" he said.

"You don't remember?"

"No, it suddenly escapes me."

"You haven't met Gertrude Lawrence?"

"No."

"And you can't remember the name of the play?"

"No, it just evades me."

"I'll bet you have an unconscious crush on Gertrude Lawrence," she said assertively.

All Tom could think of now was that he had been very lucky that Martha had turned him down years ago.

"But Gertrude Lawrence doesn't have anything to do with you and me, Tom."

"No. I guess not." There was a mild note of irony in his voice.

"I really did love you, but I was afraid. I learned that too in my analysis. But I didn't let you know. I didn't surrender to you because I was afraid of my father."

"I didn't know it was that complicated," he began.

"It always is. You're that complicated. If you got yourself analyzed, you'd be surprised to know what you'd find out about yourself. You ought to, Tom. Maybe that's why you never became creative. I wasn't creative then. I am now."

"Are you writing?"

"No, don't worry," she quickly said.

"But Martha, I wouldn't be worried if you were writing."

"I didn't want you to think I was an aspiring literary lady coming to you for help."

"Oh," he exclaimed, "I never thought of that. If I could help you, I'd be only too glad to do it."

"I study dancing."

"Do you like it?"

"I love it. It permits me to give expression to all my frustrated subconscious drives."

Tom went on eating.

"You never saw my figure, did you?"

"You have a very attractive figure, Martha."

"Thank you, but I don't think so. But I meant—saw me naked. I never took my clothes off in front of you."

He smiled again to cover his embarrassment.

"You did take me swimming. Well, then you would know that I have a good figure and good legs and good leg muscles for dancing."

"I wouldn't know anything about that."

"I'm going to be a good dancer."

"I'm very glad to hear that."

"I always was artistic, and this is the art I always needed. It may sound screwy to some people, because of my age. After all, telling you, Tom, that I'm no spring chicken—well, you're in the family. And my age is against me. But my muscles are as limber and as flexible as they ever were. My leg muscles are as good as those of a young girl."

She seemed to be gazing at him invitingly. It made him uncomfortable. He was unexpectedly tempted. His sense of the present grew vague. An illusion took hold of him. For a moment he believed that they were in Chicago, and still young.

Her leg touched his and she held it against his. He wanted to pull away. He didn't.

"Well, Tom," she said, "now you tell me about yourself."

"There really isn't a great deal to tell. My life seems dull and ordinary, I guess."

"But Tom, I don't believe you. You're an influential literary editor. Why, young writers and lady poets must dote on you."

"It's just a job, and when I finish it, each day, I usually go home."

"And don't you go to many literary cocktail parties?"

"Not when I can get out of them. And when I can't, I leave as quickly as it is polite to take off."

She was rubbing her leg against his. His rush of desire bothered him. He forced himself to seem calm.

"Tom, you were so romantic. If anything, you were too romantic. You used to quote Walt Pater to me, and talk about the colors on the lake, and paintings. Do you still love art and go to galleries? What do you think of Miro?"

"I don't get to see any paintings any more. In fact, it must be two years or more since I've gone to an exhibition."

"I'm ashamed of you, Tom. I'm saddened to hear it. And don't you go to the concerts?"

"Sometimes I listen to WQXR on the radio, but it is hard for me to get it in the country. I play records at night now and then."

"Yes, you should be analyzed. You need to be taken out of your rut."

And as she said this, an inviting smile crossed her face, and her leg again pressed firmly against him.

He was confused. He was growing inwardly tense, and increasingly uncomfortable.

At this moment, the waiter came with their coffee. Tom was glad, and quickly put cream and sugar into his cup, stirred and drank. It seemed to relax him a little.

"If I lived in New York, I'd help you."

He gazed at her quizzically.

"I'd help you not to grow stodgy."

"It seems to me, Martha, that you have to take stock of yourself, recognize your limitations, and make the best of yourself within your limitations."

"You surprise me."

"I do? Why? Do you think that that is too stuffy and too defeatist a thing to say?"

"It's mature. It's mature. Tom, you surprise me because you are mature. Most men are little boys. They want women to be men so they can be little boys. They want their sweethearts to be their mothers."

Tom had never thought along these lines. He nevertheless felt uncertain. Maybe what she said was so. Maybe he was that way. Still, he had managed to live happily with Louise, and to raise a family. Did it make any difference? Did all she was saying make any difference?

They finished their coffee and dessert, and Martha asked for brandy, assuming that Tom always had brandy after his meals. As she sipped her drink, she said:

"Well, tell me, have I improved?"

"Yes," he told her politely.

"I'm not the frightened girl you used to know, playing at being sophisticated."

"I'm glad to hear that."

"Can't you tell the difference?"

"Yes, yes, I can."

"I imagine I'm as sophisticated as many women you know in New York."

"I don't know too many, except perhaps as passing acquaintances."

She showed her disbelief, and took another sip of brandy.

Then, suddenly, she got up from the table, walked around to Tom's place, bent down and kissed him. He was taken by surprise. He said nothing as she returned to her own chair.

She quickly took still another sip of brandy.

"Did I embarrass you, Tom?"

"No, not at all."

"Do you know why I did that?"

"It flatters me, whatever the reason."

"Do you have to go back to your office this afternoon?"

"Yes. I really do. I have appointments all afternoon."

"Do you have to go home for dinner?"

"I do. I'm very sorry, but I have a friend coming, and I can't get out of it."

"You married men!"

He wanted her to finish her brandy. He had seen enough of her. Still, impatient as he was to get away, he was also sad. It was sad to meet an old sweetheart this way. She was really mixed up. She wanted something, something that perhaps no one could ever give her. Most certainly, he couldn't give her whatever it was she wanted. A little while ago, he had, in fact, been toying with the idea of going to bed with her just to find out what the experience would be like. He wouldn't. He wanted to get away from her. But she dallied over her brandy.

"Maybe I was too aggressive," she mused. "Men don't like women to be so aggressive, kissing them in public that way."

"Maybe they do."

"Did you?"

". . . . Yes, but . . . ."

"I was too aggressive," she interrupted.

He said nothing. He decided to be as polite as possible, but not to see her again.

"You aren't revenging yourself, are you?" she asked.

"For what?"

"Because I gave you the gate years ago."

"Martha, it all worked out for the best."

She glared at him. Then she forced a smile.

"Tom, I've been trying to tell you to take me all during lunch."

"Martha, it wouldn't work out."

"You don't know unless you try."

He shook his head.

"I knew I was too aggressive."

He noticed that she had almost finished the brandy, and his eyes strayed anxiously in search of the waiter.

"You want to get rid of me?"

"No, Martha, not at all. I'd very much enjoy to just sit here and talk some more to you, but I have a very important appointment back at the office, and I must be there."

She gulped down the rest of her brandy, and looked at him in sulky silence.

He paid the bill. They left the restaurant. Outside, he stood with her a moment.

"Don't be so polite. Tell me to get the hell out of your life. Kick me out of it!"

"Martha, what's the matter?"

"Goodbye, Tom. Don't hate me . . . . too much."

She strode away. He gazed after her, puzzled, full of pity.

IX

Riding home on the New Haven that evening, Tom looked out of the window at green trees and a fair sky. After having had lunch with Martha, he had been unstrung all afternoon. He wondered if she were really a mess or not. He was glad that he'd had enough sense not to accept her invitation. But more than that, he was sad. Years ago, she had meant something to him. Years ago, he had thought of her as beautiful and superior, as a creature he wanted wholly. How had he changed? How far away he was from youth. And how she had changed! How lucky he was that she'd not accepted him!

He didn't like her now. And yet, years ago he had thought that he was in love with her. Tall and young, lithesome, she had strode along beside him in Jackson Park. They had laughed together and kissed. He had felt as one with her. She had seemed extraordinary. It had been a dream. Dreams. Youth was only a matter of dreams. She must have been a lot different then from what he had imagined her to be. And he, he hadn't known it. He had seen her in his own dreams. And these were gone, gone with youth. Now, he was middle-aged and practical and content Yet, he still knew that there was a longing in him for those dreams of youth.

He got off at his station. Louise, plump and simple-looking, kissed him, and asked if he had had a good day. He said yes. They drove home to the dinner that was waiting for him, and the slow contented evening, when he would talk with his family, read and go to bed.

He kept thinking to himself that his youth was gone. He looked at his gray hairs in the bathroom mirror. He still felt that there was something good in those dreams he had had years ago, when he had known Martha. He went down to dinner, wistful and quiet.

HIGH SCHOOL

Fifteen, and going to High School and a blazing, scintillating career of glory. Danny felt good. Walking down the steps of the graybrick apartment building on South Avenue and a few doors down from Fifty Eighth Street, he felt good and liked the sunny September morning a lot, and told himself that it was going to be one of his days. He told himself that living was certainly a fine thing, and repeated that it was going to be one of his days.

Danny halted at the bottom step, and dreamily gaped at two round-shouldered, clerkish-looking young men, who walked as if in a daze, their sallow faces thrust forward, and cigarettes drooping from their lips. He wondered why so many people looked so mopey when they went to work in the morning. Always when he was on his way to school he saw them moping along like that, Funny!

He breathed deeply, obeying the instructions for breathing that he remembered from the articles he had read in the Chicago Evening Post. Les Darcey, the great Australian middleweight, had written them just after coming to the country, and before he had died so sadly after not being allowed to fight and being called a slacker. He had died . . . *so sadly*. Danny forgot about breathing, and sorrowed over Darcey, because Les had been such a great fighter, and they had played such dirty tricks on him, and he had licked Jimmy Clabby, Eddie McGoorty, Chip, and K.O. Brown, and he'd have even whaled Mike Gibbons, and Batt. Levinsky, if they'd have let him fight.

Poor Les Darcey!

He said a Hail Mary for the repose of poor Les Darcey's soul. And it made him think of how sadly another great middle-weight had died, Nonpareil Jack Dempsey. He started reciting to himself, the poem that a San Francisco sport's writer had written about Dempsey's grave;

> Far out in the wilds of Oregon
> On a lonely mountain side,
> Where Columbia's mighty waters
> Roll down to the ocean tide,
> O'ergrown with firs and lichens,
> I found poor Dempsey's grave.
> No rose, no shamrock could I find. . . .

He breathed deeply, letting the air slowly seep down to his lungs, holding it there as long as he could, and then permitting it to Phuh out, all at once. An athlete had to have good wind. Good wind was necessary if you wanted to keep in condition. He stood and practiced breathing, because he wanted to keep in good condition.

In self-propelling wheel chairs, three gray-heads rolled by.

Danny swung south along South Park Avenue.

The fine sun seemed like a diamond that had broken and chipped off many little pieces that had dropped and lay sparkling all over the street. He walked along. A woman, her belly out like a big egg, passed him.

He glanced sidewise at Washington Park, ending in wire-fenced, yellow clay tennis courts at the other side of the street. The shrubbery in back of them was thick and indistinct. There were low thin patches of bushes before the nearer side of the courts, and a line of leafy trees stood erect, their leaves slightly agitated in the light wind. A patch of grass ran along the curb, green now, sun touched, and with still a few sparkles of dew. It was nice all right, and the air was as nice as it had been up in Michigan where he had gone on his summer vacation for two weeks. And it was just like the kind of a morning he would have liked for going barefooted in the dew, with his Airedale, Liberty, yapping at his side.

He felt suddenly sad. He was going to high school, and that meant that he was growing up, and growing up meant that there were things he wouldn't be doing much longer, like going barefooted in the park with Liberty.

He thought of going to High School, and started to lose his nerve. He tried to tell himself that he shouldn't be so afraid, but there he was, with a sinking feeling in the pit of his stomach. He imagined the place to which he was going, the brick schoolyard of the Carmelites High School, full of kids he didn't know, and some of them older than himself, and tough, and ready to rag the daylights out of newcomers, and maybe even to kick them around the block a few times. And many of the kids starting like he was, would be from tough mick neighborhoods all over the south side, and they might mean a lot of trouble to him too. He was always a bit leary about meeting new kids, because they might be liable to start a scrap with him and clean him up, or maybe treat him rotten, and make him eat dirt. Right now, he might be just walking into a place full of kids who were just waiting and ready to make a big goof out of him.

He felt a physical sensation of shrinking and horror.

"Hello, O'Neill!"

"Hello Slops," Danny replied, surprised at seeing Slops Murphy, who had graduated with him from St. Patrick's last June.

"Going to high school?" asked Slops.

Danny said yes, he was going to the Carmelites school over near Jackson Park.

"I wouldn't go to school. You couldn't get me inside a school again on a bet. You couldn't get me in one of them even if you hired a team of horses and tried to drag me in."

"What are you going to do?"

"I had a job, office boy, McGregor, Cohen, Schmaltz & O'Toole, Lawyers, but they gave me the gate. I was supposed to go and roust up another one, but I been hunting for a couple of weeks, and I ain't found nothin'. Today, I'm jus' goin' over in the park and sit in the grass."

"I don't know that I'll like it, but I gotta go," said Danny.

"Maybe you can play on the baseball team," said Slops.

"I hope so," said Danny, modestly.

"You'll have a uniform and you might even play a game in the White Sox Park. Sometimes they play a Catholic League game there for charity or something."

"I hope so."

"I wouldn't mind the baseball part, but you couldn't get me into a school room again," Slops said, pulling a butt out of his pocket, and lighting it.

Slops adjusted his cap at a tough, crooked angle, and said so long. He walked on.

Danny turned and looked at him, walking along, his clothes old and poor looking. He remembered that Sister Magdalen had told him that Slops wanted to go to high school but his father was too poor to send him. And Slops was a sweet little ball player. He would make good in high school baseball. And his old man was always getting drunk and kicking Slops and his old woman around. Slops must have gotten hell beaten out of him for losing his job. He watched Slops snip a butt, and he walked on.

He was afraid again, and wished he could run after Slops. But he had to go to school. He started losing more of his nerve.

The Carmelites schoolyard became a huge eye, growing inside his head. It watched him, a timid, four-eyed curly-haired kid, small for his age, approaching it slowly. The eye grew into a cruel, sneering, deadeye dick's villain face, as big as the four-story school building. A four-story face slid the word *cockeyes* out of the side of its first story mouth. Danny had that midnight sort of feeling that he slowed down, like something automatic. He felt himself getting smaller, and miserable, and smaller, compressing into the size of a midget, or of the Teenie Weenies who were always in the Sunday paper. The schoolyard got bigger, and multiplied with tough kids, the school building changed back into the big eye, and came towards him big and even powerful, like the way a train seems to come up on you in the movies. It got closer and closer. He tried to shag the thoughts and fears out of his mind, and they wouldn't go. He looked across the street at the vacant courts. He told himself that the White Sox were sure winners of the pennant, and they were going to clean up in the world series, just like they had two years ago in 1917. He was afraid. He thought of Sister Magdalen.

She came to him, a cooling, dark figure of consolation, dismissing his vision of the terrorizing eye. But she pointed a finger of accusation at him. He felt guilty, ashamed of himself, sorry for himself, and for Sister Magdalen, because he had betrayed her. It seemed as if she was really right there beside him, telling him that he was disloyal to her, to himself, to God. It all seemed like an awful dream. He had promised her that he would go to Quigley Seminary, and

study for the priesthood, and here he was, breaking that
promise, and he hadn't even told her. He wondered about
vocations and the priesthood. Maybe after all he didn't
have one, because if he did, he wouldn't want to do things
as much as he did now. But he felt and knew that he really
did have a vocation, and that he was willfully being heed-
less of God's call to him to study and join the consecrated
ranks of the priesthood. He wondered, too, if God was going to punish him with unhappiness and failure at the Carmelites school. If God took away all his baseball ability,
spoiled all his dreams, and his wanting of success . . . . it
would be terrible. And his conscience told him that God
would do this. He tried to ditch his conscience, because it
kept telling him that he had turned his back on God. But
he couldn't give it the slip. He had no excuse for his dis-
loyalty in not going to Quigley like he had signed up to go.
It was his own fault, and his own weakness, and he would
be punished for it at the Carmelites school. He had only
been goofing himself when he had felt that it was going to
be one of his days.

He drooped along. A blind man came forward, tip-tap-
ping his cane on the pavement, his face strained and hollow looking, tiptapping his cane, zigzagging, swerving over
to the right edge off the sidewalk onto the grass, almost
tripping, steering back onto the stone, tiptapping before
him, and wavering from side to side.

Danny paused at the south corner of Fifty Ninth Street.
He started jumping back and forth over the three foot iron
railing, and he even imagined a little game of jumping. He
talked to himself about how he wished that he was still a
grammar school kid back at St. Patrick. He remembered
how on graduation night last June, he had cried, and he
had wished that he was still back in the eighth grade, where
his friend, Sister Magdalen, had taught him. He was somebody there. The best fighter, ball player, and wrestler in the
class. And one of the best pupils, too. And that was where
Roslyn had been. But she had graduated, too, and it
wouldn't be any use to be back there unless she was there
also. He told himself that he better give the Chutes to such
thoughts, before they made him sad.

He looked across the street at a snappy tennis game
between a young fellow, and a girl dressed in white in the
first court this side of the park entrance. They were

cracks all right, and what a sweet serve she had. She even shot them over like bullets on the second serve. And wowie, the way both of them could loft them over the net. And she had a bangup backhand stroke too. They were cracks all right. And boy what form the girl had. Gee, if he and Roslyn were good enough friends to play tennis together in the early morning, and if Roslyn could play like that, they could become even better friends.

Moving on, he thought of Roslyn. A Washington Park Hospital ambulance clanged through the north bound traffic on South Park Avenue. He thought of Roslyn. He imagined her before him, green sweatered, sharp-tongued, blond Roslyn. She was not so awfully pretty, but that didn't matter, because. . . . *he loved her*. His feeling for her was sacramental. Nobody could ever know how much he loved her. Nobody could ever imagine that he loved her with such a sacramental feeling. Nobody could imagine that he felt Roslyn, a sacred statue in his mind. He was afraid, because his love for her was so sacramental and religious that it might even be sinful and a sacrilege. It was sinful, because the First Commandment said I am the Lord thy God and thou shalt not bear strange gods before Me, and he thought of her like he did of God, and he was afraid to tell it to the priest in confession because he couldn't tell anyone about it. And he had the sins of many bad confessions on his soul, and would go to Hell sure because he loved her. But he couldn't stop himself. And sometimes, he imagined that the whole world was as a huge cathedral in honor of Roslyn, St. Roslyn, who smiled from above where she stood on a mile-long altar of sunny clouds. And all the people in the world knelt and genuflected before her, and himself, a priest, celebrated mass, in her honor, and God was there, kneeling, praying, genuflecting, swinging a censer before her, and the sun burned in the censer, giving off incense all for her—Now how could he tell that to anybody?

A paddy wagon, with a cop, standing nonchalantly on the back step, rushed across Sixtieth street, heading East.

He turned east at Sixtieth, and walked along the park edge. He loved Roslyn, she thought he was a boob. She hardly ever spoke to him. At St. Patrick's he used to see her nearly every day, but they had scarcely ever even said hello to each other. And he had always wanted to say something to her when he saw her; he had wanted to tell her how he felt about her, the things he pretended and imagined because of her, how he was going to become the greatest baseball player in the world just for her. But whenever he had seen her, he couldn't think of anything to say, and they had passed each other by on the street, as if they were strangers. They had always acted as if they were too proud to speak to each other, and it wasn't at all true. He loved her. And he knew that she liked him, he knew that, because her cousin, Glenn, had once told him so. Since they had been in sixth grade, they had liked each other, but they had hardly ever even said hello to each other. Every day, since they had gotten to like each other, he had gotten up in the morning hoping that it would be the day when they would get to understanding each other better, and becoming sweethearts. And every Saturday morning, even when it had rained and snowed, he had gone walking, even too when he had bad colds, he had gone walking out in the slush and wet and everything, and he had strolled by her house, hoping that he might see her. And now they were graduated and starting to different schools, and they were no ways closer to each other, like they should be after liking each other over two years. They wouldn't see each other so very often now, and maybe she would soon be old enough to go out to dances with fellows, and well, she would get farther and farther away from him, and she would forget him. Well, he would never forget her. It all got pretty dark, and he wished that a guy fifteen years old could cry. But he wasn't supposed to, so he walked along, passing on the other side of the street from the Washington Park Hospital, where there were a lot of sick people, and deciding to hope and pretend that everything was going to turn out all right. He'd once read somewhere that if you wanted something bad enough, and pretended you would get it, and had enough faith behind your pretending, and you kept demanding to yourself that the thing would come to you, well it would. Once, last spring, the thing had worked for him. He had demanded to himself on a Monday that he would be able to kiss Roslyn before the week was over. Well it turned out that on Friday, Glenn ran a party, and they played post office, and he was able to call her into the post office, and he had gotten his chance, only she had only let him kiss her on the cheek. Sometimes this business of wishing hadn't worked, but if it had worked once, it would work again this time, so he wished that everything would turn out right, and he knew that it would, and that he and Roslyn would get to seeing each other regular, and speaking to each other, and well she would be his girl.

He turned south on Eberhardt Avenue, and walked along the west side of the street. A crippled little girl, her left leg too short, labored on ahead of him, her strapped books slung over her shoulder. When he came to the middle of the block, he stopped and gazed up at the blue scraps of sky just over a modern-looking, redbricked, three-story apartment building, as if he was really interested in the sky, with maybe an airplane in it. He slyly dropped a nickel in the grass, and searched for it. He saw it, glinting in the sunlight, but he kept looking for it in places where it wasn't.

He stole looks up at the second floor north of the building, and at the entrance way, with its brightly polished brass door knob. He imagined a blond greensweatered girl emerging from the entrance way, and he pretended that a blond head appeared in the window after the curtains were flipped back. He imagined the girl coming out of the hallway again, and crossing the street, holding her head pert, tossing it from side to side, and stopping by him to ask, very friendly, what he was looking for. He imagined the two of them searching for his nickel that glinted before him in the sunlight. And he saw her find it, and hand it to him, saying;

Here booby, if it was a dog, it would bite you.

But of course the booby wouldn't be said in a spiteful or mean way. And they would walk slowly towards the Sixty First Street carline, taking their time so they would have longer to talk to each other. They would speak of schools. She was going to St. Xavier, and he would tell her that it was a good school. He would tell her that he was going to the Carmelites school, and she would say it was a good school.

Maybe they would walk along, silently for a few moments, and suddenly she would say, girl-like, dropping her head, and swinging her shoulders a little with being shy;

just the same way the heroines did in the movies he saw every Friday night. . . . she would say;

I won't be seeing you so often.

No, he would say.

But I want to, she would say, again dropping her head, and swinging her shoulders, girl-like.

And he imagined himself asking her to go to the Trivoli Theatre at Sixty Third and Cottage with him next Saturday afternoon, and of course she would say she would be glad to.

The sound of fire engines and sirens came from a nearby street.

Everything always happened all right in a fellow's pretendings. If things only sometimes did the same for him really and truly. But they would go to the Trivoli, and it would be nice. The Trivoli was supposed to be the grandest theatre in the city, with all kinds of draperies and things in it, and fine music, and a big pipe organ. He and Roslyn would sit, side by side in the darkness of the theatre, holding hands, happy, listening to the pipe organ, and looking at the pictures, and they might maybe hear someone sing or play Mickey. He demanded all this to happen and it would, and he demanded that they hear Mickey . . . *Mickey lovely Mickey,* Roslyn was in real life, like Mickey had been to him when he had seen it at the Michigan Theatre with Mabel Normand . . . *With your hair of raven hue* . . . It was all going to turn out just like he pretended and demanded that it would . . . *And your smiling so beguiling* . . . And if he went without lunch all week, and saved his money, he would have enough to take her to the Tivoli in style, and buy her a sundae or a banana split afterwards, and maybe buy candy to eat in the show. . . . *Mickey lovely Mickey.*

No one emerged from the entrance way. He picked his nickel up and moved on. It was a damn shame all right that kids of fifteen weren't supposed to cry, because he wanted to. . . . *There's a bit of Kilarney, bit of the Blarney too.* He walked along. Well there were other days ahead of him.

He told himself it was too bad. He gritted his teeth. He held a dialogue with himself, and proved that after all, she might not be so much, and someday she would come to him, begging and sorry. . . . *Mickey lovely Roslyn can you blame anyone for falling in love with you. . . .*

He was walking along right now, starting to high school, where he was going to become such a scintilating baseball player, whose playing would bring four straight championships to the Carmelites school. And he would be signed up direct from high school by the White Sox and Roslyn would see his picture in the papers and the articles about him when he signed the contract . . . *Mickey lovely Mickey.* . . . Fame and glory would be his, and the future was blazing with what he would do and be. Playing the White Sox Park against De La Salle, he would win the championship by hitting a homer with the bases full, and he would do it batting left handed, the ball going over the fence into the right field bleachers, and Roslyn would be there and see it, and she would hear everybody cheering with the name of O'Neill on their lips, and then she would see and be sorry. And after bringing his left spiked foot down on the rubber, he would tip his hat, and without a smile on his face or anything, trot back to the dugout. And he would make his big league debut against Walter Johnson, and he would bat lefthanded and smack out three hits off of the Big Train, and he would have more pictures of himself in the papers. He would play like Eddie Collins and Ty Cobb combined, and be a great batterfielder, and he would bat both ways, and be able to play every position on the diamond. Then Roslyn would be sorry and humble . . . *Mickey lovely Roslyn with your* . . . . and she would beg him to be nice to her, and he would be cold and distant, and make her see her mistake, and let her swallow her own medicine in big enough doses . . .

He moved on along towards Sixty Third, not seeming to know where he was going. He was sad. He did not want to be going on in the world like he was going. He wanted to be a kid in St. Patrick's for another year anyway. The Carmelites High School was the big eye, and his future made him afraid, because he didn't know what it was even if he did pretend a lot of things . . . *And your smiling so beguiling.* . . . He was afraid. He wanted to turn back and not go to High School today. A sweat and a sinking feeling got him. He tried to tell himself he was walking down the road to his glory. He wiped the sweat off his forehead.

At Sixty Third Street, he noticed the time in a store window, and decided to take a street car, because the school was over near Jackson Park, and if he was late on the first day, it would look bad, and get him in dutch, and maybe cause some of the priests to be getting a grudge against him, or even taking a poke at him.

Roslyn lovely Roslyn. . . .

Riding on the street car, he found that his thoughts were all mixed up, and he didn't even know how he felt, but he told himself that someday, anyway, he was going to be a great man . . . and it would all be for. . . . *Roslyn.*

GEORGE LONG

I

He had run out of seconals but had taken a non-prescription sleeping pill which Cissy had bought at the corner drugstore. It wasn't working and he tried to control his restlessness lying in the dark bedroom. He'd be beat up in the morning again, and at the start of a new week. The most sensible thing for him to do was to lie as quietly as he could and to think of something innocuous. But the damned trouble was that some screened-off emotion took hold of every innocuous subject he used to fall asleep and this trick didn't work. He had used to use baseball to achieve this result. Now, it was failing him.

What time was it? It was early morning. He could hear the trucks rumbling. He and Cissy should have moved out of New York. If for no other reason, then because they would have gotten more rest and relaxation. You took more of a licking than you realized living in New York. You never knew one moment of perfect quiet, of that silence and quiet which you could know living in the country or in a suburb.

The trucks. In the daytime you often got so that you didn't hear them. But at night when you couldn't sleep they could rub on your nerves like a cheese grater. You had an impulse to jump.

—Lie quietly, George.

If he couldn't sleep, he could nonetheless get some rest.

In 1935, he'd seen Babe Ruth strike out as a pinch hitter at the Polo Grounds. Ruth had been with the Braves. How had he swung? George closed his eyes and tried to recapture an exact memory of Babe Ruth swinging and missing, swinging under the ball in a lofting movement. He visualized Ruth in a gray suit with red trimming. But he could not visualize the swing clearly. Each time, the imagined Babe Ruth swung under the ball, either too quickly, with a jerky graceless movement, or else he had some block in envisioning Ruth bringing the bat around. This trick was no-go. What about work tomorrow? He had a luncheon appointment with Alvin Carter. Carter, their most aggrieved and complainingest author. Christ, he wouldn't sleep if he thought of this.

The straining, bursting noise of a truck motor, a shifting of gears. The trucks must have awakened him.

George closed his eyes again. He heard Cissy's even breathing. Perhaps if he woke her up and made love to her, then he could sleep. But he was tired. Desire was, at the moment, cool in him. This wouldn't be right.

He sighed, and pulled his arms out from under the sheet and blankets. Cissy had warned him to keep his arms and shoulders covered up before she had passed off into sleep. Her devotion to him was more than he was worth, more than any man was worth in this cynical age. At least during these periods of insomnia, he was gaining enough control over himself to avoid the terrors of sleeplessness. He didn't become as anxious as he'd used to. But how boring it was, and then, you were washed out the next day. Your mind didn't function well. You stimulated yourself on too much coffee. Or you'd have two or three martinis at lunch to pep yourself up and that half-ruined your afternoon. It's hard as hell to like your job and do it well unless you go to it rested. The zest was lacking. Without zest for your job, you felt that you were working at something stupid and were wasting, squandering the most valuable goods in the world, your own time.

George kept tossing. Finally, he became so bored and restless that he got up, found his robe and slippers and went into the living room of his apartment. It was better to get up and read. He went through the darkened corridor to the living room in the front of the five-room apartment. He was too washed out to enjoy reading. His anxiety, he knew, had been dulled by the two pills which he had taken, but he was left without the will to concentrate. A sense of personal helplessness and of a lack of meaning in life swept through him. He was tempted to feel sorry for himself. Men, some men anyway, received these undeserved psychological punishments.

He went to the window of the long, narrow living room and looked down on the street, ten stories below. The air was blue, and full of flying, scattered snow. Electric lights brightened the shining white snow on the sidewalk. Across the street were low old apartment buildings, solid and heavy. In the blue night and caught here and there by rays of light, the buildings were less drab than in the daytime. Here and there, a window was lit up. He kept staring down on the scene and it evoked a nameless or vague nostalgia in him. Rarely any more did he pause like this and look at something, some scene. He sometimes thought or suspected that his capacities for seeing and experiencing were wearing out. You came to care less about so much that was in life and about one's own feelings and development. The continuing effort to live was too much to bear, and you closed in on yourself more and more. This was what it meant to grow old. But he was not as yet an old man. Rather, say that he had or was coming upon the threshold of old age.

A lone man was straggling along on the opposite sidewalk. The fellow was drunk. Or was he? Was he lame? The fellow twisted through the snow on the sidewalk. Yes, he was drunk. The fellow stopped near a garbage can, swayed a few times but slightly, dug a hand into his pocket, and then on uneven keel, he walked up a step and disappeared in the entrance way of a building. The scene had been fascinating. No, not fascinating, but interesting. Better, it was highly interesting. Who was the fellow and where had he been? A drunken man alone on the streets and going home at 5 A.M. was pathetic. You saw such waste and loneliness. A man didn't stay out that late, drinking, unless he was unhappy. He'd done that a few times.

Even though there was some noise and pounding of trucks, the street now seemed to be weighted in silence. The snow had ceased and everything was fixed and immobile, deserted with all life having gone from it so that it reflected an absent life.

George turned from the window, switched on a lamp and dropped heavily into a big comfortable chair. To read. The book before him had just arrived in the mail, *A Carnival Buncombe,* H. L. Mencken at his best in politics.

He'd read it. Mencken was dead now. The way the French expressed it. Mencken's writing had excited and roused him in his youth and he had always hoped that he'd get a chance to meet Mencken. It had never happened although he knew many people who had had this honor. Still, he felt as though he had known the man.

Looking at the picture of Mencken on the jacket with his hands on the keys of a typewriter, his glasses down on the nose, a cigar in his mouth and his expression one of concentration and, also, of ironic amusement, George filled up with newly stimulated sadness. Hell, you had to die and as often as not, it didn't matter when you did. But the fact of death, the idea that you could and would be destroyed, obliterated, wounded and mangled your pride.

George began to read the book.

II

George sat at his big desk, and outside the air was growing dark. The sun had already gone down. He was all done in today, but lots had happened and he'd had to keep his mind fixed on business. There had been ads, a hitch at the printer's about a book which had already been postponed once, an unpleasant scene with one of their authors, Dewey Lewis, a boring lunch with a stupid woman author, who had written a best seller, and her business man husband; the fellow was a nonentity who should be led around with a ring in his nose.

Especially since he was tired because of his sleepless night, the day seemed to him to have been stupid and meaningless. He didn't have much hope or even concern about the future. It didn't mean much to him. Other than Cissy there was no one. If their daughter had lived, they'd be grandparents by now and that might have given new meaning and significance to their lives. For a year after Geraldine had died in a fire, he'd been disconsolate and for the first time in his life, he'd drunk heavily. He had never gotten over that tragic accident. It had affected Cissy as much. But he tried not to think of that nightmare. It had happened fourteen years ago during Christmas week.

Geraldine, Gerry, had gone to stay away from home for the first time in her life.

George winced and pressed his teeth into his lower lip.

He recalled Gerry as a little girl, with her deep blue eyes and her blonde ringlets. Her eyes had been so shiny. Her toddling walks. The way she ran to the door and kissed him and called him Daddy. He had used to take her out on Sunday afternoons. Sometimes the three of them would go out. Until she had been eight or nine, she had liked to go to the zoo in Central Park. She had used to laugh at the monkeys, and she had always liked to stay for a long time, watching the sea lions.

Rubbing his face, he shook his head as if by doing that, he might shake these memories and their pain out of mind.

Miss Jenkins, his secretary, came in with a stack of the letters he had dictated that morning. Looking at them, he wanted to tell her to sign them for him and send them out. He couldn't care about them now. He couldn't care about anything. Since Gerry had died in such a stupid, senseless, tragically unnecessary way, things hadn't mattered.

He took the letters and pulled the black pen out of the holder on his desk. Miss Jenkins stood about three feet from him, stiff and silent. Bending over the letters, he was aware of her presence, of her eyes on him, and he knew that she was trembling within herself in fear that he might find mistakes in her work. Poor girl, to be afraid of so unimportant a matter. Unimportant a matter? What was important any more?

A letter to Eustace Rowe, the reprint publisher. He was offering Eustace two novels. He signed it. Usually, he handled the reprint rights. And he did pretty well. But he did everything well and knew that he did. And a letter to their author, Skimp Cushings. Skimp was old and sick now, an old man. He'd spent all of his money, and his books no longer sold. The firm published Skimp merely out of sentiment. It was a sad business, a hell of a goddamned thing to see Skimp ending up like this. He'd dictated a sympathetic letter, ending it with "good luck old man." Yet he wasn't at all certain that he had actually felt and meant the sympathy which he'd expressed.

And other letters. A polite rejection of a novel by an

unknown writer, an answer to an inquiry from Yugoslavia about one of the firm's novels, letters to three of their authors, a letter to a book reviewer in Milwaukee, two letters to old friends, another to Hallie McGann, one of his old flames. Hallie must be gray now. He half-choked up for a moment.

When he'd gone through the letters and signed them, he handed the stack back to Miss Jenkins and thanked her. She smiled but with lightness and restraint. How had she become such a grim girl?

The phone rang as he watched her leave his office. She didn't at all have a bad figure and would be rather attractive if she weren't so grim and shy. The world was full of drab creatures, many who were a hell of a lot more drab than Miss Jenkins.

Lighting a cigarette, he thought how he shouldn't think and feel as he so frequently did. Where was his pride? And if he continued to remain depressed, and so frequently lacking an interest in life, wasn't he the only loser? This was a way of throwing away some of the final years of his life before he became an old man. He remembered when he had been young, there had been so many things in life which he had wanted to see, so many places he'd believed that he'd see, and so many books that he'd read. Now he knew that he would one day die with many of these ambitions neglected. This was not because of his grief over Geraldine. He was changing.

Squashing out his cigarette, he knew that he was allowing his curiosity and whatever curiosity and zest for life which he had once had to dry up. Working here was largely a matter of habit and routine. It no longer gave him any of the old pleasure and excitement which it once had. There were times, at least, when he even believed that publishing was a dying business. It didn't seem important to him as it once had. Hell, he wasn't an old man, old enough to feel and to keep thinking as he did, and neither was he young enough. But this was not precisely disillusionment, nor was he tormenting himself about the purpose of life. This was not life, but himself. His old capacities were gone. They had died or possibly only gone to sleep. He didn't throw his emotions into his work. Nothing mattered because he did not feel that things mattered. And he had been feeling this way for a year or two. Why did he keep thinking of his daughter Gerry? At times, he believed that it was because of her death that he had come to be as he now was, but she had been dead all of these years. Was it really because of Gerry that he now lived in feelings of emptiness? The thought of his dead, dark-eyed daughter, of her pretty round face, her smile, her straight white teeth, her face and eyes shining, and of the way she would laugh with such suddenness—all this choked him up. His body shook in a kind of silent sob. But what good did it do in thinking about his loss?

George took a manuscript from the side of his desk. But as he read, his mind dwelled also on his dead daughter. He remembered how he had used to look forward to getting home from the office at the end of the day. And how empty his home had been that day when they had come into it after having buried her. It had been empty ever since.

George realized that the manuscript was good, and it held him, his other thoughts sliding away. It was a story of marriage, and the people were real. When they spoke you believed that actual people had spoken. What this young author put into their mouths—he assumed the author was young since he had never heard of him before—seemed to be just what they should say. If the author sustained himself, they had a writer. His interest quickened more and he read for about an hour, uninterrupted. This usually didn't happen, and he had to do much of his reading at home. It was five o'clock. Getting up from his desk, noticing the dark outside his window, hearing now the steady noises of traffic, his mood changed again, and he became aware of how tired he was. At least, tonight, he would sleep.

III

"Is that you, George?"

"Yes, dear," he answered after hearing Cissy call when he'd let himself into the apartment with his key.

He took his coat off, and put it and his hat in the closet off the entrance.

Walking heavy-footed to the bedroom in the rear, he

found Cissy seated in a chair. She was a very good looking woman of forty-seven who didn't at all look her age. Like George, she had begun to grow gray, but her figure was still firm and compact. There was something both warm and sad about her.

"I just got home, and I sat down for a moment. It's been one of those days when you feel it's a tremendous effort even to do so much as to lift your finger. How are you, dear?"

"Oh, all right, Cissy—done in."

"You didn't sleep last night."

"I will tonight."

"I brought home a steak. I'll cook dinner in a minute. Darling, fix me a drink. I need one."

"I can do with one myself."

He hung up his jacket, took off his tie, and his shoes, stuck his feet into his slippers, and yawned. His eyelids were heavy with tiredness. But the day was over. He could fall asleep when he wanted to.

"All right, darling, I'll mix you a martini. Do you want it here?"

"No, we'll sit and sip it in the living room. George, I've felt very blue all day."

"O.K., dear," George said, feeling some quick pangs of sorrow and qualms of guilt.

Going to the kitchen to make the drinks, he silently told himself:

—It's not my fault.

But there was no real assurance in telling himself this truth. Cissy had never been the same since Gerry's death. She had not only changed but she had seemed to begin aging, not caring, not showing too much interest in life. She was like a person going on a schedule.

—Hell, we're both playing the schedule, he told himself, as he made the drinks.

When George brought the drinks into the living room on a tray, Cissy was sitting back, half lounging in an awkward position. She was almost gray now and shreds of her old hair fell across her face, and there were crows' nests under her eyes and little wrinkles around her mouth. It had once been such a pert mouth. He wanted to wince or sob as he bent down and held the tray in front of her.

"You're a darling, a sweet angel, George," she said, taking the drink.

Her words pleased him. They came like a release from the feelings he had had in the kitchen.

Setting the tray on a small table, he took a chair. Perfunctorily, they raised the martini glasses and took sips.

"It's good—but you always did make good martinis, George."

"It's a small accomplishment," he said in a murmur.

Running her hand over her face, she said with disturbing bitterness:

"Today I could have screamed."

"Why? What happened, dear?"

"I had a star baseball player in."

"Who?" George asked with a slight quickening of interest.

She named a well-known star who had retired from active play about two years previously.

"He was damned good."

"I suppose he was. But darling, you know that I know simply nothing, nothing whatsoever about baseball. I know that there are hits, runs and errors, and that some batter is always in the clutch, and some player is always a shade to the left—and oh yes, it's always the top of the seventh. It's never anything but the top half of the seventh."

George smiled indulgently, but with amusement.

Cissy shook her head from side to side, slowly and with an air of assumed bewilderment.

"Tell me about him."

"Well, of course the idea was for us to arrange some lectures for him. The next thing I know, I'll be arranging a lecture tour for a chimpanzee and do you know why?"

Cissy had become histrionic for purposes of emphasis and George was both charmed and sad. This was the old Cissy. God, when she had been young and beautiful, he'd loved her when she was in moods like this one.

"What?"

"The chimpanzee will lecture not to make money— nothing as vulgar as that. God no. He'll tour the country in order to solve the problems of delinquency and, of course, *naturalement*, to fight Communism."

"Fight Communism . . . ?"

"Oh, Smacker—did you know he's called Smacker, darling?"

"Yes, of course."

"You know everything, darling," Cissy said, finishing her drink.

"I wish I did," he said wistfully; he believed that he had almost ceased really learning.

"Darling—I'm so low, finish your drink and make us one more. Then I'll rustle up our dinner. Can you wait?"

"Sure, sure," George said. "There's enough for another drink for us in the martini pitcher."

"You were sweet to think of that."

George finished his drink. It was warming and pepped him up a little.

"You were telling me about Smacker, dear," George said, returning with their glasses filled.

"Yes, Smacker," Cissy said, pronouncing the nickname with a touch of irony. "On Communism, Smacker wouldn't know what it is unless it turned out to be a breakfast food he'd endorsed."

George smiled. Cissy was becoming gay, yes, like the old Cissy and his spirits were lifting. The drink tasted good, and he did make a pretty fair martini, even if he did have to admit it to himself.

"Tell me more, my dear."

"Oh, it isn't really interesting—what could be interesting working in a lecture bureau, selling stupid people and ladies' clubs men like so many hunks of cheese?"

George nodded, going along with her in his thoughts and in the tone of his feelings.

"But your friend and hero, the Smacker, is a hunk of cheese. No, dear, pardon my inaccuracy. Your martinis are a wee bit too strong. They'll make me tight. The Smacker is a hunk of beefsteak. He must eat an entire cow for breakfast."

George burst out laughing, and suddenly noticed how his wife's face was changing, beginning to shine with interest so that she looked younger. Softness of emotion flowed through him as the martini had a few moments previously. He shouldn't be so continually downhearted. Life wasn't over for Cissy and himself and with the love which bound them, they had something to live for. It was corny or mere indulgence in sentimentality when he thought in this fashion that they had each other. He stared at Cissy, holding his drink half in the air.

"Is there something wrong, George?"

Her question surprised him and he was a trifle slow in answering.

"Why no—I was . . ."

"You were looking at me—peculiarly, a bit strangely."

"You're still beautiful, Cissy," he said and then he took a big drink.

"Oh, George, darling, don't flatter me or try to soothe my feelings. I know that I'm not beautiful."

"You are—when we talk like this, your face changes. It lights up and your eyes brighten."

"It's the drinks you're plying me with, George. But you are darling to tell me such things. No woman can be insensible to them, even at my age."

"You look fifteen or twenty years younger than your age, Cissy."

She laughed nervously.

George knew that now she wanted him to make love to her. He didn't really have the desire. He wanted to sit here drinking and talking to Cissy. But if he continued drinking he'd get drunk and pass out, or who knows but what he'd get it into his head to do some damned fool thing.

"Want another?" he asked, downing the rest of his drink.

Cissy didn't answer for a few seconds but she stared at him, her glance softening up with both affection and desire.

"All right, darling."

George acted as though he had not sensed her changing mood. With a feeling of embarrassment he rose, took Cissy's glass from her outstretched hand, and went to the kitchen to mix them both another drink. He took a long time doing this.

His disinclination to respond to Cissy's desire troubled him. He believed that he should and in a sense was obligated to. But there were times when it was distasteful. Tonight he had to. Cissy was in the mood. Good God, there had been many times in the past when he had not been able to have enough of her. It was saddening to think this way and to recognize the truth of his thoughts.

But what was he to do? It made no sense to pretend to yourself that you did not have feelings which you knew you had. He was full of sympathy for her.

"Is everything all right out there, Georgie?"

"Yes, yes."

"It's taking you so long."

"I'm coming, right away, Cissy dear."

George quickly finished mixing the drinks, and then returned to the living room, handing one of them to Cissy and keeping the other for himself. Taking a drink, he told himself that there was no reason why he and Cissy could not be happy, reasonably content and happy, during the remaining years which they had together. There was no necessary reason to give way to passing moods of black despair which sometimes came upon him. No, there were many opportunities in life left for them. And Cissy would be happier and she would respond more to living if he did. They had gone through their great sorrow and tragedy together and they had survived it. They could not live in that sorrow forever. Time was passing fast now, and time was all they had.

But already so much of his life was gone and in that, how much waste had there been? But what was and what wasn't a waste of time and life?

"I was just thinking, dear, wondering if we might take a long vacation and go back to Paris?"

"Why, George, what a darling thought," Cissy exclaimed.

The idea had come to him suddenly and he could not have predicted that he would suggest anything like this. But it was attractive, and if they went to Paris and did nothing but live, they could just about make new persons of themselves.

"It's over twenty years ago, since before the War."

"I know it," Cissy said, moodily; she took a sip from her glass.

"We enjoyed it, remember?"

She shook her head in agreement. Cissy seemed very sad now and this began to trouble him. Possibly he might have been able to have made her less sad.

George did not know what to say. The room was very quiet.

He drank.

IV

They sat in the kitchen eating, George in shirtsleeves and Cissy in the pink bathrobe which he had given her as a present on her last birthday. Glancing at the clock, he noticed that it was already ten o'clock. The evening was pretty much gone.

"You like it?"

"Yes—much," he said with double meaning.

She playfully reached across the kitchen table and slapped his hand.

"I meant the steak."

"So did I."

"Don't call me a steak," she said, teasingly.

The scene and their mood brought back something of the feeling of their earlier years. Often after being in bed together, they would eat like this in the kitchen. Sometimes they had eaten at two, three or four A.M. He had always remembered such times with emotion and regret. But now why should he have regrets or feel sadness? He had not, had he, in the past in times and moments quite the same as this one? Why should he now?

"You didn't think I had stopped and bought you a steak as good as this one, did you?"

"No, I didn't. It's damned tender."

"A beefsteak eating male," Cissy said, her eyes twinkling with merriment.

George ate, relishing his steak and the salad which Cissy had prepared. He did feel content, fulfilled but perhaps, also, a little empty. The few drinks tonight had made the difference. They had loosened him up. And Cissy, yes, he still loved her. Hell, they had plenty of basis for living and for living on together.

"George, do you really want to go to Paris?"

He hesitated for a few seconds before he answered: "Yes."

"Do you mean it?"

"Yes, of course I do," he said, continuing to eat, but he was doubtful that he did.

The change, the effort, all of the small details which would have to be attended to before going abroad—all this loomed large in his mind.

"You didn't quite sound as though you meant it, George. t seems like one of those ideas you sometimes get, one of your brain storms after you've taken a few drinks."

"I wasn't drunk, Cissy."

"I know that—you don't get drunk."

George looked. He had finished his plate.

"Do you want more, George? There's plenty."

"No, I had enough. I had a big piece."

"When a man makes love, he gets quite hungry," Cissy said.

George wished she had not said this. It gave such a tone of familiarity and even casualness to the evening. And yet what should he expect? They were not bride and groom any more.

"Cissy, it will do us a lot of good to go away—to go back to Paris."

"I'd love it, darling—if you want to go."

"Yes, I do. It's a way of getting out of a rut."

"George, do you feel you are in a rut?"

"Routine, that's a better word. We've been doing much the same thing, going to Maine every summer. We can afford it. God, how much have I read and heard about Paris in these last twenty or so years since we were there."

"George, it's more than twenty."

Neither of them spoke for a moment, and a sense of embarrassment crept between them. Cissy's remark had reminded them of Geraldine. They believed that it had been while they were in Paris that Cissy had become pregnant.

"Yes, it has," George said, moodily.

Would going to Paris seem like a grotesque and ghastly anticlimax?

"I loved Paris," Cissy said, wistfully.

"I'd like to sit in that cafe on the Left Bank—the Deux Magots, that's it."

"Had you almost forgotten the name of it, George?"

"No—we've just published a novel in which it's mentioned ten or fifteen times."

"I remember how we went there for breakfast."

"We'll do it again."

"When can we go, George?"

"The spring. Can you get away then?"

"If I couldn't, I'd quit."

"I can get away—we ought to spend three months in Europe."

"Paris in the spring," Cissy said with joy and feeling.

Bill's eyes became dreamy. He was growing happy with expectations. And Cissy was happy. She had just sounded as she had used to when she had been his young bride. He should have thought of doing this sooner.

"I'll have to get an entire new wardrobe," Cissy said enthusiastically.

"We'll fly—you aren't afraid, are you, Cissy?"

"No, I'll love it—and that will give us more time in Europe."

"Remember Notre Dame—how much I liked it, the stained glass and the sight of it with the flying buttresses when you stand at that quai and look at it."

"Yes, and I was thinking, now, that we'll go to the Louvre and see those Chardins that I loved."

"We'll do a hell of a lot. With three months, we could rent a car and drive around France."

"Oh, let's," Cissy said.

Her enthusiasm seemed to take years off of her life. She looked as she had used to during all those first years of their marriage, and she had come alive with energy. Her gestures, too, brought back his old memories. And this was lifting the gloom which had hung upon him like an oppressive but inevitable spiritual burden.

Rising, Cissy said:

"I'll make some coffee."

Lighting a cigarette, George leaned back in his chair. He was more deeply contented than he had been in a longer period than he could remember.

V

"Paris was different years ago when we were here."

"Yes, but I don't care. I love it," Cissy said. "It's the most beautiful city in the world."

They sat on the terrace of the Deux Magots, facing the Boulevard St. Germain. It was about eleven o'clock on a sunny spring morning. The cafe was more than half empty, but near them was a group of young Americans, two girls in dungarees and two young men, one of them wearing a full beard. There was much traffic on the street and many people passed along.

"What was it Chekhov wrote about Paris in one of his letters?" Cissy asked. "Paris is full of little Frenchmen who give you the impression that they are at home in the streets?"

"It was something like that," George answered meditatively as he continued to gaze off idly at the passing street scene.

It was not sufficient to say or to think that Paris was not the same as it once was or had seemed to be. Neither were you yourself.

"You can't tell me, dear, that you don't like Paris?"

"Oh no—to the contrary, Cissy, I like it better."

"But not as enthusiastically."

"That's true—I like it more quietly. It gives me or I find here a feeling of inner quiet."

Perhaps he could best describe his feeling about Paris as one of resignation to aging and fading beauty. He turned to glance tenderly at Cissy. She was aging, and she, too, had been beautiful to him, once. Cissy returned his glance with a smile which was wan but affectionate.

"Let's stay two or three more days before we drive to the Loire Valley, dear?"

"Oh, George, I was hoping that you'd say something like that—I want to stay a few days longer before we set out."

"D'accord."

"I suppose everyone misses many things in life which no one ought to miss seeing and experiencing," Cissy remarked, reflectively.

"Yes, they do."

"Well, at least, we haven't missed Paris. Paris in the springtime. That phrase has always meant much to me. And today is a divine day, darling."

George nodded but did not speak. His mood remained quiet, full of a pleasing sadness. This, he thought or guessed, was a reflection of a sadness or melancholy of spirit which had settled down as an abiding but bearable part of his nature. When he had been a young man, whatever had stirred him as an object of beauty had impelled him to want to look beyond and beyond. But now, there was little looking beyond. Had he spent part of his youth in Paris, he would have been stimulated by Paris to look beyond. Now he saw Paris as beautiful by reflection. Paris induced you to want to look and think backward, backward beyond. One of the most obvious facts in the life of many men, perhaps all men, was that they looked forward so long as they had something to look forward to, and then, when they had nothing really to look forward to, they looked backward. *C'est la vie.*

"Where will we eat tonight?" George asked.

"Let's be adventurous. Let's walk out of our hotel and discover a restaurant—a wonderful restaurant."

"All right. I wish I didn't know that restaurant on the Ile Saint Louis. It doesn't classify as a discovery."

"I love it—but it isn't a discovery. It wouldn't be Hoyle to go there."

"It's not a dangerous adventure to go out intent upon discovering a good restaurant in Paris."

"I know—but it's fun. When we were young, we always used to do that whenever we could. We don't do the things we did when we were young, George."

"Let's go over to Montmarte and look for a restaurant there."

"Oh, that would be wonderful—and afterwards we'll go up on the hill to Sacré Coeur."

They sat. George was content. They both looked at the casual and passing street panorama.

"Oh, I just love Paris—the streets of Paris."

"Yes," George said.

He knew they were happy and would be happier than they had been during these recent years. There was still a beyond. It was too soon for him to be looking backward.

"Cissy."

"What, dear?"

"I was thinking of you—I still love you as much as ever."

"George, you're a darling."

WAR WIDOW

In the evening Elizabeth liked to sit looking at the trees and the sky while twilight seeped away. In her sadness she would feel a deep and incurable loneliness. Sky and trees but especially the sky, which seemed so much more vast here in the country than in New York City were symbols of permanence, but even in this permanence there was loneliness. And loneliness was aloneness, a word she liked and which possessed special emotional connotations for her.

There were times when she hoped, but mostly she did not hope. She knew that many men survived in war and that they might return, well, undamaged, able to pick up their lives and to re-kindle their loves and restore their marriages. But she had no faith, no conviction that this could happen in the case of George and herself, even though she was unable to find reasons or to explain and clarify to herself why her faith had seeped away. It had disappeared as did the light each day while she sat and watched the silent change into night and darkness. She sometimes thought that people enjoyed sitting in front of the small wooden house in the country because the fading of the twilight suggested to her that her faith had faded like the end of a day, slowly, and at every moment imperceptibly, but yet with an inevitability like that which turned day into night.

These changes, this succession of day and night, had been happening all during the years of her life with George; these changes had always been happening. Always consisted of all of the time that day had been evolving softly into night, and night in turn slipping away into day. And always in the future would be marked by this same and ever-recurring change. There was no always for her, and there had not been an always for her love. A madman living in Germany had brought an end to it. But nonetheless that love had been good in its season and she had been happy. Possibly it would be more precise to say that she had been content, very content, so content to say that she had not desired or envisaged any change. Happiness was different from contentment, and most frequently she believed that happiness was merely an illusion.

How monotonous and yet appealing was the chirping of the crickets. There was joy in this chirping. It seemed as if there was a world in the grass, in the trees, and in the woods behind the house, a world that was breathlessly alive and singing over and over again its one note of joy. But to her this only spoke of sadness. Crickets could sing their note of joy and die. Human beings could think and hope for what was not and would never be. They sang, they laughed, and they loved against the backdrop of death. But it was not the fear of death which was most awful, at least not to her. She was not afraid of death. What was most awful was longing. To long for something intangible, to long for more love than human flesh and the human spirit was capable of giving, to long for more happiness than anyone was able to find . . . this was the deepest of the reasons for sadness and melancholy. And to retain the habit of longing after you had come to know in yourself that there was not and never would be any appeasement of it, this defined the melancholy, the sadness in her own spirit.

Perhaps it was tiredness, a weariness with life which had come upon her, but this was not merely a condition of recent vintage: she had begun to feel this way before George had gone into the army. Slowly, like seconds ticking away heard but not heeded or thought about, her faith in life had ebbed out of her. It seemed to her that this had begun to happen to her after the coming of their first and only child with so much expectation, but also they had both hoped for a boy, not a girl. And even though it seemed unreasonable and unscientific for her to think that she had let George down, had failed because she had given him a baby girl instead of a boy, she had nevertheless begun to believe this of herself. Now and then, she had told herself that it was her fault, and there had been times when she had snapped at George and quarrelled with him because she had been condemning herself. She regretted this, but now there was no longer any great capacity for sorrow and remorse in her nature. Once there had been, she told herself with a sigh.

The sweetness of the country, especially at this quietly dramatic twilight hour, charmed her and was also a source of great calm. Only music could give her as rich a sense of calm, for she was not a serene person, or at least, she had not been one. Was she changing? She was forty now, and no longer a girl. Once a thought such as this would have stricken her with horror, but now, looking at the sky with its fields of blue, its growing sense of depth, she was not horrified. George might die. She might never see him again. If George could face death with courage, couldn't she do likewise? But she did not want to think of George in the fighting. He had landed in France with the invasion last month, and she had received one short letter from him. He spoke of missing her and Georgette, and his letter had been very affectionate. Reading it she had wept. But, the war, even with all of its horror and danger, exhilarated him. He had not written this, but nevertheless, it had been there in his words, between the lines of his letter, and she knew positively that she was not imagining this.

Home and family, work and comfort had proven insufficient for George, she could understand and sympathize with him. It must have grown dull for him. When he had been young and they had first gone together, George had still dreamed of writing; he had been one of how many hundreds, how many thousands of young men of more than one generation who had dreamed of writing the Great American Novel. Dreams! She had had her own dreams too. She had wanted to dance. Why had neither of them gone on and worked to fulfill their artistic dreams and ambitions? Once married, they had gradually abandoned them, and had even come to stop talking of all that they had aspired to achieve in youth. For some years now, any allusion to George's forsaken literary ambitions used to touch off sensitive points in him, and also he had become bitterly critical of most living writers, especially the Americans.

A few tears collected in her eyes. She continued to gaze
off, thinking of the vast sky. It was a sky of glory beyond
the touch of men. They dreamed of the glory in the sky as
though if they lived there, in another universe, they could
be happier. They wanted to make love under that sky. And
it was not as far away as some of the dreams of men.
Thinking of this she could cry; she was crying even though
she had learned how futile tears could be.

Her maid, Miranda, was putting Georgette to bed now.
In a moment, she would have to go inside and kiss her
daughter good night, send the little girl to sleep with a feeling of love and security which she, herself, had never
known in her own girlhood.

Her own girlhood! She wanted Georgette to have a happier childhood than she had had, but now, with the child
only seven, her father was gone off to war, and he might
not come back.

Georgette could grow up a fatherless child, just as she
had. How patterns of life were repeated. Her own father
had not left for war; he would not have been brave enough,
man enough to do that. But he had left in order to escape
responsibility. And what troubled her was the fear that possibly a parallel desire to escape responsibility had been
George's true motivation.

She could remember how she desperately had wanted a
father, even though she had never breathed a word of it to
her mother. The bewilderments of those days when she
had been seven, eight, nine and ten, had affected her entire
life. Yes, she had wanted a father almost desperately, and
because she had, she would often even think or convince
herself that she hated all men. This had probably caused
the shyness which was still such a definitely formed trait of
her character. She would not have married George had he
not been so gentle in those days when they had first known
one another and had begun to go out together. He had
seemed to understand her, and he had been shy himself.

Those had been years of happiness. Never again would
she know such happiness. It had been like living on a peak
and then slowly, gradually descending until you were down
on a level ground and you gazed up at the peak and it was
no longer there; it had vanished into air, into nothingness.
Those years! George had used to tell her how beautiful she
was, and though too shy truly to believe him, she had used

love these words and she would sometimes tell George
at for him she wanted to be beautiful. She and George
d been happy once: they must have been. But how much
mained of joys and happiness? There was left a dull ache
her, a regret for what was gone, and a suspicion that
ere had always been something wrong in their marriage.
oking back now on all of those years, she thought that
obably her life as well as George's had been misdirected.
It was strange for her to think this now. However, the
ought had come to her like one of those insights or in-
ition which come to one, as if by accident and the truth
which one at first resists. But how could it be true to
ink that she and George had led a misdirected life? They
d seemed so well mated. From that first excited and
xual period when they were first married, they had gone
o a period of deep contentment. So it had seemed. And
s once again, they had been happy. But even in their best
oments, she could recall her occasional hidden doubts,
though vague, and scarcely articulated to herself at the
ne, but they had, nevertheless, been real doubts. One al-
ays knew more than one truly knew, and there were such
wer surprises in life than was usually believed. Even that
ght when George had unexpectedly told her that he be-
ved it to be his duty to enlist, she had not been surprised.
le moment he had told her, she had become instantly
vare that she had been expecting him to do precisely this.
She heard Miranda calling her, and went inside the small
ouse. Georgette, a golden-haired, shy and beautiful little
rl with blue eyes, was already in bed. The mere sight of
e child, who looked so transparently innocent, touched
ıd saddened the mother. There was a catch in her throat,
ıd she experienced a quick upsurge of guilt.

"Mommy."

"Yes, my darling."

"When are we going to hear from my Daddy?"

"Any day now, my angel."

"But you keep telling me that, Mommy. Any day. Mom-
y, what day is any day?"

How easily she could have cried, but she knew that she
ould not. She would confine her pain to her heart and
ep it imprisoned there.

"I know, honey—but Daddy can't write every day. I
ow he writes us as often as he is able to."

"When is my Daddy coming to us?"

"When the war is over."

"Why can't the war be over quick in a hurry?"

"Maybe it will be now—soon."

"Soon, any day. How soon is any day? Mommy you can't answer that question."

The girl's face broke, and for a fraction of a second, she stared at her mother hurt, deeply wounded, before she sobbed.

She felt a wrench, a deep feeling of sorrow and of pity at the sight of her child in the throes of such suffering.

Georgette wailed and through her tears, she said in a wounded voice.

"I want my Daddy to come home."

Sitting at the side of the bed, she took the little girl in her arms and held her tightly.

"Daddy will come."

She could have broken into tears herself, and she felt as though she, also, was responsible for the bewildered and confusing sorrow and sense of loss of her little girl.

"Don't cry my darling and tomorrow we'll. . . ."

"But I want my Daddy home."

"Yes, I know and as soon as the war is over, he'll come back."

"But maybe he'll be killed."

Georgette now shook with sobs. The mother held her more firmly and stroked her hair, very softly.

If George were to be killed! Oh, the suffering of this innocent child! It could rip her heart out.

"Mommy," Georgette said in a low voice as her hysterical tears began to subside.

"Mommy does Daddy love you?"

The question cut like sharp edged glass, but she did not show her feelings to Georgette, except possibly by a slight delay or hesitation in responding to this terrible question.

"Of course he loves me. And he loves you."

Silent, the child looked at her mother with hurt and unbelieving eyes.

She continued to hold Georgette tightly to her for some moments. Then she kissed the girl fondly.

"Good night, my sweetest. Sweet dreams."

"Good night, Mommy."

She left the bedroom, feeling a heaviness of heart.

II

"Are you chilly, Miranda?"

"Oh, sorts, Miz Stone."

"Maybe we might have a fire in the fireplace."

"I fix it, Miz Stone."

George had used to sit silently for hours looking at the burning logs. Sometimes, they both had sat here in this room each of them musing and staring in fascination at the fire, listening to its cracklings and other noises, watching the licking, lapping flames.

What had he thought?

There had been times when she had been dull, as though he had wanted neither to think nor feel. She would occasionally glance over at him and notice the melancholy, the sadness on his face, and she would wonder if she were responsible for it?

One night, sitting here by the fire, she had asked him if anything were the matter?

—Why—no—nothing at all. Why do you ask, my dear?

She could remember him saying that, and also she could clearly recall an alarmed expression coming into his eyes.

—We hardly speak to each other some nights.

—I come home from the office tired—it's a rat race, my dear, and at night, I'm done in.

—George, if you are unhappy, quit your job at the advertising agency. We can live out here all year around—we'll have enough to keep us for two or three years. You can write then.

He hadn't answered her immediately. But hadn't there been fright on his face?

—We couldn't do that.

—George, remember before we were married? You used to say that if a man worked at anything he hated, he was throwing away his life.

Perhaps she shouldn't have said that to him. It was tactless, and it had hurt him.

—I'm not unhappy, he had said but with no conviction in his voice.

—You seem unhappy and frustrated, George. We could live more simply.

I'm not at all unhappy—no more unhappy than most people. Who can be happy in this world?

—We were, George, once.

—We were young then. We're as reasonably happy as anyone can expect—and we're getting as much security as you can hope to get in this insecure world.

—But George, I don't care about security unless you're happy.

They had talked this way several times. Then, she had been more troubled than clear. Still she had known that something was wrong, and now she could understand what it had been. They had already begun to drift apart.

George, also, had joked about marriage. She hadn't minded it then, and sometimes she had laughed at his quips.

At parties, they had both bantered about marriage. Thinking of this now in retrospect, could she believe that there was nothing behind those jokes of this banter?

She looked into the warming noisy fire. The logs had caught on and the flames were roaring.

George had been so handsome when he was young. He had been handsome to her. And handsome, too, in his soldier's uniform, with his face tanned and lean, and his temples merely touched with grey. And they had loved so intensely, so furiously. Those days had alternately been so idyllic and fevered, and every moment of waking life had been like a dream. And then, slowly, gradually the dream had receded the way the sun might, the way that a day might end, first gorgeousness, then in melancholy but colorful grayness and finally in darkness.

But wasn't this the way of life, the order of life, the order of human emotions? Didn't love burn out as those logs now were, leaving only ashes?

George had gone to work for her, and in order to build their home. He had said that once this were done, he would write.

—Nest egg.

He'd often used that phrase. She had disliked it. Maybe she shouldn't have allowed him to sacrifice his literary aspirations. She should have insisted. But what good would it have been? Had he wanted to write deep down in his heart, he would have done so. And she had urged him to even to the point where he had become annoyed.

But then, no one was to blame. And if he did return, she just knew that their life would never be the same.

Georgette had almost broken her heart tonight.

—Does Daddy love you, Mommy?

Oh God! Children weren't fooled. In her child's way
eorgette knew.

She looked again into the fire, hoping that she would not
ry. She wanted to cry her heart out, just as she had the
ght after his enlistment. But she did not believe that she
uld weep again.

—If he should die?

No, she assured herself, she would not weep again, even
he were to be killed.

III

The days passed slowly and in dull sadness for Elizabeth
one. June became July. Each day brought more news of
e fighting, and she read of the invasion of Normandy and
battle of France trying to visualize the scenes of
ttle in her own mind. She would imagine George in a fox
le, or leading his men through small shattered French
llages, lined with broken walls. Seven years ago that sum-
er, she and George had gone through France. After land-
g at Cherbourg, they had ridden through Normandy on
e boat train. She remembered how green it had been, soft
d green, lovely flowing countryside that had been farmed
r centuries. And now, George was fighting there in war.
e thought of this often.

If he lived and reached Paris, would he think of her?
hey had been very happy then, happier than on their first
neymoon. Breakfast of *café* and *Croissants* in the morn-
g, and then they went out to wander to look, and see, just
ke any other tourists. The little streets, the old buildings
narrow streets that were more like alleys, the harmony
at they saw everywhere, *cafés* crowded with little French-
en, the Louvre, the quaint and inexpensive restaurants
ey had found. She could remember all these. And on
me days, they would buy bread, cheese and a bottle of
rdinary red wine, and she had always enjoyed such
nches.

In Paris, George had frequently spoken of books and
riting. She had believed that he would try to write a novel
hen they returned to America. Yes, he had been relaxed

and very happy in Paris. Never had she seen him so aler
and curious, noticing and observing so much. He had ex
panded in a sense of freedom which he had been unable t
feel in America since the days before their marriage.

—George, you seem like a true Frenchman, she ha
used to tell him, and he had always accepted this as a com
pliment.

And on that day when Paris had fallen to the German
George had felt and acted as if it were the end of the world
France had so appealed to him that he had wanted to b
one of her liberators. This had given him one of his motiva
tions for enlisting. But dwelling on George's love of Franc
and on the summer they had spent there, she believed tha
there was a connection between this and George's need fo
freedom. To him, France and Paris must have been a sym
bol of the freedom he had come to desire so much, a free
dom of escape.

She wondered sometimes if George had gone with othe
girls or women, and believed that he must have had a fe
casual affairs. These, she did not mind. In a vague way, sh
herself had hoped for a change, for something differen
from George. Separation, and the thought of his possibl
death had focussed a clearer light upon what had been hap
pening within herself, and it also gave her an ability t
imagine more plausibly what his own thoughts and feeling
had been. She thought of all this while the days of lif
rolled away from her in slow procession.

She played with Georgette, went to the market, took a
occasional drive and now and then visited with or wa
visited by a neighbor. Occasionally friends from New Yor
visited her for a week end. Frequently she was bored, an
there was a quiet sadness in her, persisting from day to da
Often she fed and re-stimulated this sadness with music.

Georgette played and appeared to be an untroubled,
happy, growing child. She did not again ask questions abou
her father, but every day around one o'clock, when th
mailman was expected, Georgette would become notice
ably nervous. When the mailman was late, as frequentl
happened, Georgette's nervousness increased. She clun
close to the house, and as soon as she heard the sound
an approaching automobile, she bounded out to the ma
box. On many days, Elizabeth watched this performance
and she could always tell if there were a letter from he

husband by Georgette's demeanor and the child's actions. Twice letters arrived, and on each occasion, Georgette rushed back in uncontrolled and pure joy. On other days, Georgette would come slowly away from the mail box. This scene always wounded Elizabeth. In losing these years with her father, Georgette was being robbed of precious experiences which could never be made up. The little girl couldn't understand the need for her father's absence. This was all painful, and almost daily, she was impressed with this: the scene at the mail box would cut her and she would flinch for a moment.

George might well become a hero. She was inclined to believe that he would because he was a brave man: in addition, she suspected that in having gone off to war, he was even courting death. There were times when this situation seemed close to unbearable for her. What then must it mean for Georgette? Of course, a child had great resiliency and tragedy and sorrow could not hang as constantly in a child's mind as it sometimes did in the case of an adult. A child forgot quickly, but in forgetting the child sorted away sorrows that would return in pain and agony years later. This, she feared for Georgette. Years from now, perhaps after both George and she were dead, these would come back to trouble Georgette like ghosts. And not only Georgette but also many children of her daughter's generation would undergo this same experience of long delayed tragedy.

And if George did come back, would it be the same? Would they love one another again as they once had? If not, would they, for Georgette's sake, establish a *Modus Viviendi*, living security to their daughter? George would come back changed, a different person. The estrangement that had grown between them in the last years before his enlistment could only be deepened. Now, she was fully conscious of this. Must he not be also? Must he not think often of this, and of his future? In commercial success he had found only a sense of inner defeat. She and the home she had given him had been insufficient to compensate for his own sense of failure.

His letters all suggested to her that her estimation was correct. The expressions of love, the descriptions of his loneliness sounded formal, written not because of what he felt but rather because he believed that he should tell her that he loved her, that he missed her, and that he was lonely. She could read all this between the lines of his letters.

And what was she going to do? What did she want to do with the remainder of her life? There was Georgette and she must do the best she could to be a mother, and also a father, to her little girl. Of this, she did not and would not complain. But would this suffice for her? She was not too old. Could she not again be a passionate woman? Now, passion, desire appeared to have frozen in her. Before coming here in the country for the summer, men had shown an interest in her. George had not been gone long before her telephone had started to ring. Even some of George's best friends had cast interested, vagrant eyes upon her. George's boss, Tom Ambercrombie, had invited her to dinner, presumably as George's friend and because she might be lonesome. But in the restaurant, he had kept rubbing his knees and the calves of his legs against her. And all during dinner, he had looked at her with lecherous eyes. And others, also. Sometimes there had been unpleasant situations. Friends of George and husbands of her friends had tried to paw her. When all other reasons for marriage had become meaningless or irrelevant, the protection from annoyance and pawing still remained as a valid and sound reason for remaining married. But her own desires had grown cold.

She believed, also, that were it not for the war and George's enlistment, it was more than likely that she and George would be spending the remainder of their lives together, and adjusting to the fact that their love had gone to sleep. And they still might, if George did come back.

At times these thoughts troubled her. She feared that since she had kept dwelling upon the possibility of George's death, she must wish for it. Undoubtedly, that was how Freudians would interpret in a case like hers. But then, she had no concern with what the Freudian interpretation would be, and she was convinced that she did not wish George's death. Perhaps the cruelest event that could happen in Georgette's young life would be the death of her father.

One evening, after Georgette and Miranda were both asleep, she sat listening to records, but her mind drifted. The war, she speculated, quiet had broken up her home. Except for it, she and George would have gone on together at least not unhappy even though happiness had fled their marriage. They would have raised Georgette in security, and that should have been both an achievement and a fulfillment of a duty or an obligation. Perhaps, there had been times during the final pre-war years when they had been dull or bored, but dullness and boredom must truly be numbered among the burdens of life. It had all been bearable. They both loved their daughter: definitely, George was fond of Georgette. He had always been kind to herself, and he had doted on Georgette, spoiled her. That was why his enlistment and sudden departure for War had been so cruelly bewildering for the little girl. But then, she could understand why he had seen in the War, a reason, a cause that would justify his leaving. He was fighting, risking his life in the defense of Georgette's future.

But the more that she thought on these questions, the less clear she was in all that was involved. In a more concrete and painful sense, she had come to a fresh awareness of how all people were locked up inside their own skin. And inside of everyone, there was such complexity, so much confusion, so many purposes in conflict with one another. Look at how contradictory George was, and how his purpose was so masked. He had told what he thought and meant only in an oblique way. But living with him, coming to know him so intimately, she had arrived at an understanding for him. He almost never said what he meant, but found reasons for what he wished to do, reasons for explaining and defending himself. Knowing George required the faculty of seeing shadows, reflections and images in mirrors. And was George singular, different from others? Wasn't an ability to understand people a faculty for seeing meaning in mirrors?

Her life was boring, and yet there was a kind of peace in boredom and dullness. She could lose herself in the performance of small chores. And now she felt less keenly and quickly than she once had. To feel too keenly could sometimes destroy a person, tear one's soul apart. If she broke away from her dull and settled routine, what would happen to her? And by consequence, to Georgette. She did not think that she could go through another love affair.

Before George there had been an intense affair with Dave Waddell, an actor. How humiliated she had felt. Dave was no good and had never been any good. Dave handsome with his weak mouth, his soft pretty face, his

endless, dream-like lies, his cheap romanticism! How
could she have loved him, given herself to him so com
pletely? Even today, merely to remember her affair with
Dave chilled her. He had been incapable of thinking o
anyone but himself. He had not even been a boy; he had
been a baby. His pouts, his tantrums, his silly lies had
wearied her: by force of contrast, George had seemed to
her manly and honest.

She decided that she must face the fact that she had been
unfortunate in the men she had loved, and that the reason
—or at least part of the reason—must lie in her. This
thought caused her great apprehension for Georgette. She
wished for her little girl to have a very happy life. But what
did that mean. What was a happy life for a woman, espe
cially in this age? Hadn't she seen and known many career
women? How many of them were satisfied, happy?

It was difficult for her to envisage the future, either for
herself or even more so, for Georgette. Perhaps every gen
eration ended in the same kind of a dilemma. Perhaps, the
causes of emotional malaise were deeper than the characte
of these times, but even so, the War was disrupting so
many lives, bringing into the world so much pain and death
wrenching security away from people and forecasting only
danger as great or greater for the future.

No, she didn't know what to think, and she did not want
to take any more risks, to expose herself anew in love.

Actually, she was not unhappy. Rather, she would de
scribe her state as one of sadness, quiet sadness. She en
joyed thinking of a future, continuing much as her presen
with Georgette growing up, and with herself growing old
perhaps in this same quiet and almost easeful sadness.

Twice now she had given herself, fully in love, to Dave
Waddell and to George, a third time did not seem possible

IV

Thus, the summer passed. Then they returned to New
York, and Georgette was back in school. Letters came
from George. Her thoughts about his possible death be
came less frequent. She began to think that he would re
turn, but she was not certain that he would be coming back

o her and to Georgette. The War became an accepted fact
f life. George being away and fighting was likewise an ac-
epted and assimilated fact. At times, it seemed as though
e had always been away. The years before the War sunk
way and she thought of them as one does about experi-
nces which had happened a long time ago.

Once back in the city, she did U.S.O. work, answering a
elephone: also she saw more friends. But no matter what-
ver she did, a core of sadness remained like something
ard and irremovable in the center of her being. She felt
ot only incomplete, but incapable of ever again being
omplete. Gradually, she began to believe that she was
aiting for George, and that she did love him. Her old feel-
gs for him were growing fresh and becoming renewed.
er letters to him became more warm and spontaneous.

One evening, after she had kissed Georgette good night,
d as she sat listening to a Bach record, she wept. Her
ody shook with tears as she lay face downward on her
ed, the bed in which she and George had slept so many
ights, the bed in which Georgette had been conceived.

She wanted him back. She wanted him back under any
onditions. And when he did return, she would be more
oving, more giving. She knew that she would not lose him.
ll of her capacity for love, for giving would go out to him.
he was alone and this was miserable, almost unbearable.
he and Georgette were two females alone and they needed
man, their man.

Perhaps in response to the tone of her letters, George be-
an to write differently, with more feeling, with something
f the old feeling and warmth of his first letters to her and
f their first days together. But when would the War end?
er life became focused on that one far-off, and unpre-
icted event—the end of the War which would permit her
usband to return.

And now, also, she began to interpret George's enlistment differently. He had gone to protect her and Georgette,
o fight for their future. He was a hero. When Georgette
rew up, she would have the most loving pride for her
ather. These crucial years when the child was separated
rom him would then take on different meaning. Georgette
ould understand.

The sense of happiness which she had foresworn came
ack into her, but as a hope. After these long, tiring and

dreadful years of war, there would be new joy, and a richer contentment. Elizabeth looked younger, more gay. A revived and sustaining faith carried her on through commonplace days in which there was so much repetition, even to the repetition of dreams of hope. And Hitler was losing. The end must come soon.

And then one day, not long after the Battle of the Bulge, she received a dreaded telegram from the War Department.

George had been killed in action.

She sat alone and numb. She had been betrayed and in the deepest sense of that word, betrayed. She and her daughter had been robbed. Never before had death intimately entered her private world of feeling. Now it had coldly, officially. It had come in the form of a few words cast on a piece of yellow paper.

She sat, still numbed, asking herself—Why? Why? Why? Why? Why must it be she and Georgette? Why had it to be George. He was a hero. But how much must those who remained behind pay as the price of heroism?

This was an End. Now, she would grow old, not in bitterness, but with a sadness and feeling of loss that could never be fully appeased. Part of herself, years of her life, had died when a German shell or a bullet had smashed all the life out of George. On that field of snow in Belgium two lives had died, not one.

She would go on. She would be brave. She would hold herself together. She would be father and mother to Georgette. But two lives, not one had died far away from New York in cold and misery. When George had grown stiff in the snow, far away, the best years of her own life had frozen, too.

Late that same afternoon, Georgette was brought home from school. How beautiful and how innocent she looked, rushing to her mother and kissing her.

"Mommy, is there a letter from Daddy?"

Elizabeth was silent, and frightened. The child sensed that there was bad news.

"Mommy, tell me."

Elizabeth was trying to find the softest words with which to tell the news to Georgette.

"My Daddy's been killed," Georgette yelled.

The child stood, numb for a moment. Then, her face

broke and lost its form. Tears came. She screamed. Eliza-beth held the child tightly against her.

"Don't cry, my sweetest. My angel."

After about ten minutes. Georgette quieted down. With her face streaked by tears, she looked gravely at her mother.

"He is dead, isn't he?"

"Yes. He died for you and for me. He died for all of the little children like you. He died to make you free and hap-py. He died for this beautiful country which is yours and mine."

"But Mommy, I was Happy. Now I'm not."

"We must be brave women now, my sweetest."

"I don't want to be brave. I want my Daddy."

"Other children have lost their fathers, too, my dear."

"I want my Daddy back."

"I know, my darling."

"No. Mummy, you don't know."

Elizabeth went again and embraced her child, but Georgette broke away from her mother and ran to her own room.

Elizabeth sat, too hurt to think. It would take much time, patience and love to nurse the little girl through the shock of this loss. For the moment, she must let the child be alone in her room. She sat, wanting to think, wanting to remember George, but again she was numb. She heard Georgette crying. Going quietly to the door of the girl's room, she saw Georgette on the floor, crying and staring at a picture of her father, which had been taken before he had gone off to War.

Elizabeth went into the child's room and sat with the girl on the floor, looking at the photograph. It grew dark outside.

"Come, I must give you your dinner, Sweetest."

"I don't want dinner."

"I know—darling, but you must eat. Your Daddy would have wanted you to eat and to grow strong. He was very proud of you and he loved you."

The child stood up and looked at her mother with terrify-ing gravity.

"All right, Mommy. Mommy. . . ."

"Yes, Sweetheart."

"Mommy, now you and me, we have to be as brave as Daddy."

"We must, my darling."

"We will, won't we. We will always be as brave as my Daddy was."

Elizabeth now feared that she would break. She gazed off. Her lips trembled.

Georgette took her hand, squeezed it.

"Mommy, let me help you fix my dinner."

They walked to the kitchen. Elizabeth felt empty, and with each step towards the rear of the apartment, she was reminded of George. Now every object in the apartment housed ghosts of memory.

"We'll pretend that Daddy couldn't come home tonight. He is having a dinner for business with Mr. Abercrombie, Mommy." Georgette said bravely, but with a wounded voice, as mother and daughter entered the kitchen to prepare their lonely dinner. Georgette set the dining room table while Elizabeth cooked. Then staring at her mother, Georgette said:

"Mommy, when I grow up, do you know what I'm going to do?"

"What, my darling?"

"Mommy, I'm going to kill Hitler."

TICKLE 'EM IN THE RIBS

Stanton Wadsworth was driving out of Cleveland in a depressed mood. His hair was now gray and he was pushing fifty. There were many times when it was uncomfortable to dwell upon the fact that most of his life was over, and to admit to himself that he had done so few of the things that he had wanted to. Out of the suburbs and hitting fifty along the concrete road, his mood became wistful. The sky was heavy, a dull day, one to lower a man's spirits. He had delivered a lecture on the novels of Theodore Dreiser. It had been well received and in his pocket was the two hundred dollar honorarium, a sum of money not to be sneezed at by a professor of English. But he had given this lecture God knows how many times. Dreiser had lived and still was; he had not lived—not sufficiently. For years, he had been locked up in university life. Those ambitions to write, to be a great writer were long since put away. And to be a lover.

His hands on the wheel, his eyes on the road before him, Stanton grew troubled because of this thought. He had been afraid to love much. He had been faithful to Mary. But not in his mind.

That poem of Ernest Dowson. In the classroom, he had more than once dismissed it as adolescent. But this had been insincere. These last two or three years, he had been tormented with sexual desires and he was becoming fearful that his time was short. He would be too old. Coeds sat in his class and he acted calm, poised, respectable. But his thoughts would raise the blood pressure of any wowser or Methodist preacher.

And he was afraid, afraid of Mary, of his position at the

University, of society. This was due to his Puritan upbring-
ing. But then, this was part of him. And still, just once, just
once to have a girl of nineteen, twenty, twenty-one, fresh
and in the bloom of youth, a rosebud to be plucked.

Stanton drove on at fifty miles an hour, past fields a dark
green under the towering sky. He was more depressed than
the depressive sky and the depressed day. Love, adventure,
romance, he had forever missed them.

Ahead, Stanton saw a hitchhiker. Should he stop? Sometimes a motorist was robbed or murdered by a hitchhiker.
But this needn't happen. Approaching the hitchhiker, who
stood waving his hand and pointing his thumb ahead, Stanton noticed that he was thin, medium-sized and neatly
dressed. And he had set down a suitcase at his side.

Stanton halted a few yards ahead of the hitchhiker, who
immediately picked up his suitcase and hurried to the automobile.

"Are you going far?" Stanton asked the young fellow as
the latter came up to him.

"Columbus. I'm going to try my luck there."

"That's where I'm going," Stanton said.

"I'm sittin' in luck then, ain't I?" the young fellow said.

"Yes. I can take you there; get in."

"You live in Columbus, Mister?" the young fellow asked,
getting in the automobile beside Stanton in the front seat.

"Yes, I do."

"How's things there?"

"Oh, sort of quiet. They were worse a few years ago, of
course, but they're still not any too good."

"Not much chance of getting a job there?"

"Well, I don't know. There isn't a great deal of industry
there anymore, as you know," said Stanton, starting the car
again.

"Well, I'll get along," said the young fellow.

"I can only say I wish you luck, young man," said Stanton.

"Thanks, Mister," the young fellow said.

Stanton drove on at a steady clip, and they did not talk
for a while. He lit a cigarette, and asked the young fellow
if he wanted one.

"Sure. Thanks," the young fellow said, accepting the
proferred package, lighting a cigarette, handing the package back to Stanton.

The young fellow leaned back in his seat, and looked idly ahead at the concrete ribbon of road.

"Have you done much of this hitchhiking around?" asked Stanton.

"No, can't say that I have."

"Come from Cleveland?"

"No, I come from Manchester, Ohio. Not a bad town. Lots of nice gals there," said the young fellow.

"What makes you want to go to Columbus?" asked Stanton.

"Oh, nothing in particular. I lost my job waitin' on tables in Cleveland, and I was fed up. I was fed up with a girl there. She took her hair down the other night and tried to sink the hooks into me. Wanted me to marry her. She hinted that I had her knocked up. Well, she wasn't sinking the hooks into me. I just moseyed out of town, and thought I'll try my luck some place else."

"Was she a nice girl?" asked Stanton.

"All girls are right in the right way, meaning in the right position," said the young fellow.

"There might be something in what you say there," Stanton said in order to make conversation.

"And don't I know there is. A woman has got to be treated in a certain way. You got to tell her the right things, give her the right feel, and do the right things to her. But you never want to let her get you. Say, if I hadn't been smart with my women, I'd have been hooked many a time before now. And I would be burning up the home fires, sittin' around at night with a lot of little Johnny Monks, that's my name, crawling over the floor to make life hard and uncomfortable for me."

"You don't want to get married?"

"That's the way to take all the fun out of it. I got a better policy," said the young fellow.

"What's that?"

"Well, I'll tell you, Mister," the young fellow began philosophically and as if he were preparing to utter words of profound wisdom. "My policy is to let the other guy marry. And then when his wife wants a good time, I'll come along. That's my policy. It's less expensive. And you get variety. Variety is the spice of life, ain't it?"

"Well, I suppose it is," said Stanton, half enjoying this young hitchhiker.

The young fellow threw his cigarette butt out of the window.

Stanton was slowed down behind a truck, and he maneuvered to pass it. Yes, he thought, he half-wished that he was free like this young fellow, free and with a life uncluttered either by books or morality.

"I couldn't see myself tied down to one dame for the rest of my born days. No sir, life's too short. I like to play around," said the young fellow.

"Do you get by with that?" asked Stanton.

"I ought to knock on wood. Say, you know, with all the screwing around that I done, I ain't never had a dose. I must have been born under a lucky star. Of course, I do say this. I kind of pick them careful. You see, I don't want any damn bum that comes along the street. Hell, I like a little class. Now take in Manchester. Some of the boys there, Jesus, they'd screw anything. Honest, I tell you some of them would screw two boards. Well, there ain't no man alive what likes his screwing more than Johnny Monks here. I don't just like it Mister. I love it. There's nothing in life like it. Now I practiced up on my screwing, and when it comes to climbing into bed with a dame, Mister, I don't miss a trick in the whole deck of cards. Say now, when I was in Manchester. I learned something there. There was a young dame there. She was married to the guy that used to be Chief of Police at the time, but he ain't any more. Well, I made her. Now she was a piece. I learned something from her. There ain't many I learn from. They usually learn from me. But there I was going away with her at a nice fast pace, and she says to me, hardly able to breathe you know, because you know, she went for me, but she pants to me, tickle my ribs, tickle my ribs. Well, I had never thought of that trick. But I did. Say mister, you know what a thrill is?"

"What?"

"When you're in there, going good, why you tickle 'em in the ribs. Say that's a thrill. It goes out right through the top of your hair, to make them laugh when you are in there, and doing your stuff in a man-size way. Then, you tickle 'em in the ribs. That's something. And I learned it from the wife of the fellow that used to be Chief of Police in my home town. She was one of the best tricks I ever had. Now, as I was saying, there ain't much for me to learn. I learn them now, they don't learn me nothing Mister. But I did learn that, and would you think you could beat it. She was the wife of the fellow that was Chief of Police at the time."

—And I learned about women from 'er, Stanton recited to himself.

"It's good he didn't catch you."

"Well, she liked it too much to tell him. It was a good thing for her and for me. Of course, after a while I got tired of her, and there was a waitress in the restaurant where I was slinging hash at the time. She was young and fresh, and willing, and I went for her. And say, you know, when I got her and I was just hitting my pace, I tickled her in the ribs, and she laughed. I knew it wasn't special with the other one. I tickled every one I had since then and it's always the same. I tell you Mister, try it some time. It's a thrill that you get to the top of your hair."

"You tickled many in the ribs since then?" Stanton asked, masking his interest in a very casual tone of voice.

"Yes, sir. I lost count. You know I used to keep count of the dames I laid, but after a time, I lost count, and so I figured, oh what the hell difference does it make if I can or if I can't count them."

"How many was it when you lost count?" asked Stanton.

"Oh, it was about forty. Let's see. Forty. But that was two years ago," said the young fellow.

They drove on in silence for a while. Stanton was appalled by these tales, but believed them. No, this wasn't what he wanted. Or was it? He was suddenly not sure of himself.

"Say!" the young fellow said.

"What?" asked Stanton, keeping his eyes fixed on the road.

"I was wrong. It was fifty. I lost count after the fiftieth one, not the fortieth," the young fellow said.

"I guess that correction was important," said Stanton.

"Yes. It makes a difference. The way I know now that was my fiftieth one, she was jail bait. She was a kid. Boy, she scared me out of my pants. I knocked her up. Yeh, there I was with a kid, she was only sixteen, and she was knocked up. Jesus, I didn't know what the hell I was going to do. I got to do something, I figured. And just my luck. On my fiftieth one."

"That the first time you got in a jam that way?" asked

Stanton; he was now disgusted, but did not show his feelings.

"Hell no!"

"It was just the worst," said Stanton.

"Wasn't it. You bet it was," said the young fellow.

"What happened?" Stanton asked, interested, despite disgust and guilt.

"Oh, I took her to a doc, and he fixed her up. But I tell you, I had some anxious moments there. I tell you they were damn anxious."

"Well, it was good you got out of it," said Stanton.

"Yes, but then, that sometimes happens. It happens sometimes in the best regulated lay that you can fix yourself up with. And I know it, because, Mister, I ain't dishing you out no crap anyhow and whatsoever when I tell you that I have had some of the sweetest tail in the entire state of Ohio. That is, of course, barring what's in Columbus because I ain't never been at work there, you see. But then, I'll be adding in Columbus too pretty soon, now that I'm planning to settle down there for a while," the young fellow said.

"What else interests you besides tail?" Stanton asked.

"More tail," said the young fellow with enthusiasm.

"That all? Don't you ever like to read, or see the movies, or see ball games?"

"Oh yeh, that is I like to see a ball game now and then, and I like to go to the movies. Say, boy, I'd like to hit Hollywood. Now there is the place where I'd like to land. Now let me tell you, some of them movie queens, what wouldn't I give for *that*."

"Why don't you go out there and take a chance?" asked Stanton, smiling slyly as he asked the question; his mood had changed and he believed that he was satisfied with his life as it was.

"Say, I have had a mind to for a long time. One of these days I believe I will," said the young fellow.

"What'll you do then?"

"Oh, I'll get me a job in a joint where some of them actresses eat, and I'll fix me up that way. I'll be waiting on the table where they grab their grub, you see, and that's the way I'll make my entry. After I do that, why there isn't anything hard about it," said the young fellow.

"Well, you know, those movie actresses are rich and famous, and they might not be so easy to meet."

"That's no problem. Why what the hell, wasn't I sleeping with the wife of the Chief of Police, that is the fellow that was a Chief of Police when I was only an ordinary hash slinger in a restaurant? Sure, I was. Well, why the hell won't I get going with a dame in the movies when I make my entry?"

"I don't doubt but what you will."

"Sure I will," the young fellow said.

"Well, I wish you good luck."

"Thank you Mister. But in this matter, I'm not one of these amateurs. Say I been around. Just as I said, I have had some of the sweetest and most luscious tail that you'll find in the whole goddamn state," said the young fellow.

"What do you talk about with a girl?"

"Well, different things. Now before I get in the clutch with her, I talk about anything. You see I sound her out. If she is interested in movies, I talk about movies. If she is married, and her husband can't satisfy her, well, I try to get the subject around to hubby. Anything that helps, that's my technique before she and I get in the clutch. But after, well then I talk to her about screwing. You see, once you screwed a girl, you can talk to her about it. They like it. Mister, you know when a dame has been screwed, that subject ain't out. They'll talk. After we get out of the clutch, why then, we talk about it, and then set the stage for the next act."

"What'll you do when you're all dried up?"

"That ain't no problem now. It's a problem for the future," said the young fellow.

"I guess so. You're at your height now, aren't you?" said Stanton.

"That called the turn. I'm in my prime. Yes sir, I'm at my prime now. Just like Joe DiMaggio is in his prime as a ball player, well, I'm in my prime right now at my chosen sport," said the young fellow.

They drove on in silence for some distance. They both smoked several cigarettes. Stanton kept going at a clip between forty and fifty miles. The young fellow slouched down in his seat, lost in thought. Stanton was again nervous. Sometimes he thought that he would feel relieved when he was old and could no longer be torn by desire.

"They got a university in Columbus, ain't they?" th
young fellow said in an abstracted mood.

"Yes, there is one. It's a big one, too."

"There's coeds there, ain't there?"

"Yes."

"I guess I didn't pick the wrong town at that," said th
young fellow.

"Do you like college girls especially?" asked Stanton.

"That depends. You see, because a girl goes to college
that doesn't mean yes and it doesn't mean no. It all de
pends on the girl. Now some coeds are O.K. and som
aren't, just the same as waitresses. You see, girls are not al
alike. Some now, you look at them, why they seem lik
they're so hot that they'll burn right through steel. And yo
get them with their hair down, and they're cold, and the
make you think you've got into the refrigerator busines
And then again, some others, they ain't cold. Just as I sai
it all depends. Well, that's as true of coeds and college girl
as it is of any other ones, and Mister you know, it's just a
true of dames with the ring put on their fingers."

"You seem to know everything about it, all right," Stan
ton said, but he was thinking that coeds like it as much a
any other girls. Many times he might have. Had he really
been acting responsibly or had he been afraid?

"Well, if there's something I don't know, that's just wha
I'm out to learn as soon as I can learn it," said the young
fellow.

Stanton did not answer. He drove on, wishing that he
was back in Columbus, and rid of his passenger. Also he
wanted to be rid of his own doubts.

"We gettin' there?" the young fellow asked.

"Yes, it won't be long now."

"What kind of a town is Columbus?" asked the young
fellow after another lapse of silence.

"Well, it's a one-street town," said Stanton.

"What do you mean?"

"Why the entire town is built around one street. High
Street. It runs about twenty miles. Haven't you often heard
Columbus called High Street, Ohio?"

"No," said the young fellow.

"Well, it often is," said Stanton.

"I always work on the main street when I'm out on the
hunt. I'll have a big woods, a twenty mile main street."

"I think you will at that."

They drove on into Columbus, and the young fellow said: "Well, I'm here. I'm going to give some of the coeds some real education too."

Stanton stopped the car to let the fellow out.

"Well, I thank you kindly for the lift."

"Don't mention it."

"Now I'll see what these college girls know," he said.

"Going to tickle 'em in the ribs?" asked Stanton.

"Yes sir, I'm going to tickle 'em in the ribs all right," the young fellow said, grinning widely; then, he walked down High Street with a jaunty gait.

Stanton watched him, still cut and divided by his own thoughts. Then he drove on towards home. He still wished, wistfully, that once, once more he might dare to make love to a young girl, to tickle one in the ribs.

THE STUFF THAT DREAMS ARE MADE OF

I brought her back to me in a dream, and she stood vividly in my mind, blond, tall and wearing a black dress and silk stockings. But this is all I now remember of this dream of twenty-eight years ago. I woke up on the bench in Union Square. The air was gray in the pre-dawn. Just as I opened my eyes, I saw milk wagons moving on Fourth Avenue, more like white objects in a dream than the real wagons they were. The milk wagons passed before my sleepy eyes and I felt such an intensity of emotion and longing that I believed I must have seen them in my dream. Then, I heard the cloppity-clop of the horses, the noise of an automobile and I was fully awake.

Ed was slumped asleep on the bench beside me. Men slept on the benches and the grass, lying on old newspapers. Other homeless men sat or walked about like shadows. By choice, I had become homeless. Ed and I had hitchhiked to New York, and having only one dollar between us, we had slept in the park. Now, I was awake and my first day in New York was beginning. The air was now becoming gray with the beginnings of dawn. I was tired, stiff, dirty. But also, I was launched on what I imagined would be a life of adventure.

At the time, there was a painful clarity about my dream. Perhaps it could be interpreted most simply. I wanted a girl and I did not have one. I was physically deprived. Hence, the girl had come to me in my dreams. But there was much more to my dream and it involved something which, at the time, I did not want to admit to myself. I wanted to be back in Chicago and living in circumstances that were familiar to me. I wanted to be going out on a date with a girl in

Chicago. But I was in New York, sleeping in a park with bums and not knowing what the future would bring me. I had revolted, rejected the standards of my family and neighborhood and was determined to "live dangerously."

I had dreamed of Frances. She was but one of many girls who represented the world I had consciously rejected and left. She brought back with poignancy all that I had abandoned.

I did not think much of my dream. On awakening I was disappointed because I was not with Frances. I was frustrated and felt anguish. I sat and looked at homeless men and we went for coffee.

On and off through the years my dream occurred to me, but I never puzzled over or tried to interpret it. Now, once again, twenty-eight years later it comes back to me. Over the years, we remember very few of our dreams. But this, obviously, is one of my remembered dreams.

Why should the girl have been Frances? She was but one of many girls who had lived in my fantasies. I had managed to have one date with her, thanks to Katherine Anne, the girl with whom Ed often went. One night in 1924, when she had a date with Ed, she brought Frances along for me. We went to a movie at Fifty-Third Street and Lake Park Avenue and saw *The Birth of a Nation* which was being revived. The date was pleasant, but nothing happened on it. There was not even a chaste good-night kiss.

After that evening, I had phoned Frances several times and had asked her to go out with me, but she had always rejected me with a polite excuse. Except on the telephone, I never again talked with Frances after our one date.

Why, then, had I dreamed of her? Asking myself this question now on a hot morning when I am no longer a youth, I made a few random associations; and suddenly these lead me into a deep morass of associations, connections, names, fragmentary recollections of incidents. I am lost in an inner chaos of the past. And I see in this, the fact that the lives of others, innumerable others, become inextricably entangled in the very structure of our personality. We carry our memory of people along with us, and they come out of our past and press into our present. They are lodged in our lives like ghosts who can return at any moment to haunt us with the memory of what we never had, with shame and moral agony or with joy. We carry them along with us, and willy nilly, they are the symbols of our own pain and anguish and the objects of a bliss we wanted and only dreamed of in our sleep.

My random associations brought back to mind the names of boys and girls I used to know. Some of them, like Ed, are now dead. Others are scattered about the country, changed by time. They are no longer boys and girls except in my memory. And they will remain that, ghostly boys and girls who will from time to time re-occur to me or come back like distorted memories in my dreams.

About fourteen years ago, I saw Katherine Anne. She told me that Frances was happily married to a doctor and was the mother of two children. She was very attractive, Katherine Anne said, and she and her husband were both very nice people. Now Frances is about forty-six or forty-seven, and long past the time when she can rouse a young man's need for love and romance. She has probably forgotten that one inconsequential date she had with me, and she probably never knew that once I wanted to love her and that she was the focus of one of my important and possibly crucial dreams.

But why—I ask myself—was it Frances among all the girls I know, who came to me so vividly in an intense, painful and frustrated first dream in New York City at the moment when I believed that I was launching myself on the career that was everything, even life and death, to me. Why should she have been the first girl of my dreams at that moment?

Posing this question, Frances, the real, physical human being, becomes to me only the stuff that dreams are made of. She loses her identity and becomes the concrete image of a song, *The Sweetheart of Sigma Chi*. Often the popular songs of childhood, adolescence and youth become linked to us as personal code signs and symbols of some disappointment, some frustration, some failure which once distressed and troubled us. These songs sometimes come, unwilled, into our stream of thought and an old hurt, an old emotional pain saddens us and we feel again the distress we once felt. *The Sweetheart of Sigma Chi,* is one of the songs which has such a meaning to me.

Thus, out of the morass of association, names, partial memories and seeming chaotic recollections, Frances emerges as an image describable as *The Sweetheart of Sigma Chi*.

Associating her in this way, my long-past dream no longer seems like an enigma. The enigma resolved, this girl comes forth in recreated memory as one of those who became significantly entangled in my life and my career. Because she was tall and slim with blond hair, because she lived on the South East Side of Chicago, because she went to St. Paul's High School, because her parents were well off, because she knew boys and girls I knew, and because of other but related and seemingly accidental facts, she became the image of that first dream of mine in New York City back in the summer of 1927.

Obviously, the dream was sexual and this feature of it is sufficiently transparent; it needs no elaboration. But to me, this sexual wish, now long removed in time, is not what is significant. What is significant is that she, out of a number of possibilities, should have become the particular object of that wish.

II

The girl of my dreams is the sweetest girl of all the girls I know.

This is the line of the song which connects immediately with Frances.

In New York, on that first night, and on many other days and nights of that period, my boyhood and youth remained with me painfully. Memories of it, nostalgia for it, longing and yearning came to mind with great frequency. Boyhood and adolescent memories were most poignant for me when autumn came. There were days when the October sun was golden and glowing but without the summer heat, and the air was heavy with the signs of the changing season. The leaves had turned in Central Park and out in Queens where I sometimes went. I saw the children in New York City, going to and coming from school. I remembered autumn in Chicago, in Washington Park when I was a boy going to a parochial school. I would have many fantasies about the past, reliving it according to desire rather than fact. I would think of the girl who had been in those days, my idea of the sweetest girl of all the girls I knew.

Her name was Roslyn.

I thought of and fantasized about Roslyn more than I did about Frances.

Now, autumn had come again. Slowly these memories come back to me, and I think of autumn in Washington Park, autumn in Paris, autumn in many places where I have been. The seasons come and go more rapidly when one has lived more than half of one's life. Time is relative and felt in terms of intensity as well as measured in the even span of seconds. When gray appears in one's hair, time seems to move more swiftly. Boyhood, youth sink further and further away into the past. You know that now you belong to the generation whose hair grows gray just as the leaves turn. You have moved toward the autumn of your own life. The seasons pass by more rapidly, and each new autumn with its moods of melancholy depth. The turning leaves, what are these but the hair of the trees changing color before winter comes. Yes, autumn is coming again, now. At its fresh onset, I sit and remember. I sit and puzzle over sunken memories, and over this long lost dream.

Frances and Roslyn! Frances was a prettier girl than Roslyn. They both went to St. Paul's, but Roslyn was one year ahead of Frances. Frances was more popular and had more dates. In her late teens, Roslyn was thin and somewhat bony. Socially both of these girls and their friends were above me. Their parents were more successful in life than mine had been. With them, I often felt like an interloper, one who did not belong. I dreamed of them. I wanted one of them.

And then I had passed twenty-one and was a young man in determined and uncompromising revolt. I was angry about all of the injustices of the world, and also about my own frustrations. I throbbed and thrilled with visions of freedom, of a life and a world beyond that youthful social world of the South Side of Chicago to which I had once wanted to belong and in which I had been a gauche and awkward failure.

And following my revolt, my changes of mind and the awakening of my ambitions, I put girls like Frances and Roslyn below me. When I thought of them or daydreamed about them, I punished them. I felt sorry for them, but in a deceptively insincere way. They had once meant all the glory of the world to me. Then, I came to believe that they

never would or could know all the glory of the world.
Sometimes, I wished them ill. Because they had not responded to me as a boy and a youth, I even wished them
unhappiness. Roslyn had been to me the sweetest girl of all
the girls I know, but she had rarely spoken to me. I believed
that with me she had been proud and haughty. For her, I
had wanted to be brave and great. I had wanted to lay fame
at her feet. In my daydreams I had performed countless
deeds of heroism, all for her. I had imagined myself an ad-
venturer and the bravest of the brave . I had slaughtered
Germans and won medals in the First World War. I had
imagined myself to be a baseball player, greater than Eddie
Collins or Ty Cobb. I had succeeded Jack Dempsey as
Champion of the World. I married her and kissed her many
times. But I had never really known her, and had usually
been too shy even to say hello to her. She had been a symbol to me, not a real person. And after I had gone to high
school, I had transferred my dreams and yearnings to other
girls, but almost all of them, like Roslyn and Frances, had
been St. Paul girls.

A little more than a year after that one date with
Frances, I had matriculated at the University. I had forgotten much of what we had said on that date and also, had
forgotten what Frances looked like. At the University, I
wanted to fall in love with a beautiful and popular club girl.
At first, also, I hoped to become a fraternity man. But I
was a hard-working and determined grind, also bent on the
quest of knowledge and hell-bent in my desire to become
some kind of a success in this world. My ambitions, were
if anything, grandiose. Socially at the University, I should
not say that I failed. I never even got off the ground.

Frances was a student at the University in my day, and
I knew that she was dated by frat boys and invited to fraternity parties. Often, I would go to the campus in the
morning, hoping that I would run into her. I would imagine
the two of us in the same class, sitting side by side, and myself impressing her with my knowledge and also helping her
with her studies, if she should need help. She would be the
girl I met and loved. But I never saw her. Occasionally, I
would meet Katherine Anne. I was almost a straight A student. Katherine Anne knew this, and I hoped that she
would tell Frances about me and the scholastic success I
was having.

I used to see a cute blond girl on campus, and having forgotten exactly what Frances looked like, I began to imagine that this girl was Frances. Every time I passed her, I used to stare waiting for a greeting. Sometimes I would convince myself that the girl was Frances, and then, I would doubt it. She was smaller than Frances and it was a case of my mistaking an identity out of wish and need.

Before I had dreamed of her in Union Square, Frances had already become a mixed identity in my mind. It was because of this that she was the girl of my dream. I was dreaming of a dream in female form, the sweetest girl of all girls. The fact that Frances had gone to the University was important, also. It reveals continuity in my inner life. Intellectual emancipation had not erased the aching and never forgotten pains of frustration and loneliness of my boyhood. And out of that boyhood had emerged the dream of a girl. She had at various times, a different face, and figure: her name changed, and so did the color of her hair.

In my first days at the University I had wanted a girl who would be popular enough to become idealized or sentimentalized as the sweetheart of Sigma Chi. Then, I became a Bohemian. My values changed, I came to scorn social position. With this, the song acquired a new connotation for me. Then, the song referred to a girl who could be the sweetheart of Sigma Chi, not in the sense of popularity, but rather because she would have sexual relationships with an entire fraternity. And in this new period of my life, I met Texas. Jokingly, we used to think of her as the sweetheart of the marines. She became involved in the associations which clung to the song. Before leaving Chicago, I had had a brief affair with Texas. Had I been in Chicago on that night I was in Union Square, I well might have been spending it with Texas and should not have been physically frustrated.

Hiding behind the song, there was Roslyn, Frances and Texas.

Frances was substitute for both Roslyn and Texas. As such she was a link between purity and innocence, on the one hand, and experience and sexual knowledge on the other; she concentrated the contradictions between the pure dreams of boyhood and the frustrated dreams of adolescence and early young manhood. Because I knew no other girls at the University, I had fastened my hopes on her. She was associated with my pre-college past. She was a figure of fantasy who marked the persistence of one fixed dream and desire through a period of intellectual growth, change and revolt. I had dreamed of fame and success since I was a small boy. I had always associated this with some girl. The shift from Roslyn to Frances was marked by my attendance at the University, and my fixing on the ambition to write. I quit college and left Chicago in order to achieve my ambition as a writer. But by becoming a writer I would not only express my won feelings and prove myself: I would also show them.

Whom would I show? Everyone who had ever hurt me, insulted me, ignored me. All of those who had ever indicated that they lacked faith and confidence in me. Most especially, I would show girls. How many girls, during my years of bewildered puberty and adolescence had refused to go out with me on dates? How often had I not felt on the outside, unloved and possibly disliked by girls? At one time, I had apprehensively imagined that they talked about me and laughed at me behind my back. I had believed that they had given me a bad name as a goof, a dope, and that because of this, I could not get dates as my friends, did. And sometimes I had believed Frances was one of the girls who laughed at me. All of this was at best only partly true. But it served to deepen and harden my ambition and my will. Out of the vanity I felt concerning these girls, I found my purpose in life.

I reasoned that at some time or other, Frances must have seen me on campus, but had not spoken to me. This must have been a way of cutting me. This had happened many times with Roslyn when I was a boy in grammar school, and the year after my graduation from grammar school, Roslyn had given a party. I, alone, of our old bunch had not been invited. My vanity was wounded by what I interpreted as having been slighted and ignored. And I had carried that wounded vanity along with me to the University. I had nursed psychological wounds and my need for self-justification had become urgent. I believed myself misunderstood. I imagined that my virtues were unrecognized. And I saw my own need to love as a pure and adoring feeling which was not recognized.

I have already mentioned that Roslyn and Frances were both St. Paul girls. And the girls at this school always "rated" as we used to say. The boys I knew back in 1922, 23, and 24 all said that Frances "rated." Roslyn did not "rate." But all during that period I held many different attitudes towards Roslyn. There were times when I would decide that she was homely. Then, I would change my mind and think her attractive. I saw her only once during my last two years of high school, and that was when she was coming out of church after a Sunday Mass. She seemed well-dressed and beautiful. I wanted to phone her and ask her to go out with me, but I was too shy, and too fearful of being rejected.

And then, when I was going to night school, I had, on New Year's Day, 1925, gone to a small party at Natalie O'Reedy's. She had been Roslyn's closest friend in grammar school. At the party, I had danced with Roslyn's younger sister, and with the other girls, but not with Roslyn. I had scarcely spoken a word to her, nor she to me. However, when I danced, I had shown off for her benefit. Likewise I had talked of night school, my studies, my good marks, my progress, and my ambition, all for her ears. She had seemed cold and uninterested in me and in what I said. All over again, I felt the same old hurts of boyhood. My ambition and determination grew more firm because I was hurt.

From night school I went to the University, and intellectually I began to come into my own. I started to feel that I was on the way to fulfilling my destiny. Frances, also a student, could have been the messenger to my past, telling of my growth and success. Had I met her and gone with her, Roslyn would sooner or later have heard of it. I should have avenged those boyhood wounds. And, I convinced myself, Frances was more desirable than Roslyn.

Now, across the space of crowded years, this dream becomes clear. At that time, I was not fully confident. I was afraid that I had taken the big chance, the big gamble, and that I would fail as a writer. Believing that I had burned all of my bridges behind me, failure meant emptiness. I was sleeping in a park with homeless and destitute men. Were I to fail, I could become like them. I was unproven and was assaulting the gates of fame and immortality. And I was still unsure of myself with girls. I felt inferior and that if one of them rejected me, my vanity would bleed. I had dreamed of being Ty Cobb for Roslyn. In college, I ha dreamed of being a writer. Frances had taken the place of Roslyn.

I recall that as I woke from my dream, I was putting my arms around Frances to kiss her. Roslyn was the girl most deeply embedded in my consciousness. But in the dream, I was treating both of them as though they were Texas. They were all amalgamated and became my sweetheart of Sigma Chi. And I woke up before I had them, these three girls fashioned into the dream image of a beautiful and tall and blond Frances McTeague.

Such was the first dream of a young writer who went to New York penniless in order to put dreams on paper.

And then, there were those milk wagons, seen in my sleep and then when I was awake. Intense and yearning, I looked at their whiteness which glowed for me. I thought of the milk wagons as white dreams. And whiteness is a symbol of purity. I washed my dream of sex, anger, and revenge by turning milk wagons into the white dream-like quality of angels. And in my boyhood daydreams, I had often thought of Roslyn as though she were a saint or an angel.

Lurking further behind this dream were deeper layers of memory—memories of family, home, mother and grandmother. All this, I had rejected and left. I had gone away from it. But in my dream it remained, and haunted me. It haunted me mostly in the psychically intense white of milk wagons, rattling by Union Square as the first gray of dawn heralded my first day of freedom in New York City.

And such is the stuff that the dreams of writers are made of.

THE OLD FLAME

Arnold Benton had been anxious to meet his ex-sister-in-law but, at the same time, uneasy about it. He hadn't seen her in seven years, and he had begun to grey, to grow flabby, to show the signs of middle age. He knew that Genevieve had seen a totally different person, the Arnold Benton who had been young, slim and unconquerable. That had been while he was going with, and later married, Genevieve's sister Ella. Though he'd been more attracted to Genevieve. He remembered the afternoon in Minneapolis. . . he had been alone, waiting for Ella to return from shopping. It had been just before their marriage. Genevieve had been resting alone in her room. He went in and spoke to her for a few minutes.

He felt his pulse racing, his breath coming faster, and he went back into the living room, pretending to read. Suddenly he had wanted to kiss her, seduce her. Since then he had thought of that afternoon often, imagined himself seducing her.

Genevieve had always seemed to like him; even during the most painful first days of his separation from Ella he and Genevieve had remained friendly. He remembered her now as a pretty, laughing girl of seventeen. Dressing to meet her, he imagined the times he had kissed her, openmouthed and passionate. The fantasies he had created for himself. He had been disappointed at himself because he had not seduced her; he knew she hadn't been an innocent. Even at seventeen, he had known, she had been far from innocent.

Arnold Benton dressed carefully. He tried to hide the

act that he had aged at all; though he was only forty-one, he had a painfully acute sense of himself as old. He wanted her, also, to be awed by his success. He was no longer the old Arnold Benton. He was—Arnold Benton, the famous news commentator, the national figure. Millions of people had heard his news analyses on the radio; millions knew his name, the sound of his voice. But his success and fame added to his feelings of uneasiness while he put on a new stylish suit, carefully tying his bowtie, smoothing down the hair which was already beginning to streak with grey, patting his cheeks with aftershave lotion and, with a feeling of rectitude, using the very lotion which was manufactured by his sponsor.

He hadn't told Louise that he was meeting Genevieve. That made him a little worried: sometimes, there were slips. You saw someone you knew, uttered some chance remark that created suspicion. He could have told Louise. But he knew why he hadn't.

He had, surprisingly, hopes. Definite hopes. Genevieve had gotten a room in a hotel. It would be easy to go upstairs with her. . . .

But why should he? He was Arnold Benton. She was a girl from the smalltown fringe of poverty.

But for two days he had thought of Genevieve. Over and over he had seen himself in her room, kissing her, making love to her. He had imagined countless conversations, trying to work out the one best approach. He hoped that she would invite him up, in fact, proposition him. He could imagine that happening, imagine her flinging herself into his arms.

Uneasy, he left his Park Avenue apartment and took a cab to meet her.

Soft music came from the radio in the wall. Arnold and Genevieve sat in a corner. To Arnold, the music brought back memories, the old memories of all he had been cheated of, the love he had wanted and, somehow, never received. It startled him for a second to realize that he was sitting, listening to the songs of his youth, talking with Genevieve here in this exclusive New York restaurant—he, Arnold Benton, who earned five thousand dollars a week!

He told himself he would sacrifice that salary, sacrifice

his fame and his success, if only he could have the last twenty-three years to live over again.

"I'm very happy you called me up," he told her.

"I always liked you, Arnold. I looked forward to seeing you." She smiled.

He was unsure about how to interpret that smile; instead, he was measuring Genevieve against Louise, against the chic women he met in New York at theatres, parties, night clubs. He couldn't decide how attractive she was. He remembered thinking her beautiful as a girl, and imagined her beautful now, but he couldn't be sure. He simply could not see her objectively enough to judge. He felt certain, though, that she was attractive enough so that he wasn't ashamed of being seen with her. She dressed well, and she had her black hair done up in the latest style. She could, he thought, well be New York rather than Minneapolis.

"It's been a long time, hasn't it, Jenny?" he said with a sigh.

She laughed, "Too long."

He raised his Scotch and soda. They touched glasses. "To Jenny," he said.

"That's sweet of you, Arnold," she said. "But you always were sweet."

"Was I?"

"I thought so," she whispered.

For no reason at all he said, loudly, "Yes, it's been a long time."

"And you haven't changed much," she said. "You seem the same."

"Did you expect me to be changed?"

She shook her head, no.

"I don't think I'm changed," he said. "None of this has gone to my head," hoping he wasn't showing her how self-conscious he was.

He decided finally that he wanted her. He didn't care how dangerous it might be, he wanted her. But how could he know? She might repulse him—repulse him and then going home, tell Ella.

"We never thought we'd be living in the kind of world we are—did we, Jenny—in the old days?" he said heavily.

"No," she answered slowly, and repeated: "no."

"Never knowing. Wondering when war will start. Always on edge."

"You're doing everything you can," she said.

"Everybody does his bit, if he's worth his damned salt," Arnold said bitterly.

Then they sat. Neither spoke. After a time she said, with a tone and a smile that reminded him of Genevieve at seventeen: "Gee, I'm so glad to see you."

"I'd have been disappointed if I'd heard you'd come to own and not looked me up."

"But Arnold, darling, you know I wouldn't do that," she said.

Arnold wondered how he could interpret her calling him darling. If the world really knew him, he thought, really knew Arnold Benton, how they would laugh. On the radio he seemed so confident, calm, able to talk, sure of himself. And here he sat with this—girl from Minneapolis, and didn't know what to do next.

Self-consciously, he yawned, then quickly said: "I've got a tough time."

"You must have," she said. "With the work you do. But Arnold, it's wonderful to think of your making such a name for yourself."

"I work hard, harder than a lot of people think," he said. "Got to be on my toes all the time. I usually work more than ten hours a day. No, a radio commentator's life isn't a glamorous one."

"I know, I know, Arnold," Genevieve said sympathetically.

He grinned. "Well, these aren't easy times. We're fighting for survival." He took another sip of his drink. He stared around the restaurant, to see if he would recognize any faces. He saw no one he knew. "And you," he said. "Tell me about yourself."

Ella? he wanted to ask, but hesitated.

"Here I am," Genevieve said and laughed.

He felt her laugh was a little self-conscious. But then, she was probably trying to impress him. "Are you happy?" he asked.

"Oh, yes. You never met Sandy, did you."

"No. No, I didn't" he said absently, then added quickly: "I'd like to."

"I'd like you to meet him," Genevieve said. "He's nice."

"How long have you been married now?"

"Five years. Gosh, the way time flies."

"Yes," Arnold agreed wistfully. He wanted to say more, but hesitated.

"And how are you?" she asked. "Married again."

"Happy," he said shortly, not wanting to talk about his own marriage. He finished his glass. He pointed to her glass and said: "Drink up, and we'll have another."

III

"We used to have fun, didn't we?" Genevieve said.

Arnold nodded.

"Ella said for me to send you her love," she continued.

"That was nice of her. Thank her for me," Arnold said.

"She's changed."

"How?"

"She works hard. In a veteran's hospital."

"Will she ever get married again?"

"I hope so, I think she will. She's been going with Adams."

Arnold raised his eyebrows in a question.

"Oh, he's a doctor. In the hospital. He's very nice."

"That's good," he said. "I'd like to see Ella married. I guess our marriage was a mistake. But we all make mistakes."

"Ella only wishes you well. I know it."

"I wish her well," Arnold said quickly.

"And my mother, even my father, they talk differently about you, Arnold. Really, they're proud of you. They both said I should say hello for them. They are proud of you."

It was dull; but, Arnold realized, he was interested.

"Aunt Kitty had to be put away. She collapsed," Genevieve said.

"Sorry to hear that," Arnold said, again taking a sip.

"She never really forgave you. She always said you ruined the life of her niece."

Troubled, Arnold asked: "How is your father's busi-
ess?"

"Oh, he's doing fine."

Arnold wanted to ask: Does he hear my radio program?
ut he kept quiet for a minute. Once, he recalled, he'd
ad such contempt for her father . . . and now he wanted
e old man to listen to him. He shook his head vaguely.

"Yes, it's a long time," he said suddenly, his thoughts
nfused.

"It is. But it's good to see you, Arnold, dear."

He reached across the table and, shyly, squeezed her
nd. She smiled at him. He thought: Perhaps I might . . .
t I shouldn't try. Now he was free of connections with
 family. Better stay that way. And if he tried and failed,
pose she went back home and told that to Ella. He
uld imagine Ella's knowing that, feeling happy, justified.
, he'd better not try.

He looked at Genevieve and she seemed beautiful. He
alized that for years he had regretted not having tried
 do anything in the old days—especially on that afternoon
hen they'd been alone.

The radio was still on, and he heard a dim orchestra
aying, *Three O'Clock in the Morning.* He'd danced to
at song, with Ella. Waltzing, he had the only girl in the
orld in his arms and they would be happy together
r years. And now, here he was, divorced and the famous
rnold Benton, talking with Jenny, and Ella was miles
vay in another city and their life was ended. And he knew
at he was bitter, and he wished they had never been
arried.

"I always like that song," he said moodily.

"Yes, it is nice," she said.

He wished he could take Jenny in his arms and waltz
ith her to the tune.

He began to feel cheated. Life had not given him what
 had hoped for, what he could have had. He remembered
mself in his late teens and early twenties, hopeful and
ger and expectant. He had wanted love and fame. And
 had gotten—love and fame. Thinking of this, he realized
at Ella had given him what love she had to give. But it
ad not, somehow, been enough. Often, in the last few
ars, he'd thought of this, imagined that there was some-

thing hollow and empty in his life. And now, the old son
seemed to tell that to him; for a moment, it almost fille
something of that empty hole at the center of his person
ality.

Quickly, he took a drink. He had to talk. If he sat her
like this, Jenny would think he might not be happy, she
think something was wrong and she wouldn't have th
impression of him that he wanted her to have. He didn
know quite what that impression would be, other tha
that he wanted Jenny to admire him, to think that he wa
unchanged and unspoiled by money and success and prom
inence, and that he was happy and satisfied.

"You don't have any children?" she asked him.

"No," he said, shaking his head.

"I should have thought you would want children,"
said.

"Why?" he asked.

"You're so kind; you'd make a good father."

He smiled. Pleased, he was getting somewhere. Perhap
he could risk something here.

"Tell me more about yourself," he said.

"Oh, there isn't so much to tell. We're all happy, we g
along fine. Ella gets on well with mother."

"How is your mother?"

"Oh, she isn't so well. She has attacks of rheumatism
But she does get around, and she and dad are so happ
together."

"That's good," he said, sentimentally thinking that h
parents were, after all, examples of the real virtues of th
American Way of Life. He had been wrong about them i
his youth, wrong in the contempt he had felt for them
Theirs was the real life, the kind of life he wanted. An
yet, he thought, people like himself were needed, tho
who were more sophisticated, and who not only receive
more of the rewards of life but also sacrificed mor
worried more, carried more burdens.

"I like your parents," he said.

"They'll be happy when I tell them that," Genevie
said.

"Let's have another drink," he said.

"All right," she smiled at him. "Arnold I like you," sh
said, still smiling. The smile seemed inviting, liquid, willin

He reached across the table and took her hand, squeezed it.

"You're a darling, Arnold," she told him.

He signalled for the waiter. If they had a few drinks, everything would be easier, and then, if anything uncomfortable or troublesome did happen, he could always say that he had had some drinks, and that he had done what he had because of the drinks.

IV

She took his arm.

"Gee, it's nice to be with you, to see you again," she told him.

He smiled, puffed up with pleasure. It was a Spring day. The air was fine and balmy. The fine quality of the Spring air stirred him. He had always felt so hopeful in the Spring, and now, he was too old for that. And yet, he asked, why was he? He was with Jenny, and they were going back to her hotel, and they would have an attractive adventure. Jenny was married; she wouldn't make any demands on him; there was no danger. He was going to have just the kind of adventure he had always wanted, especially in the Spring.

They walked along Fifth Avenue, past Rockefeller Center. The avenue was crowded and noisy. He saw many well-dressed people, well-dressed and stunning women. And Jenny was well-dressed, and he could walk with her as one of the crowd on Fifth Avenue. He wanted to be recognized but, at the same time, he was afraid that the wrong person would recognize him. He felt a part of this Fifth Avenue crowd; it was part of his world. The shops on the avenue were the shops in which he and his wife bought. Nearby were the nightclubs to which they went, and the studio from which he broadcasted. He was one of the famous men in the land, and Fifth Avenue stood as a background to his fame. He imagined how proud Jenny must feel, hanging on his arm, walking down Fifth Avenue with him.

He had told her that he wanted to get out, and then he

had said he would go back to her hotel room with her and talk there. It would be so much more pleasant talking there than in a restaurant with music playing. . . .

And she had given him that same, inviting, liquid smile. He was sure they understood each other. In the old days he had imagined a rivalry between Genevieve and Ella, and he guessed they must be rivals still. Perhaps that was why Jenny was willing. . . .

He walked calmly, head erect, his face rather solemn. He had an air of importance about him, and he imagined that his posture, his gait, his expression, as well as his carefully selected clothing, all bespoke his importance.

They walked with long strides.

"This is nice. It's nice seeing you, Arnold, you nice old thing," she said girlishly.

V

"This is a nice big room," he said, taking his hat and grey topcoat off and setting them carefully on a chair.

The hotel room was large, and it had been furnished carefully, in a manner suggesting a Hollywood hotel-room setting. The walls were a pure white, and most of the furniture, modern in design, was blue. The curtains were white with blue dots. The room was sunny.

He sat on the bed and sighed. He had felt nervous for a moment as they had come up in the elevator, afraid he would be recognized.

She sat on the bed beside him, ran her hand through his hair, and said: "It's wonderful to see you, Arnold, you darling."

"Is it?" he asked meaningfully.

"For me it is," she said.

He took her hand, put his arm around her shoulders. He kissed her, at first shyly and tentatively. But she did not resist him, and they kissed passionately. Then he knew that he had her as a conquest and, holding her in his arms, their lips sealed together in a long-drawn-out kiss, he thought of her as a conquest and grew tense. He had made a mistake, he didn't know how to get out of his error. . . .

Suddenly she laughed.

He shrank from her laugh. She was making a fool of him, and when she went back to Minneapolis Ella would know everything. The famous Arnold Benton had been trapped and made to look like a fool.

"I forgot to lock the door," she said, and she immediately got up and went to the door.

He heard her locking the door.

He lay waiting indecisive. He tried to convince himself that he was drunk, at least slightly drunk. He knew better. He wanted her, but he did not want to be held responsible. He wished that he were more drunk, drunk enough so that he could really feel convinced that it was not he making any choice.

She lay beside him, put her arms around him. Suddenly he reached out with a hand and pulled her to him brutally. His hand ripped the dress down her back, and against him he could feel her shudder.

"Arnold," she said. "Arnold. . . ."

VI

He was less nervous now, seated with her in the little bar. He could not understand way he had wanted to get out of her room so quickly, why he had not wanted to lie there with her, perhaps take her again, relax, fall quietly asleep.

He raised his glass, tipped it to hers, and smiled weakly. He didn't know now what to say. He thought he should have said: To us.

He couldn't. They were no "us."

"I never dreamed this would happen," she said.

He smiled again, "It did," he told her, but without spirit.

Yet once more he grinned. Nervous, having to do something distracting, he took a drink and then lit a cigarette. "Are you sorry?" he asked finally.

She shook her head.

"I'm not," he told her.

It was untrue. In the very act, he had been sorry, and so agitated that he had found no enjoyment. Now he wished that they were back in the room, and that, relieved somehow, he were enjoying her.

"You always were sweet," she said.

"And so were you."

She said: "You married the wrong sister, didn't you Arnold, dear?"

He shivered. For a moment, he was speechless. He was her victim. She wanted him, now. He had been trapped.

"I was young," he said evasively.

"When I go back home, Arnold, I'll think of you—nicely," she said.

She pursed her lips in a kiss that she blew to him. She was beautiful. He relaxed, slumping a little in the booth, and realized that she was not trapping him, that he could permit himself to smile. He felt a flood of tender feelings for her. They had given each other a few minutes of forgetfulness. Now, he thought how he worked, under such a strain, how he carried a burden of worry and how he needed forgetfulness, the forgetfulness that came with some new and adventurous experience. And this was something that he could thank her for.

He could have had her years ago. Regret for the lost opportunities, for his past years, his lost years saddened him. He imagined the people who listened to him: to them, he was only a voice. Behind that voice, he told himself, there was something very lonely, so lonely that he felt separated from people. But he had been close to Jenny—hadn't he?

He felt sorry for himself as he lifted his glass and drank.

"You're very quiet," she said.

He nodded his head, wanting to say something but unable to think of anything he might, appropriately, say.

"I always knew I gave satisfaction,' she said with a grin.

The sentence disturbed him, even though it gave him more ease. He saw from it that this time was not the first since her marriage. He remembered that she had been free, perhaps promiscuous, as a girl, and he had no need to worry. She wouldn't cause him trouble.

He nodded, reached across the table, took her hand and squeezed it. He was grateful to her; but he could not shake off a gloom, a nervous anxiety that had begun again to trouble him. He needed to be alone.

He fumbled for his watch, looked at it and, trying to conceal his embarrassment, told her: "I have to go now, darling."

She rose. She was casual. He paid and they went outside. He shook hands with her. "You're here how long, Jenny?" he asked.

"Until Friday."

"I'll phone you." He paused. "The day after tomorrow. I'm tied up tomorrow."

"I'd like to see you again," she said.

"If I can, you will," he said, squeezed her hand, and left her.

VII

He had plenty of time before he went to the broadcasting studio. He only needed to be there an hour before his broadcast. That would give him plenty of time to go over the dispatches and prepare his script; he'd learned how to put his reports in shape in the quickest possible time.

He walked back to Fifth Avenue and started uptown, pleased at being an anonymous part of the crowded procession of people. It was between four and five. The day was warm, and the noise and movement of the street seemed friendly. He was where he felt he must belong. Yet, there was something which suddenly began to gnaw at him.

Suppose she became pregnant? She had a husband, of course, but if she should make charges against him he could be ruined. He remembered one case he'd read of, a long time ago . . . he stood in the center of the sidewalk while people passed him, and he blanched. He felt the perspiration under his armpits. He was, temporarily, incapable of controlling himself, and he stood terrified, the color gone from his cheeks.

He suddenly realized that he was standing still in public, and that if anyone who recognized him saw him, he would become an object of gossip. He took a few steps, wanting to walk briskly. But he walked very slowly, his mind filled with visions of disgrace and scandal. He told himself he

would be mentioned in the gossip columns. He walked on,
and suddenly everything became much worse as he realized
that he had always wanted to have an illegitimate child.
Now he didn't, and yet he had often imagined himself as
the father, not only of one illegitimate child, but of many.

He walked on. The noise of traffic was muffled by his
fears, and he grew more afraid. He crossed a street with
a crowd, not knowing where he was. He shook his head
as though that little gesture would restore a sense of inner
balance, and walked on in terror.

VIII ·

Louise was more beautiful than Jenny. Why should he
have wanted Jenny?

"Arnold, you seem strange," Louise said to him.

They were seated in a large restaurant, and soft music
was playing somewhere.

"I was thinking, I was absorbed," he said.

"I understand. But you shouldn't take the world's
problems so hard, so personally. We'll win out, finally. We
have to."

He nodded, "Yes. Life would be unbearable if we didn't
believe that. All the misery, the suffering . . . if only we
could really do something." And he felt guilty; he felt he
should be doing more than talking.

But men such as he were indispensable, he told himself.
And besides, there was nothing anyone could do, nothing
more than he was doing. The Cold War would drag on,
but there was nothing he could do. He realized why he
had felt guilty; it was because he didn't know whether he
wanted to do anything. He had been sure; but now he felt
that if he did anything he would ruin all chance of success
for everyone. He wouldn't dare to do anything.

He had to cover up, for Louise. But he wasn't doing
anything wrong, was he? He said: "I need a drink. This
strain is killing me."

"Yes, I know, dear," she said, but her tone sounded too
casual.

He signalled to the waiter with an air of authority and

NOT FUNNY, NO, NOT FUNNY

I first saw her sitting with her Great Dane dog in the garden of my hotel on the Right Bank. She was tall with a stately figure and long auburn hair which glistened in the sunlight. She was dressed as though for a resort; her clothes looked out of place, exaggerated and possibly in bad taste when worn in a Paris hotel.

People came and went at the Hotel Sylvia and I assumed she was transient, staying for a day or two before going on someplace else. My attitude towards her was principally one of curiosity. And then, too, she seemed over-dressed in the way which often leads one to believe that a woman might be cold. Her dresses were always a shade off in color and sometimes were rather garish. She wore bright colors and looked especially well in red. Also, it seemed possibly significant to me that she should have such a big dog. Tall herself, she and her dog could not but be stared at, especially in Paris around the Etoile and on the Champs Elysées.

For a couple of hours a day, she would sit in the garden or the hotel dining room. Seeing her sitting alone several evenings, it occurred to me that this was odd for such a girl. It is as apt to use the word creature as girl in designating her, and to add that on occasion, her appearance was sultry. Seeing her about the hotel, one would assume that she led a quite interesting and exciting life and that she had a lover or perhaps lovers. The fact that I never saw her with a man did not mean anything; I only saw her occasionally, taking a sun bath in the garden, with her dog beside her, his leash tied to the chair, or else eating alone in the dining room. Every time I saw her, she was wearing something different. She wore bright colored, low-necked dresses

133

which exposed the cleft between her breasts and th
upper portions. She was tanned, almost bronze, a
walked erectly with a proud gait. And her long hair v
luxuriant, gorgeous, especially when she let it fall dx
her back.

After a week or ten days, she disappeared, like one
those guests who came and went. But two weeks la
in early July, she was back again. She was in the lob
the dining room or frequently the garden. I would see
talking with some of the guests. One evening, she was w
an English engineer who did not speak French. I had s
him at the hotel the previous year, when he had sat a
table next to mine. One morning, we had struck up a c
veration. He did not fancy Paris, and was quite lonely.
wanted to be back home in London and did not know w
to do with his spare time in Paris. Business was detain
him, and the French were so slow about business det
that he had to remain longer than he had expected.

I did not give her much thought, but assumed that
was a girl of experience and sophistication, one who li
gaiety and fun, had lovers and went out to good restaura
and night clubs. The Englishman, I guessed, must h
been too slow and uninteresting for her.

She sometimes talked to Mike Friedland. He wa
chubby little man of about forty-one who came to Eur
every year; he was in the jewelry business. Mike, a ba
elor, was having an affair with a French girl whom
always saw on his European trips. He was not interes
in the sights of Paris and did not go about a great d
He was simple, naïve and friendly. Sometimes we wo
talk about baseball, or about business. He waited
letters from his secretary, spoke of how he missed her a
how she took care of him. Unlike a number of Americ
I saw at the time, he was not bothered by or antipath
to the French, and he did not think France was decad
Perhaps wages could have been higher in France, and
people could live better, but he did not give much thou
to these questions. He was always jolly, and he kept try
to order his meals in French, but his accent was atroci
He and the girl sometimes ate together or they would t
in the dining salon. He introduced me to her and I lear
that her name was Irene.

About three o'clock one afternoon, I had coffee with them in the garden. Irene wore a bright colored print dress with a low neckline; her beautiful hair glistened in the sun as it fell down her back.

"You speak English."

"Only a leetle. I learn it from Americans, soldiers during the War," she said in a harsh, twangy accent.

"Do you live in Paris?"

"No. I live with my sister. We live at Nice."

"Isn't she too fine a girl to be in Paris all by herself?" Mike joked.

I agreed.

"You, American?"

I told her that I was.

"I like Americans."

"Well, that's why you can like me, Irene," Mike said.

"You—you nice man."

"See—she appreciates quality."

Irene did not understand his remark; she was silent.

"Yes, Irene is from Nice—the flowers of Nice. They talk about the flowers of Nice."

The daughter of the hotel owner passed us. She was a dark-haired and very pretty girl of seventeen, just in bloom.

"Nice girl—educated—a nice girl," Irene said. "Very well educated."

"They're nice people here—a nice family. It's one of the reasons why I always come back to this hotel," Mike Friedland said.

"Yes, my friend, he like it."

"You're speaking better English, Irene."

"Oh, no," she laughed.

"Yes, yes, you do. I wish I could speak French as good as you do English. After you're in the States a little while you'll be speaking English fine, fine."

"Are you going to America?" I asked.

"Yes, in what you call it, autumn?"

"That's right," Mike said. "Autumn, or fall."

"My friend, I wait for him. You have met my friend here?" she asked.

"No."

"He's colonel, American colonel with the Air Force. I wait for him. He's all the time travel."

"I met him," Mike said. "He's a nice fellow."

"Yes, very nice, very well educated. He live in Akron, Akron, Ohio—you say?"

"I've been there," I said.

"It's a good town," Mike added.

"We go there in fall and marry. I live in America. But all the time he travel. He go to Spain now. I wait. He come back in week and we go on *vacance* va . . ."

"Vacation," I said.

"Yes, vacation. You go away with your friend?"

I was surprised because I had not thought that she had noticed me.

"Yes."

"Where you go?"

"Turkey, Greece, Yugoslavia, Italy."

"Wonderful. Wonderful. Your friend, she is very pretty. Is she nice?"

I nodded, not wanting to discuss this.

She turned to Mike.

"You need friend, nice girl, nice friend."

"Oh, I'm happy."

"Everybody needs friend." She turned to me. "Your friend, she nice, nice to you?"

"Yes."

"My friend nice, too, but oh, he so busy. All the time travel."

"You're going to like America," Mike said.

"Americans, I like Americans. My friend, he's très, très gentil. French. . . ." She paused and shook her head from side to side. "French, not good. Bad. I no like French."

"I don't know. They seem all right to me," Mike said.

"No. Nothing here. French, all the time, money. France bad country."

"But you're French, Irene," Mike said.

"Yes, French and Italy—Italian."

When she said this I realized that she looked more Italian than French. And also, listening to her speak, especially with her nasal accent, she seemed quite unglamorous. But at close range, I could see that she was more youthful, younger than I had believed when I'd first spotted her in the garden.

"You should get out more, Irene," Mike said, his manner quite fatherly.

"I go out for walk every day in Bois. Every afternoon with my dog. But the men. Terrible. Terrible men in the Bois."

"It's your attractiveness, Irene, you're a very attractive girl."

"Me—Oh, no."

"You are too."

"Me, no, but the Paris men, terrible. My dog, he no make 'em afraid."

"I'll take you to dinner. You shouldn't stay at the hotel here so much."

"My friend, he be angry if I go with man."

"But my proposal is only platonic, Irene."

She looked at him bewildered.

At that moment, I had to keep an engagement. I excused myself and left.

II

The guests kept coming and going, but there were a few of us who were regulars. We came to know one another, and each of us had our own pattern of living. And Irene had got to know all of the regular guests.

The hotel was owned by a family of Balkan exiles. Besides the husband, wife and daughter, there were a sister and brother. Also, there was a distant relative, Mr. Enesco, who owned a share of the hotel. He was a man in his late forties, and was a pushing, aggressive man whose excessive concern with food caused constant comment among the guests. Although a relative of the owner, he never ate with them, but usually by himself. He sat at a small table with his back to the garden, and frequently I would sit at the one next to him.

Mr. Enesco spoke English very well and usually tried to talk with me. The year before I had talked to him frequently, but he had begun by bluntly asking me intimate and personal questions, and when he talked politics, he had been wearisomely anti-American. At one time Mr. Enesco had been a salesman, and he had often gone to

London. Now he did nothing, hung around the hotel most of the time, and he talked Marxism, proclaiming that he was a Marxist. Whenever he could buttonhole me, he would repeat Marxist clichés. According to Marx, there had to be a continuation of race prejudice in America and also a depression. Marx also explained for him the Rosenberg case of the year before and the Oppenheimer case, which was, at the time, receiving much attention in the French press. I had long since expressed my own views to him and had learned that he was not interested in discourse or discussion. If I answered a question about America, he would switch the issue and as a last resort, he would bring up the Sacco-Vanzetti case. The Sacco-Vanzetti case proved to him whatever he wished to have proven about contemporary America.

Mr. Enesco had had an ailing wife with whom he had lived in the hotel for several years, but she had never come down from her room. From the little he had said of her, it seemed clear that she had been mentally ill. She had died during the previous winter, and it seemed that Mr. Enesco's antipathy to America and his—if not enthusiasm, because he was not a man with any capacity for enthusiasm —admiration for the Russians became more pronounced following his wife's death. A refugee who had become a French citizen, he tried to be more French than the French. He had picked up many of the current conceits and clichés of the French intellectuals and the Parisian press. Uncultivated and boorish, he took on the airs of a cultivated Frenchman and spoke about books he had, undoubtedly, never read.

I saw Mr. Enesco speak twice with Irene. They sat in a corner in the lounge. I didn't hear what they said; however, it was clear that he was trotting forth his entire repertoire of clichés. He pointed several times to his newspaper and talked for some time. I wondered would he get anywhere with her, for I knew that he was on the make and had failed in the approaches he had made to several women.

It was a cold day. The sky outside was gray and it was chilly in the dining salon. I had been working, but it had not been easy, and, in addition, it was cold in my room. The dining salon was full for lunch, and the guests were all talking. I sat alone at a small table and Mr. Enesco was by himself next to me. As always, there was a note of officiousness in his voice when he ordered. He sent back the salad and the veal, dissatisfied with both.

"I have an article in the newspaper to give you," he said. "I want to give you an article on anti-Semitism. Oppenheimer was a Jew and the Rosenbergs, they were Jews."

I looked at him coldly.

"The French don't want Dien Bien Phu," he said.

"Why are they fighting for it then?" I asked.

"The Americans want them to. The American capitalists want war. No one else does. Russia," he shook his head "Russia does not want war."

"Who told you all this?"

"The capitalists need war for profits. They do not want a *crise,* depression."

I went on eating. I had spoken with him enough to know that discussion was meaningless.

"Wall Street," he began.

I turned towards him.

"It's capitalist, isn't it?"

"Wall Street," he said, "it makes the cold war."

"Maybe so,' I said, and finished my soup.

The owners of the hotel were gathered about a table across the room. I wondered why Mr. Enesco never ate with them, but of course I actually knew why. The family owned a black French poodle named Guit-guit; the dog sat at the table with them. Every so often one of the family group would say something and then exclaim:

"Guit-guit."

"The French people," Mr. Enesco said to me, "want to be let alone."

"By whom?"

"Please?' he asked, leaning towards me: he hadn't understood the sense of my ironic question.

"Who is taking advantage of the French?" I asked.

"They think the Americans are."

"What do you want me to do?"

"Please?" he asked, leaning forward.

"I think maybe you're right," I said. "Perhaps the Americans should get out, cut all aid and tell the Russians

they can have you. Then you could be happy in a salt mine
and free of the oppression of Wall Street."

Mr. Enesco grinned patronizingly at me, but he shut up.

Just as I finished eating, Irene entered. Mr. Enesco
invited her to sit with him but she excused herself and
left immediately.

III

About four-thirty that afternoon I was having tea alone
and Irene happened in and sat at the table with me.

"That man, you like him?"

"What man?"

"That man, what's his name, he sit at table next to you
today for lunch."

"No, he's a bore."

"Is he Communist?"

"I don't know. He could be."

"I no like him. I no eat today because he want me to
sit with him."

Mike Friedland joined us.

"It's no fun out—do you know it's cold?"

"I freeze. I live at Nice. I no like this weather in Paris."

"Maybe you'd be better off back at Nice. It looks as if
there isn't going to be any spring or summer or anything
but cold weather in Paris," Mike told her, his voice kindly.

"You're nice Mike, but you need—friend. Everybody
needs friend. My friend, he no come back for ten days. He
write me, I get letter today—he go to Africa—Dakar for
Air Force."

"That's too bad. You should have a boy friend who
doesn't travel so much."

"He travel—lots, all the time."

"Is he going to keep on travelling when you're married?"

"I no don't know."

Mr. Enesco looked in, and noticing us, he bowed.

"Tell me about that guy," Mike said. "All he does is
talk about money, food and women. How does he earn a
living?"

"He, he own part of this hotel."

"Oh, that's it. I don't like the way he talks. I heard him talking about Karl Marx," Mike said.

"He ugly, I no like." Irene grimaced.

"Ugly, beast man."

"Whatever he is, I don't like him particularly. He's not friendly."

"Beast man. No education—he's not educated."

"I don't know what education he has . . ." Mike began.

I explained to Mike that the French used education in the sense of manners, and he exclaimed, "Oh."

Looking at me questioningly, she asked:

"You go away with her, your friend, on *vacances, vacation?*"

"Yes, in July," I answered.

"By then, I'll be back home in New York." Mike said.

"With your secretary?" I asked.

"She's all right. She runs everything for me when I'm away—I don't have to worry about my business."

"She good to you—your secretary?" asked Irene.

"Best there is."

"Maybe you should take her with you in travel."

"No, that would spoil her, and I need her back in New York."

"New York, I think I will like New York."

"Of course you will."

"I like Americans—French, I no like. It's nothing here. Nobody cares here, nobody cares about nothing. With French people, it's only money."

"I think all people are the same, French or American, or anything else," Mike said.

"No, no, not French people. I know French people. I count the days before I go to America and marry my friend in Akron, Akron, Ohio. Next week now, he come."

"You must be lonesome, Irene," Mike said.

"Yes—but I have my dog. I sew. I sew all my own clothes. I make my dresses. You like my dresses, like this dress?"

It was low-necked; the color was bright red.

"Yes—yes. You're a talented girl."

"American women, they sew, make their own dresses?"

"No—they can get anything they want in the stores and it's cheaper that way," Mike said.

"America—big rich country? Yes?"

"It is. It's so big, there's many parts of it I've neve
seen. I've never seen California, and I've never been i
Akron, Ohio," Mike said.

She looked at him in surprise. Then she rose an
excused herself, saying that she had to feed her dog.

IV

I left on a two-week trip through Belgium and Hollan
Irene was then expecting her fiancé the day after n
departure. One day shortly after my return I saw Irene
lunch time and we sat together.

"You have good time?" she asked me.

"Yes."

"My friend," she said, "he no come. He write, car
come. He fly to Rome, *Vienne, Frankfort,* and now h
come next week. I wait here all the time, and he no com
Air Force business."

I wondered if it were really business and orders whic
were keeping her fiancé away.

"He have no time for me now. Meetings. He ha
meetings. But he love me. He writes me every day . . . a
most every day, he love me."

"Well, maybe it will change soon and you'll see mo
of him."

"I wait—I wait—I wait."

"It must be hard on you."

She looked off sadly.

"I wait today, tomorrow, every day . . . but he writ
me letter, wonderful, wonderful letter."

I suspected a feeling of hurt in her voice and was ve
sympathetic. And looking at her across the table, s
seemed younger than she had on any of the previo
occasions when I had talked with her. Her hair hu
down her back.

"But he write, next week, very sure, for sure, he com
here."

"I'm very glad."

"Now, I wait for next week."

She became silent. I felt a certain shock, perhaps cha-grin, because my original impressions of her had been so irrelevantly wrong. She could almost be called a girl, although she was twenty-six. Her clothes had misled me. She was a provincial, and her taste in clothes conditioned by this provincialism. She dressed as though she were always at a seaside resort. She possessed no Parisian sophistication and was not interested in love affairs and the seeming excitements of night life. She was here in Paris only because she loved a man, and she was beginning to pine for him in loneliness.

"How old have you—I no know English—how you say it?"

"How old are you?"

"How old are you?" she asked.

"Fifty."

"Fifty—you young. My friend, he have fifty-one years. I like a man, fifty, fifty-one. His hair—gray. You never see him?"

"I don't think I have."

"He comes here. He's handsome man—looks . . . *dis-tingué*—distinguish. Colonel, military man."

"Well, I hope he comes back soon."

"I hope. Next week. If he no come back soon, I go home and wait. I live in Nice. You know Nice?"

"I was there for a few days once."

"I not like Nice. I live with my sister. She's older, married. All the time, she tell me what to do. She no like my clothes. She do not like my friend. My father dies in War. My mother dies, *trois* years ago. My father was Italian, doctor born in Torino. My mother, French. Me, French-Italian."

"You look Italian."

"Thank you."

"Last year with my sister, we got to *Venise*. You know *Venise*? How you call it English?"

"Venice."

She tried to pronounce Venice but it came out closer to "*Venise*."

"In Venice, my sister tells me everything to do. I not do what she tell me. No, I don't—you say that?—I don't?"

"Yes."

"I don't like to go back home to Nice. But Paris . . . Paris too big, too much noise. Much automobiles, noise." She smiled wanly. "But I wait here and next week my friend, he come and we go on vacation to *Suisse* . . ."

She shrugged to pronounce Switzerland as it is in English, and I helped her. She pronounced it after me.

Then, she looked off. Her smile was very sad and somewhat apologetic.

V

For a while, I saw her briefly every day. We met in the elevator, in the lobby or in front of the hotel. She continued to take a walk every afternoon in the Bois but for the main, she remained about the hotel, and spent much of her time in her room sewing. She was making her entire trousseau.

Another guest at the hotel was Donald Lindwich, a big, gray-haired American business man of fifty. He had been born in Helsinki, and now lived in New York, where his family resided, but he spent much of his time in Paris because of his interests and investments. He was a friendly and intelligent man but, other than business, his serious concern was women. He had a red-haired French mistress, a married woman, but he kept talking of dropping her. Lindwich had occupied various rooms in the hotel and liked to tell me of the love affairs going on in it. He enjoyed speaking of the noises he heard through the walls.

At breakfast one morning, he asked me:

"Who's the dame I saw you talking to in front of the hotel yesterday afternoon? The one with the big dog."

"Oh, she's from Nice. Her name is Irene."

"You after her?"

He laughed in a cordial and insinuatingly masculine manner.

"There'd be no use in anyone being after her, Donald."

I told him something of her story.

"I wouldn't want her, anyway. She's too skinny."

We then spoke of France, of moods of the people, of anti-Americanism, of the profits made by French business and of the war in Indo-China which had been ended at the Geneva Conference. Irene came into the dining salon.

"No, she's too skinny," he remarked after giving her a quick but sharply appraising look.

"I guess she isn't for her Colonel."

"Is he giving her the air?"

"I don't know. But I don't think so."

"Hell, I'm a busy man and I have conferences and travel —but I've never been so damned busy that I had no time to see any dame I really wanted."

"Maybe he is jilting her—I wouldn't know—but she's in love and more faithful than a dog to its master."

"That's curious in a French woman. It's not like the ones I know."

"She doesn't come from the kind of background of the French women you meet."

"Maybe that's so. I've learned never to trust a woman. Damned near every one of them will be unfaithful to a man." He laughed. "But that only means that they're like us."

He glanced past me and at Irene.

"Yes," he repeated, "she's too skinny. But if that colonel of hers wants her, he'd better come back. I can see that she's getting in heat. If she hangs around Paris, some fellow is going to lay her and make her forget her colonel."

Mr. Lindwich had to leave for a business appointment. I went upstairs to my work.

I saw Irene again on the day after her fiancé had been due to arrive in Paris. She looked wan and haggard, with a torn expression on her sun-browned face, and with rings under her eyes.

"My friend," she said in a low voice. "My friend, he no come. He send me telegram. He go, he must go to Frankfurt. Air Force business."

"I'm very sorry," I said, not knowing what else to tell her.

"He say he love me, and he come for sure Saturday."

"Well, that won't be so long a wait."

"No, I know. He tell me for sure, he come Saturday."
She smiled apologetically.

"I wait," she said, leaving me to go up to her room.

VI

I was eating alone the following Friday evening, and when Irene came down to dinner, she joined me.

"My friend, he come for sure tomorrow morning. He write me, tell me he love me and come for sure."

"That's good news."

"Yes, good news. I wait and wait for him. You see me, I wait, but now for sure, he come. I count the days for September, when I go to America. France," she made a face, "France, nothing in France for me. No ambition— the French," she shook her head from side to side. "No ambition."

"France is in bad condition," I said.

"Yes, terrible. There is nothing, nothing in France. And no generous," she said. "I do not come back to France. No, I do not come back here. For what? My father, he is dead. My mother, dead. Nothing, there is nothing for me in France."

"I hope there will be much for you in America."

"Americans, young. The French, no. Nobody cares in France."

VII

Irene's friend came on Saturday, and there was much excitement in the hotel. Two elderly Americans, the Stonehams, were guests and they had established a cordial acquaintanceship with Irene, and I had also gotten to know them. He was a retired engineer and they lived on the East Side of New York. They were both simple and sympathetic. Mr. Stoneham had begun to wonder if Irene's fiancé would really come back to her. He and Mrs. Stoneham were most delighted to learn that he had arrived.

Irene and her colonel ate in the hotel that Saturday evening, but I dined out and did not get to see him. She wanted me to meet him, partly out of pride in him, but she also wanted me to speak with him about her visa. He had been slow about helping her to apply for it, and inasmuch as I happened to remark that sometimes there were delays in obtaining visas, she was beginning to worry

hat she wouldn't receive hers in time to go to America for
her marriage.

At breakfast on Sunday morning, the Stonehams spoke
about Irene's colonel, declaring that he was real and not
an illusion. Irene had gone out with him after dinner on
he night before. Then, as I was standing in the lobby by
he desk after breakfast, Donald Lindwich came up to me.

"Say, that skinny one from Nice hasn't been down for
breakfast yet. Her boy friend came back for her. If you or
I had the room next to them, we'd be hearing something."

"She loves him."

"Whether it's love or a girl you pick up on the Rue
Washington, it sounds the same."

On Monday afternoon, I again saw Irene in the salon.

"My friend is here. He come back for dinner, and we go
tonight."

"That's very good news. I'm pleased to hear it. I'd like
to meet him."

"I want you to meet him. You'll like him. He's dignified,
gray hair, dignified, very well, much educated."

"Are you going away with him on your vacation?"

"Yes, but he postpone it. Friday, he must go away to
Spain, Madrid—more Air Force business."

"How long will he be gone?"

"I don't know. He says few days. I hope it's few, few,
very few days."

"He must have a very responsible position."

"Yes. He tell me nothing, almost nothing. He always
say, 'Top Secret.' "

Then, a moment later, she said, "But he tell me he love
me. I know he speak the truth. He is fine man. I want you
meet him."

"I'll be here in the hotel tonight."

"Oh, tonight we go out. Tomorrow, maybe at break-
ast."

"Very good, I'll look for you then."

I went back to my room. I was staying alone and working that evening, but about nine-thirty I went down for a
cup of coffee.

Irene was sitting with the Stonehams. At a big table,
he two women of the family that owned the hotel were
playing bridge with friends.

Irene's smile was sad and defensive as I sat down with them and gave my order to the dark-haired waitress.

"You not go out tonight and see your friend?" she asked

"No, I was working."

"We're sitting here and just talking—we're not doing anything exciting, or saying anything brilliant," Mr. Stoneham said.

"At your age, Daddy, do you still think of doing something exciting?" Mrs. Stoneham teased.

"After that walk of ours around Paris today, Mother I'm tired, darned tired."

"You walk much?" Irene asked.

"For hours," Mrs. Stoneham said.

"It was mighty interesting, even if it was just a day the life of two tourists. We looked in store windows, we went all the way to the Place de la Bastille."

"You did—good," Irene said.

"But when you go into certain districts," Mr. Stoneham said, "you can see people are poor by the clothes the wear."

"Yes, many of the working people can't afford decen clothes," I said.

Mike Friedland joined us.

"Where's your friend tonight, Irene? You look lonesome," he said cheerfully.

"She is, but you don't have to remind her," Mrs. Stoneham told him.

"Irene and I are friends. I can joke a little with her

"Yes, nice people here, all nice people in this hot, except that awful man, what's his name?"

Irene looked about and then at me.

"Enesco," I said.

"Oh, that guy," Mike said. "Whenever he talks to me I can't understand what he's talking about."

"My friend, he has meeting. I wait but he no can come. She shook her head from side to side in a gesture expressing confusion. "Meetings. All the time, meetings. He say meetings with the French are most long. The French talk too much. I wait for telephone call."

She waited long and at 10:30, when I went back u to my room, Irene was still waiting.

Her Colonel had to leave a day ahead of time for Spain

She was alone again for the next ten days. She was still waiting for her Colonel when I left Paris a couple of days later.

VIII

I was away for over two months. When I returned to the hotel towards the end of September, Irene was once again waiting.

She told me that she had had only a week's vacation with her friend, and that since then he had been away. She looked worn and was very nervous. She kept moving her hands, and twisting her body while she talked.

"My marriage is postponed. I go to America now in January."

"That's too bad."

"He love me. But work, Air Force business, makes him travel and go to meetings all of the time. I wait and wait. I wait for letter now. It's not funny."

"I know it isn't."

I was at the hotel only a week before leaving Paris to begin my return journey to America. Two days before my departure, Irene left the hotel and returned to Nice. No one knew if she had been jilted or not. The last time I saw her was the day before she left. I met her in the elevator and she looked haggard and despairing. She said to me:

"This is not funny. No, not funny."

THREE AMERICANS IN PARIS

I

The Paris night was as mysteriously seductive as the subtlest of perfumes. The three American men sat in the Royal St. Germain, across from the Deux Magots at the Place St. Germain. None wanted to return alone to their hotel rooms. Harry Bowman was with the Embassy, Nathan Eidelman was a journalist, Dan O'Neill a writer.

"How come you smoke French cigarettes, Harry?" Nathan asked, as they smoked and sipped coffee.

"When in France do as the Romans do," Harry answered.

"But don't forget that we're the Romans. The French are the Greeks," Dan commented dryly.

"Let it be that way if they like it. For my part, I'll take the Greek restaurant owners in America," Harry said.

"You're getting it bad—the disillusionment," Nathan remarked.

"Maybe," Harry answered, puffing on a *Gaulloise jaune*. The three of them turned reflective and were silent for awhile.

Harry was tall and lean; Nathan and Dan were stocky and of medium height. Nathan was getting fat; his hair had grayed, but his large face was tanned, youthful. He was forty-seven. Dan, at fifty, was only beginning to turn a little gray at the temples. He looked young, almost boyish. Harry was fifty-three, a sombre, brown-haired man with the stamp of middle age upon his character. He wore glasses with very thick lenses.

"'*Les Américains*'," Nathan exclaimed, in low-voiced anger.

He nodded to the left, towards a group at a nearby table, at which a plump man in a gray suit was talking to two young men and a girl. Both Nathan and Harry recognized the plump man and told Dan that he was Gregory Movena, who had gained some fame and notoriety in the period of Da-da; he had even been described sometimes, along with Tristam Tzara, as the leading Dadaist poet.

"He plays with the Commies," Nathan said.

"Who else could he play with?" asked Harry, rather dismissingly.

"He's a footnote in the history of post-World War One literature," Dan said.

"The way he says *'les Américains'* makes me boil. He's aking fun of Dulles. He says that Dulles was just about riven out of Geneva. There he goes again—*'les Américains.'* "

The young French people laughed at what the Dadaist poet had said.

"What burns me up is that they know better. They know that if it weren't for us and our support, they wouldn't be sitting here like this."

"Nate, our illusion was ever to believe that we could do anything with France," Harry said.

Dan burst out laughing.

"What's funny?" Nathan asked.

"We are—I've been over here a lot during the last five years and we've been talking about the French problem. What the hell ever gave us the idea that we could do anything with France?"

"Or the French," added Nathan. "There he goes again —*les Américains.*"

"The ones like him are the worst," Harry said. "They sit in cafés and condemn us and Goddamn it, they'd be in a concentration camp somewhere if it weren't for America."

"Harry, at your age, do you expect gratitude?" asked Nathan.

"Gratitude. Don't imagine that I expect gratitude, especially from the French."

"We all loved France once," Dan mused.

"Let's not talk about France as if she were a mistress who betrayed us," Nathan said. "There he goes again—

boasting that at Geneva it was a defeat for 'les Américains'."

"It is a disillusionment. I first came back in '49, following the War. There was a hell of a lot of idealism and hope poured into the effort to revive France," Dan said.

"God helps those who help themselves, Dan," Nathan remarked.

"We made two big mistakes," Harry explained. "We acted on the basis that France is a great power—and we tried to make France over as if we could turn it into America. The French have always been the same as they are now. Now, it's decadence. Perhaps they are right—they might be the Greeks of our time. There is decadence here—beautiful women, good living, brilliant conversation . . ."

"But the conversation I'm hearing isn't brilliant," Nathan said, nodding towards the next table.

"Don't let that get you," Dan said.

"It's not getting me—except that it gets me sore," Nathan answered. "Well, this is June. In August I'll be going home. It can't be too soon for me."

"I'd like to spend about two weeks in America," Harry remarked, wistfully. "I'd get a car and drive around—see the country. I'd like to meet the new labor leaders and the men who are doing things back home."

He looked off, absorbed in a dream.

"You're a fixture here, Harry."

"No one knows how lonely it sometimes gets to be."

"I no longer feel as I used to in Europe," Dan said.

"You're the same as we are, Danny. You're getting old."

"We're all getting old," Harry said.

"There he goes again—'les Américains'," Nathan snapped.

II

For a while, they sat, smoking, speaking only occasionally. Each sensed the loneliness in the other two.

"The New Deal—those were good days," Harry exclaimed. "Things were happening, and a man had a feeling of faith. Something was getting done. . . . That's when I started to work for the Government.

Harry spoke with nostalgia. But those days seemed so

ar away now. They were gone, and his youth was gone,
oo. The irrevocability of this lost time of his life hurt
im. Then, he had lived in days of hope, days when there
vas reason to hope and when a man did not hope alone.

"There's more to fight for now," Dan said, his remark
cutting in on Harry's thoughts.

"Yes, but how many people know it?" Harry responded.

He lit another cigarette and looked off. Tonight again,
ie would go home alone and sleep alone. He knew that
ie would do this for the rest of his life. He had no illusions
about this. At times, he believed that he was probably as
disillusioned as any man could be. But even so, there were
iis moments of hope; if it wasn't hope, then it was wishing.
Hoping and wishing were mixed up with other emotions.
iere was always regret. Regret and loneliness were
always with him.

A deep sadness came upon him. It was spring again in
Paris and he was an old man. He felt himself to be an old
man. He was not so much older than Dan and Nate here,
but he felt that he was immeasurably older than either of
them.

He looked at the sky over Paris. It was blue and clear,
a beautiful sky, a beautiful night.

"No, things aren't going to get any better in France,"
he said to Nathan and Dan, who had been talking about
French politics.

III

Harry had been born in the Mid-west. His parents were
well-to-do and he was an only son. As a boy he had been
shy and somewhat awkward. Girls had filled his thoughts,
but he had been timid in their presence and his timidity
had always troubled him. In college he had met Julie. She
had been as shy as he. She had been pale and beautiful,
a red-haired girl with bright blue eyes and white skin. And
he had fallen in love with her on sight. Later, he had
learned that it had been the same with her.

They had gone together for four years and during that
period, he had not made love to her. His feelings for Julie
were too akin to worship. Then they had married. He had
gotten a promising job in the office of an advertising

agency. This had not been what he had wanted to do in life. His ambitions had been of a more intellectual order, to write, to teach, to work in some field where ideas would be involved and in which he could feel that he was making a contribution towards the common good. But also, he had wanted Julie and she had been a sickly girl. She would need care, attention, and some luxury or at least great comfort. Because of this, he had forsworn his ambitions and gone into an advertising agency. They had married and had spent a two-week honeymoon on the Maine coast. And two weeks after they had returned from their honeymoon Julie had died of consumption.

Harry had feared that Julie's life would be short. But her death had been a shattering blow to him. Life had then become empty and meaningless to him. His faith in happiness had been ruptured. Everything had seemed hollow. The hurt had been deep. It had threatened his sense of his own dignity, and given him a feeling of weakness. It was not a mere sense of personal weakness, but rather an awareness of the fallibility and weakness of all human beings. Julie's death gave him a concrete, a specific sense of the cruelty of nature. He was left with a saddened morbid feeling of the insubstantiality of living. Only youth was important, and youth was brief.

Harry had lived in a state of shock and depression for some months. He knew that Julie was gone and gone forever from him, but his knowledge of this fact could bring no comfort or surcease. He wanted to live by lingering in his remembrance of her and by keeping alive within himself as much of the feelings and as many of the memories of the days when they had been together. Friends advised him to go away to the East but he would not do this. A few advised him to look around and to remarry. This likewise seemed impossible. Julie was framed in his mind. She remained there like a statue.

His major consolation had been to visit Julie's home and to sit there in the rooms where he had known her. Her old home seemed to be vivid with her and when he would visit it at night, he would have the illusion that he could feel her physical presence near him. It could not be that she was gone forever. It was true; but what was true just could not be so. These thoughts would cast him into deep melancholy, and at times it would seem as if her loss caused him physical pain.

But he said little of the despair and agony that was in him. He rarely ever mentioned Julie's name. In fact, he would often seem to be so calm and composed that others would be deceived and would think that he was taking her loss well. His sadness and melancholy were self-evident, but his friends thought that time would cover this. For Harry, such thoughts and notions were irrelevant. He wanted to live as though fixed in the days when Julie was alive. On the street, he looked at girls and women with searching, seeking eyes, wanting to find someone who looked like Julie, who resembled her in some feature or characteristic, who in some way reminded him of her. The strain was all the greater because he held it in himself. He did not want others to know his feelings, to have even an inkling of how sad, frustrated and despairing he was.

Harry knew that he must find release from his emotions. He was clearly aware that he was living in an unhealthy state. The best thing that he could have done would have been to leave, to strike out elsewhere. Now and then, he thought of doing this, and would imagine himself finding a new life and career far away, in New York, or Washington, or even Europe. Sometimes he would dream of going to Paris. Possibly, he would tell himself, he could find some surcease and even happiness in Paris. But he could not make the move.

Julie's older sister, Edna, would often sit with him. Edna had been Julie's senior by two years, and they resembled one another in physical make-up. Edna had none of the delicacy of feature which had given to Julie a quality of rare beauty, but she was a very good looking girl. Often, she looked like Julie, but healthy and sound. Harry had never particularly cared for her when Julie had been alive. There had been a rivalry between them and he had clearly sensed that Edna had not been pleased with Julie's marriage to him. But once Julie was gone, he began to see her older sister in a different light. Edna, more than any other human being he knew or saw, reminded him of his dead young wife. He would sit in the living room talking to her about books, life, his work. She would listen. Rarely would he speak of Julie, however.

One year after Julie's death, he married Edna. He did

this knowing that he did not love Edna, and seriously doubting that she loved him. Marrying Edna even seemed to him like a betrayal of Julie and of her memory. Yet he went through with the ceremony like a man driven and compelled to do it.

The marriage was a failure from the beginning. Edna was nervous, anxious and demanding. He had overlooked all this because he had seen her as a mirrored image of her sister. But once married, he was terrified and depressed. She was cold to him and he was stricken with guilt after their first night.

They lived together as man and wife for only three weeks. By this time, the depression had deepened, Roosevelt had been inaugurated and there was excitement in Washington. Through a friend in the Democratic Party, he landed a job in Washington with the N.I.R.A. He did not divorce Edna, and she was perfectly agreeable to this and to his leaving her. He agreed to support her. He went to Washington with a feeling of liberation. He believed that he would become a new man, a new person. He felt elation and he was eager, but he did not consider himself to be a happy man. Perhaps he would find another woman, but he still held Julie fixed in love in his mind.

III

Harry gazed off at the street, and thought of Julie. All these years she had been dead, and now he was becoming an old man. But it was still Julie who had been the woman of his life. Julie had been a girl, not a woman. He thought of her often and whenever he did, his disillusionment and hopelessness rose to quench all other thought and feeling.

Nate and Dan had both had their tough breaks.

"Yes, I'm going back for good in August," Nate stated.

"You're lucky you can go—both of you are lucky," Harry said.

"Dan here is the lucky one—he can go and come whenever he wants—Dan, you're a free man. Don't you know it?"

"Yes," Dan answered, concerned with his own train of thoughts. There was this struggle to care. Did Harry and

Nate feel it? The three of them had gone through personal experiences that had left their hopes for a personal life in ruins.

"I've reached the point where I can scarcely trust one Frenchman. It isn't the individual. Many of them are O.K. individually," Harry said. "It's the way they are, and their culture."

"I don't like them," Nate stated. "To me, the French are not *sympathique.*"

"France has not gotten over her defeat," Dan remarked.

"That's true," Harry said thoughtfully.

And, Dan asked himself, could not one draw a parallel between the feelings of so many of the French, and his own feelings? And also, perhaps the feelings of Nate and Harry? He resisted a positive answer to his questions because he, also, wanted to beef about the French.

Dan was struggling with himself. He knew that he was full of inner contradictions, but often forgot to take into account the fact that others were the same. His second marriage had broken up after Ruth had had a child. She had grown so anxious and, at times hysterical, that daily minute-by-minute life had been too much of a struggle. Every least little detail had been swollen into significance. He had loved her, and sometimes he even still wondered if his love had wholly died or gone to sleep? After years of petty trouble, he had finally left. They had been separated for a little over three years, and he had lived in hotels, travelling and wandering much, and looking, always looking. He had invested his emotions in his family and his work, and they had emerged from debt, and it had seemed as though they were among the most fortunate people in the world. And then his life had blown up on him. No, rather than a blow-up, it had been erosion. It had all just worn away. The storms of Ruth's emotion had caused wind and rain to wear away their love. And once, he had thought that it had been as solid as rock.

"We can't call the French our allies," Nate said.

"No, if there is war, we can't rely on them," Harry agreed.

A conversation the three of them had had before.

"Sometimes, I am in favor of clearing out," Nate said.

"I'm not," Dan intervened.

"You don't still think that France can be reformed do you Dan?" Nate asked.

"I merely think that you don't give up positions—especially if they will be of benefit to an enemy."

When Ruth had been at her most troubled and her most hysterical, he had used to tell himself that you don't give up. Now, at least for tonight, he felt hopeless about almost everything. He recalled that when Ruth would fight and scream and rage in tantrums about every little detail of their boy's life, he would strive as best he could to hold onto his own judgments and to retain his clarity and directness of perception. It was the same here in Europe. Every fact could be interpreted ten, twenty or more different ways. You could flounder and wallow in confusion.

"If war comes, what is going to happen to all the American women and children over here?" Harry asked in a sudden burst of feeling.

"War isn't coming—this year," Dan stated.

"The Russians are doing well enough without war," Nate said.

"I've seen everything change over here. As you know, Nate, I came in with the liberating forces, and we reoccupied the Embassy. I had hopes then." Harry paused a moment. "Yes, I had hopes."

"I know—we're just the suckers," Nate said.

"And when are we going to stop being suckers?" Harry asked.

"At least they are going now," Nate said, nodding his head in the direction of the ageing Dadaist poet.

"Now we've gotten occupancy of this café," Dan joked, and they laughed.

"I suppose we'd feel the same way if we were in the shoes of the French and they were in our boots," Dan mused.

"Even if they had more reason to like us, they wouldn't," Nate said.

"This nation is like a woman. It's unstable and hysterical," Harry remarked.

IV

Unstable and hysterical. The words burned in Nathan's mind. Six months ago, he had buried Yetta. Once, he had

ed to call her his Yetta. He remembered the scene in the
ematorium. The silence of his friends as they sat in the
ean, domed room had been like fright and fear. To think
Yetta, even the remains of her poor, sick disturbed
ody, being burned to ashes had produced one of the deep-
t depressions of his life. If he left France, he might get
ver his melancholy thoughts. She had died here. He had
ved here a number of years now since the War and she
ad been back in America, in and out of an institution. His
emories of her, his thoughts about her during these years
ad sometimes rankled and sometimes cut him. Their love
ad died years ago. So he had thought. And yet something
n him, some feeling for her, had not died. He never could
ve imagined that her death would come as such a blow
d that the shock of it would have been so great.

Harry and Dan now were talking about France. Harry
vas sounding off. He had gone stale over here. Any Ameri-
an would go stale, living too long in the Europe of the
ld war. He himself would go stale.

He wanted to go back. He yearned now for America,
nd kept building up pictures of a new life there. In New
York, he wanted to write and read and study the Bible.

When Nathan had first met Yetta, he had dreamed of
ecoming a writer, a novelist, a literary man, the American
Belinsky or Plenkhanov.

He and Yetta had been married in 1931. They had met
t the Proctorian Writers Club on Sixth Avenue. God, how
ng ago that was. And the very memory made Nathan
most squirm inside of himself. Then, he grinned.

"I was just thinking of the early thirties. What crazy
ays," he said.

The French Commies and some of the intellectuals over
ere are sinking back to that level now," Dan remarked.
Have you read anything that's been written about socialist
ealism?"

"Both of you fellows were mixed up in all of that,
veren't you?" Harry asked.

"Dan wasn't very much, but I was. I never joined the
arty, but I was a Communist, just the same. I wanted to
ntroduce Belinsky and Plekhanov into America. I still
dmire Plekhanov."

Nathan pronounced Plekhanov's name with warmth.
Yetta had been rabid, more so than he. But how pretty

she had been. And her youth had so appealed to him. A beautiful rebel girl. She had been a spitfire, a firebrand ready to picket and to fight the cops on Fourteenth Street and in Union Square. They had not been cops in those days: they had been Cossacks.

"Remember the Cossacks?" he asked, amused, but there was a sense of pain hidden behind his levity.

A sudden weariness came into Harry's face, also. The mere reference to the early thirties aroused his own painful memories.

"We were young then, Harry," Nathan said with softness in his voice; he was really saying to himself that then he and Yetta had been young.

Dan's feelings became poignant. None of them were really old as yet, but they had reached the point in life from which they would begin to slide. Enthusiasm was not as easy now as it had been ten or twenty years ago.

He looked off thoughtfully. Take almost any three people, once they had lived a little and passed their first flush of youth, and sit them down to talk and you would get sadness and melancholy. Death and time and impermanence were part of living, and when people were vis-à-vis themselves, death and time and impermanence all asserted themselves.

"You look profound—are you still worrying about the French, Dan?"

"No—I'm not worried about them."

"Damn it, some Americans should. Not many of them are going to be with us if the war comes," Harry said.

"There isn't going to be a war—unless it's a little one."

"I don't know. There could be."

"The Russians are getting what they want without it, why should they want a war," Nathan put in.

"If we want peace, we have to take the risk of war," Dan said.

"What is American policy?" Nate asked.

"I don't know," Dan answered.

"Neither do I," Nathan concurred.

"Most of the things we do, we do wrongly," Harry mused.

"Sometimes I think that's an understatement," Dan said.

"Some of this crap about psychological warfare burns

me up. My God, how does such damned foolishness impress people?"

"That's one of your particular peeves, isn't it, Harry?" Nathan said.

They went on talking about international politics, but more in the form of lament and of repetition than of an exchange of ideas. What they said was deeply colored by their mood. And they shared a common mood of melancholy.

They sat for sometime longer, still reluctant to go back alone to their hotel. Their talk was casual. The café was almost empty. Nearby, a group of young Americans sat and they heard an occasional remark about Henry Miller.

The night seemed to grow softer as it became late. They felt the lateness of the night as if it were a quality in itself. It was just comfortably cool and the sky appeared vast. It was blue and full of stars. They sat under the shining bright stars, and running through the mind of each of them were memories of his own youth.

Two American midshipmen passed. They were tall, young, scrubbed-looking; in their dark uniforms and white hats, they looked clean-cut and upstanding. And with them were two old and somewhat frazzled looking French women, their faces painted so much that they appeared inhuman, close to ghastly. Obviously, they were prostitutes. The two midshipmen passed by with the French whores. Spontaneously, the three men burst into exuberant laughing.

Bent over with laughter, Nathan said:

"Christ, has our prestige sunk so low that that's all the uniform can get?"

They laughed again. It was as though they washed their systems of depression by laughter.

Then they went home in Harry's car. After dropping off his two friends, Harry parked his car and rang the night bell at his hotel. A sleepy-eyed little man in a rumpled blue uniform slowly came and opened the door.

"Bon soir, monsieur."

"Bon soir," Harry answered.

"Bonne nuit," the night clerk said as Harry got into he elevator.

Harry pressed the button, and the elevator rattled and shook as it climbed slowly upwards. A profound loneliness took hold of Harry. Would he sleep? He thought of America, miles away and across the ocean, and he wished he were back there. Working in the Foreign Service cost a heavy price in loneliness. At times, and especially on nights like this, it seemed unbearable. But it was bearable, he assured himself as he got out on his floor.

Walking to the door of his two-room suite, he wondered if his life would have been different had Julie lived.

He let himself in. The outer room was large and full of books. He looked at it. It was utterly empty to him.

Would he sleep tonight or have to read for an hour or two, poring over more French newspapers and magazines? And Nate and Dan, he liked them. A few friends like them were all that made his personal life bearable. They came and went, but he stayed on, watching and reporting, the eye that saw the slow erosion of decadence in a country once great, a country he had once loved as a man might love a beautiful and fascinating woman.

SHANLEY

Shanley had loose folds of sloppy fat, which caused him to appear bigger and heavier than he actually was. But he was big and heavy. In his socks, he was six feet one inch, and his weight was ouncing up from two hundred and twenty five pounds to two thirty. His face was puffed out to bloatedness, and his neck was thick with a flabby excess of flesh. His hair had turned gray some years back. He was forty-nine years old. His eyes were pale blue and clear, a contrast to the grossness of flesh that he had become.

Shanley's walk was loose, as though he had never learned well to command and use his limbs and torso.

It was a hot Friday night, after five, and the month was July. The homebound crowd was all over the sidewalk. The streets tired you with their grating clash of noise. Shanley wanted to get out of all this mobbing confusion, and he wanted to sit down and catch his breath. He was miserably uncomfortable with perspiration, and depressed with fatigue from the heat. But he was only at Clark and Randolph, and the distance ahead to the Illinois Central Station was still three long blocks.

Shanley stopped in the middle of the block, between Clark Street and State Street, and, after fumbling in the pockets of his very light gray flannel suit, he lit a cigarette, but with a feeling of clumsiness which he had felt about many physical movements and actions almost all of his life. Then, puffing and inhaling, he continued to move with the throng. He was as restless in feeling as almost any of those who were walking around him, nervous, and even compusively in a hurry. But he slowed down, and let himself droop along, now and then taking a puff of his lighted

163

cigarette. And he was breathing as though he were panting and out of breath from too much exercise.

Tired, yes, damned tired he was. He almost ached.

And there was a pain in his left arm. It was tracing down the arm; it must be nerves, or a muscle, maybe.

It had been a hot, wearing day. He ought to be tired. The whole week had been hard, a tough one, and he was done in from it.

Shanley slackened his gait for a second time. He walked on with cautious slowness.

Yes, he was pooped out and he was drooping, and dragging his can, yes, drooping, pooped out, petered out, done in.

Suddenly, he thought of years ago, when he was in high school at St. Stanislaus. Golly, God, to be back there again, in 1921, 1922, 1923. No use wishing for that, no use, no, but he wished.

Now, it was 1956. And then—1923 was the year he'd graduated. 1956. 1923.

He pressed his teeth against his lower lip. He was melancholy for what used to be, for what was gone, and melancholy—more than melancholy, he guessed—for what had never been, but perhaps could have been, or perhaps should have been.

Shanley was sad, and fat, and tired, amidst the Randolph Street crowd of people of many ages who were going home, just the same as he was himself, going home, going away from another week of work, going away from another day of life, another week of living.

He flicked his cigarette away, and it fell behind the moving high heels of a young brunette with mighty neat, neatly shaped shanks.

His breath was very short, his fat chest burned a bit under his limp, dampened white shirt.

1923. And now, 1956.

Yes, then, years back, he had fancied that he would become a journalist. Father Geraghty had thought he would, too, and that he had good promise. That's what Geraghty used to tell him, and Father Geraghty would always grade him between 95 and 100.

What use was it now to remind himself of that ambition, yes, what use?

—I could have. And I could have gone farther than Danny O'Neill.

Thinking of Danny; no, he had nothing against O'Neill. Once in all of these years, only once had he see him. It must have been just after the war ended. O'Neill had been much different from what he had expected him to be. Not a fire-eater, and Danny hadn't talked big. He'd been quiet, soft-spoken, but awfully damned sure of himself. And there hadn't been one gray hair. But he, himself, had already grown gray. And now he was about to turn white.

There was no use of thinking about it all. He could put himself into a dither—and for what? A couple of times he had gotten drunk on beer, and it had been because of such thoughts.

Shanley told himself that he must look like a fat old man. He must look like nothing at all to look at, and possibly even something to laugh at. But those times back in his twenties, and up to about when he was thirty-five, when he'd kept planning with real hopes, and kept resolving to take off weight. But he never had. He'd never done a hell of a lot of things. He'd never gone to Washington and he had only once been to New York. That was when he'd been Secretary of The Society of the Little Rose of Jesus Christ.

This was a remembrance that had often brought him pangs of nostalgia, and, more, real sadness. Now, however, it had been so long ago, and, well . . . there were times when it had been difficult for him to accept the fact that his youth was long ago, and his hair was gray; that had given him regrets full of pain, real pain.

—I'm not so old, Shanley told himself.

Forty-nine. But it was not a question of being old, not at least in the sense of being an old man. He wasn't a young man, either, and he hadn't achieved in life what he had hoped to achieve.

—Shit, he told himself.

That awful pain of disappointment!

And now, too, Father Geraghty was dead.

Thinking of his old teacher at St. Stanislaus, Shanley wanted to stop in the middle of the sidewalk and let the crowd sweep by him. For about a second, it was as though he had lost his sense of where he was. He felt much as he had a few times when he had dreamed that he, himself, was dead, and had then awakened from a lousy, frightening nightmare.

Walking on again towards the I. C. station in that Friday night crowd, Shanley knew as though with urgent sharpness the pain of thinking about his own death. But heck-no, Hell, he told himself, he was healthy. Maybe he was a little short of breath, but that was nothing. One day he would die. But there was no reason for him not to expect many, many more years of life before his time should come. Yes, many years of life, and of happiness!

Oh, Hell, what was it that he had been thinking about? Oh, yes, Geraghty. Sometimes, in fact usually, it was hard for him to think of Geraghty dead. He would never forget that winter morning four years ago, when he'd opened *The Morning Clarion* when he had gotten seated in the I. C. train, and had seen Geraghty's picture on the obituary page. It was a picture that he'd seen often. It had been taken when Geraghty had been in the prime of his life. The big face, with that expression of strength and intelligence, the short nose, the intelligent mouth—Father Geraghty. And that was already more than four years ago. *Tempus fugit.* He still remembered his Latin pretty well. Hell, when he was a high school student at S. S., he had never thought that he'd wind up in the insurance business. No, he'd thought of something else, and, of course, at one time he'd wanted to be a newspaper man. That had been because of Geraghty's influence and advice. And that course in journalism he'd taken at the University. He should have stayed on in college, he, who had led his class at St. Stanislaus. He had, also, worked for six months as a reporter for *Catholic Life*. Father Robert, that was Geraghty, got him the job. And it had been then that he'd taken the journalism course at the University. He should have gone on in journalism, and he might have gotten somewhere, gotten to be big, prominent, famous. Pat Lyons, editor of *Catholic Life,* had thought so and Pat had liked his stories, especially the humorous ones. Pat used to tell him:

"Shanley, you have a talent for doing humorous feature stories. You can write darn funny stuff. You'll attract notice, and land on one of the big papers in town here."

And he would have, too, if Geraghty hadn't given him the job with The Society of the Little Rose of Jesus Christ.

Everybody has ups and downs, good luck, bad luck in his life. He wasn't complaining.

Shanley walked on to the underground pass of the I. C. station at Randolph Street; he was lost as one of the big crowd flooding into the station. Shanley was weary. He felt the slight ache of a heartburn. He walked slowly, but after descending the stairway to get through the tunnel under Michigan Avenue to the station, he was puffing from shortness of breath. But no, he hold himself, he wasn't any more short of wind than he'd been a few days ago, or two weeks ago, for that matter. He'd had a checkup a month ago, and Doc White had said that he was in good shape. There was no need to be worried. He was certain on that score. But he walked more slowly.

He would have to wait about five minutes before going down on the platform and, hence, he found a seat on one of the benches facing the gates which led, through several doors and down the stairs, to the trains. There were several men and women on the bench where Shanley sat down with sagging tiredness. He glanced at them, cursorily. He always looked around at people, hoping he'd see someone he knew, perhaps someone from the old days when he was young, possibly one of his classmates or another fellow from St. Stanislaus. Three months ago he'd met Marty Milligan, good old Marty. Marty was doing well. Most of his class of '23 were, also. They probably all had automoblies, too. Well, his would be ready again tomorrow. Grace had smashed it up a hundred and fifty buck's worth. But he should be happy rather than complaining. Grace hadn't even been scratched. She'd merely been shaken up and frightened just a little, that was all.

He wanted, impatiently, to board the train immediately. He yawned and yearned to be home already, quickly, as quickly as possible. He was more tired than normal this week-end. And something he had eaten for lunch, the grilled cheese sandwich, hadn't agreed with him.

Shanley yawned again.

He would doze off on the train. That's why he hadn't bothered to buy a newspaper tonight. No, he didn't feel like reading the paper, and applying the little concentration required for that. There were too many crises in the world, anyway, and you just became fed up reading about them.

Shanley hiccoughed. Gas in his stomach was still giving

him a heartburn. He took a Creamlin tablet from a small
bottle he carried in his coat and chewed it. It nearly always
stopped his heartburn.

Then, he decided that he would buy a newspaper. No
use merely sitting there on the train and twiddling his
thumbs in boredom. He got up and walked to the news-
stand with a slow, slack gait. Yes, God, yes, he still felt
tired. He must have bursitis or neuritis. That pain in his
arm. But now it had died down. And it wasn't serious. No
cause for worry.

But then, a dark, black mood struck him. He thought
that he might die; his fear was paralyzing. For a terrible
moment, he saw himself as dead. But this terror passed in
less than a minute.

He bought a newspaper and walked slowly to the train
gate. People were now swooping by him. The mob-like
rush of the crowd was fatiguing and disconcerting, and he
wanted to be out of it. This was far worse than driving,
even though traffic had become one hell of a bitch. Well,
his train was in and he'd be home sooner, much sooner
than if he were driving.

Shanley handed a commutation ticket to the conductor,
who punched it. It paid to use a commutation ticket even
though he used his car to come to work on many days.

Shanley began to read the newspaper. He heard much
loud, gay talk in the car, and the train rolled out of the
Randolph Street Station.

II

Dinner was a happy occasion for Shanley. When his
four girls had been born, one after another, he had been
sorely disappointed, and so had Grace. They were still a
little disappointed because God had not given them a boy.
This was a recurrent regret. He felt it, especially, when he
went to high school reunions. But girls, daughters, could be
grand, even though they were more expensive growing up
than boys were. He liked it, siring four of them, swell girls,
with their beaux and their going out on dates, and all of it,
their lives. And yes, with his four daughters, he sometimes
felt almost as though he were a king. Of course, they were
the source of many worries and they brought him cold

weats. Good as they all were, they were a big responsibility. God, how he had used to worry about what could happen to his girls! But nothing had. Now those worries were mostly a thing of the past. With a mother like Grace, with the nuns at the parochial schools, and with the Church, there was no cause for him to go into any more sweats, and he didn't, not on that score.

"You're quiet tonight, Father," Grace said.

Shanley had been sitting in silence at the head of the table. He was thinking, and he ate very slowly because tonight he had very little, almost no appetite.

"Oh," Shanley exclaimed, "it's been a wearing week, darling."

Grace was plump now, and her chin was full. But as she had taken on weight and gone along the years with him, the added rounding out of her face had given it something of a doll-like beauty. And her hair was gray. Sometimes, in moods both of incredulity and of sadness, he would keep thinking that they were both gray now. But as the hair turned to silver, there could be a deep shaft to a new mine of understanding. This was consoling.

"Don't you like the perch tonight, Father? It's fresh."

"Yes, of course I do, dear. I'm merely a little tired, and taking it slowly," Shanley said.

He started to eat more, because he didn't want to tell Grace that he really felt so worn down and fatigued tonight that eating was almost like forced labor.

"Daddy isn't eating much," Jenny remarked.

Jenny, nine years old, was their youngest daughter, and always sat on his left. She was still their baby, and he was probably most fond of her, even though he always tried as well as he could to treat all of his girls with fairness and equality.

"Jenny notices everything about Daddy," Gladys said.

She sat at his right at the round dining room table. Jenny glanced with confidence at her sister, and did not speak, but tossed her head pertly and with an air of triumph.

"Don't think she's the only one," Shanley said in affectionate irony.

"Daddy," Ethel said, "Don't you think we all would naturally watch you? After all, look who you are."

Ethel was seventeen.

"Who are you, Daddy?" asked Jenny.

"Who am I, honey?"

"You're our Daddy. Only you and nobody else is my Daddy," Jenny said. "If they want another Daddy, they can go get him."

"Jenny, what are you saying about your sisters?" Grace asked in unmeant reproof.

Jenny turned an amused smile on her mother.

"Daddy, don't let your dinner get cold," Ethel told him.

"I won't if my menagerie will keep quiet so that I can hear myself eat."

"Hear yourself eat," Jenny exclaimed, as a prelude to a joyous peal of laughter.

Even though he still felt pooped, Shanley found himself becoming very soft inside. His pride in his loving daughter thrilled him. The laughter of Jenny, the affectionate voice and attention of these three pure and pretty girls of his and the feeling of supreme importance which he had when he was home with them, all this was food for the ego. It was a proof of the unselfishness of his life, too. But it was rich, thick cream for the ego.

"You girls eat your supper and let your father have his in peace. After all, he's our breadwinner," Grace said.

"Daddy, do you want peace?" teased Jenny.

"Will it do me any good to want what I can't get?"

"Daddy, you don't have so much to complain about. You should just see what my girl friend, Betty, does to her father," Gladys told him.

"Tell me," Jenny said quickly and with great eagerness.

"Well, last Saturday when I went over to her house, he was taking a nap. She tiptoed up and untied his bow tie and that woke him up."

"I'm going to do that," Jenny giggled.

"Don't tell her any more," Shanley said, with a mock frown.

"Tell me some more, Glad. Tell me more," Jenny demanded.

"Listen, you. Eat your dinner and stop finding out new ways to torment your old man," Shanley said, still maintaining his mock frown.

"Daddy, you did have a hard day today," Ethel said sympathetically.

All during the meal she had been watching her father

osely and with a curiously enigmatic but loving expres-
on on her alive and very pretty face.

Shanley was touched. He almost choked up.

"No, not too hard."

"Tell me more, Gladys," Jenny insisted.

"Another country heard from again," Grace said.

They went on with their meal, and the girls continued
to shower Shanley with questions and attention. He ate
more than he wanted to and felt heavy in the stomach. He
had a heartburn. He belched.

III

Shanley and Grace were sitting in the kitchen. The
supper dishes were done. They heard Ethel singing from
her room upstairs, and Shanley cocked an ear for a second.
She was singing *Frivolous Sal*. Shanley turned towards
his wife, remembering how, just when he had learned to
dance, he had taken Grace to one of her sorority dances,
and the orchestra had played that song, *Frivolous Sal*. He
had never forgotten it, and even now sometimes, he would
sing a few lines of it silently to himself. He yearned for
those lost days.

His mood became one of absorption and strangeness.
There was Grace sitting at their kitchen table, gray-haired,
looking settled and almost as if she had never been young.
She had given all of her youth to him. But then, he had
been faithful to her and . . . What the hell had he been
thinking about? His thoughts had wandered. And he
believed that he had a faint pain in his heart. He had to
stop worrying about his heart. There was no pain; it was
merely his imagination at work.

"You seem down in the mouth today, dear," Grace
remarked in a loving voice.

"Oh, no—I don't know what's wrong with me. It's
nothing. I just don't feel up to par tonight, Grace."

Somehow he felt better and he lost all worry by telling
her this. He gazed at her for a moment with a feeling of
abiding affection.

"Betty phoned me today, dear."

"Yes? What did she say?" Shanley asked with a quick-
ning of interest.

"She's very well."

"God, I hope she has a boy."

"Yes. She and John wish the same, too. Betty said that after growing up with so many sisters, she'll imagine the baby is her sister instead of her own child if it's a girl."

Grace smiled. Shanley did also, but weakly.

"She's in her third month now, isn't she?" he asked.

"No, dear, it's her fourth."

"Men aren't expert at those matters," Shanley commented, dryly.

"She and John will come over Sunday."

"Oh, fine, fine."

"I only hope the rest of our girls find husbands as good as John," Grace remarked.

Shanley agreed by shaking his head. He no longer felt that wrench in his heart about his oldest daughter. But he had, even against his will, when Betty and John had first declared that they wanted to get married. At times, he still believed that Betty was his favorite, because wasn't she their first? It was so many years ago since she had been a baby. So many years ago and yet it didn't, not always seem as though it had been long ago. Time was fast and life was short. But he would not get into such thoughts. However, the years melted together in his memory, and many, too many of them, were gone. Well, there was something to show for them, a family, this home, a respectable life, decently lived. But even while thinking of this with gratification, Shanley knew that there was a core of disappointment, of unfulfillment, inside of him. He had once wanted more, aspired to be much more, but now it was too late to aspire. Heck, his disappointment was probably pretty general. Many others had the same feelings. Everyone, or almost everyone, could have done more, gone higher in the world. Yes, this was pretty true.

Yawning, he suddenly rose and went to the refrigerator for a can of beer. His thoughts were pressing within him with a threat of too much melancholy.

"You're not going to drink much beer tonight, dear?" Grace asked, with a not-unpleasant concern in her voice.

"No—one or two, that's all."

"Because you know I don't care—except as a question of your health."

As he opened the can of beer over the sink, he grimaced.

t Grace did not see this. Yes, it would be better for his
alth if he didn't drink so much beer and if he should
atch his eating very carefully.

He would do it. As he brought the glass and can to the
chen table, Shanley decided a second time that he would
it, drink less beer and eat carefully from now on. But
e or two beers tonight would put him in the right mood.
needed them. It was the end of the week and tomorrow
ght, he wouldn't want to have a few beers because he
as going to confession. It was best not to take a glass
beer after going to confession. Tonight, a couple of
rs wouldn't hurt him, not seriously.

As Shanley took his first sip of beer, however, he
ongly felt that it would have been better if he had not
ened the can.

IV

Shanley was a little guilty as he walked the half block
om his home to that of his friend, Walt Costello. He
ouldn't or need not be feeling this way because Grace
dn't objected when he'd suggested that he thought he'd
to Walt for about a half hour. She had, however, been
little bothered when he'd drunk that can of beer in the
tchen, but not because she feared his getting drunk. She
ew that the most he ever did was merely to let himself
t just a bit woozy. What worried her was his weight, and
knew that he was too heavy. He would have to take
f some poundage, in fact twenty to twenty-five pounds.
t he was going to do this. He still had time.

With this thought, Shanley blinked his eyes in sudden
rprise. That was a strange damned thought for him to
entertaining.

For a moment, he shambled slowly on in a mood of
remitting and almost total gloom. He had a premonition
impending disaster and death gripping him. More than
ar, he felt despair, and a terror that startled and shocked
m with a sense of impending eternity. But then, he shook
is mood out of him. Such fears and premonitions came to
eryone and they didn't necessarily forecast anything.
ere was no reason why he shouldn't live for many years
come, and he probably would.

The big living room window of Walt Costello's hom
was lit up, and Shanley saw the gladness of welcome
the lights. He'd have a chat and get the lowdown o
Costello's case, drink a can or two of beer, but no mor
and then return home and get to bed early.

He turned and shambled up the walk and steps, ran
the bell and waited in expectation. Walt Costello answere
the ring in his shirt sleeves. He was a big, balding man
his middle forties, and on seeing Shanley, his face brok
into a genial and spontaneous smile.

"Shan, my lad—come on in."

"Doing anything, Walt?"

"Nothing that I can't stop. Come on, come on in."

"I thought we might talk."

"Sure, sure, Shan. You're always welcome, you kn
that."

Shanley stepped in and entered the large living roor
He did not notice the room and its furniture through i
specific objects. It was sumptuous, and the furniture w
more expensive than in his own home. He envied Walt
greater affluence, but most positively, he didn't think th
Walt was the kind of a fellow who put on the dog.

Shanley slumped into a comfortable, brightly covere
chair, and yawned.

"How you been, Boy?"

"All right—I'm kind of done in today," Shanley sai
speaking very casually. "And I'm not lamenting that it
Friday night."

"I second you there, Shan. But there's no rest for th
weary or for a lawyer. How's business?"

"Oh, fine, fine enough. It always could be better, b
I have no complaints on that score."

"That's the spirit, Shan. How about a beer?"

"Yes, I'll have one—and thanks, Walt."

Walt rose and walked out to the kitchen. Shanley relaxe
in the chair. He had a slightly stinging pain in the regic
around his heart. The beer wouldn't do him any goo
Heck, it wouldn't do him any harm, either, not necessaril

Walt retuned with two glasses of beer and the ca
on a tray.

"I'm glad you dropped by, Shan. Bea went out to pla
bridge with some of her girl friends."

"That reminds me, isn't it about time that we had
another good poker game, Walt?"

"Suits me."

Then Walt went to Shanley and held the tray before
him.

"Is Bud O.K.?" he asked.

"Yes—yes, thanks. My favorite beer," Shanley answered, taking a can and a glass.

He drank and then set the glass and can on a small
table at his right. Walt went back to his chair, sat down,
drank, and said:

"How about tomorrow night?"

"No—I'm going to confession."

"What's the matter? Stud is no sin and you don't cheat,
know that. I know you darned well, you old so-and-so."

"I might be tempted, just because I'd been to confession," Shanley said with a laugh. "Sunday night."

"O.K. I'll phone the boys."

"It's too bad I didn't think of it sooner—we could have
had a little game tonight."

"We still might drum one up."

"No, I'm feeling done in tonight, Walt—let's get an
early start and have a good game on Sunday night."

"Suits me, Shan."

Shanley shook his head and lifted his glass. The two
men sat as though in contemplation for a moment. Shanley
finished his can of beer, began to say something, stopped,
and then said:

"Yes, I'll be ready for a good game Sunday night. Post-
communion."

"Hell, I played stud poker with Father Loftus."

"I know—I was merely joking, Walt. A poker game isn't
a sin—if I go to Hell, it sure won't be for poker."

"I don't think you're bound for that hot destination."

"Well, I'll do my time in Purgatory with the rest of the
boys," Shanley laughed.

"Have another can of beer first. They won't be serving
Budweiser, or any of Miller's High Life in Heaven, Hell
or Purgatory."

They both laughed and then Walt went to the kitchen;
he returned with two more cans of beer. Shanley decided
that he would have this last one and meander home.

"Thanks, old man," Shanley said, accepting the beer from his friend.

"Don't mention it," Walt answered, going back to chair

They drank, and Shanley wiped his lips and then grinned contentedly.

"How's the case moving along?"

"O.K. Too bad I can't tell you about it—as I naturally can't—but he deserved hanging. I'll save him on a guilty plea and insanity."

Shanley got excited, remembering the sensational newspaper stories he had read of the rape and murder of an eighteen-year old girl on the West Side. And from what Walt said, he could take it that all of the allegations were true. He had gotten the inside dope and this stirred him up to feeling important, in a sense on the inside himself.

—Take that Fitzsimmons case now, he could say. know Fitzsimmons's lawyer.

That would be enough. That would establish his connections and show possession of inside information with Joe in his office and the pals with whom he had lunch.

Lifting his can of beer, Walt shook his head from side to side, and spoke meditatively.

"A criminal lawyer, Shan, comes in contact with the worst in human nature."

"Yeh, yeh, I know it."

"Some things—they make you sick. But each man has the right to a fair trial and the full protection of the law. That's all I provide for my clients, if they are guilty as charged."

"Yes, I know that—hell, Walt, you're one of the pillars of the parish and of our community out here. You're the most well-known and distinguished man in St. Daniel's Parish."

"I don't know about that—I merely practice my profession as best I can. It's my living, after all."

"Some day, you'll be as famous as Clarence Darrow. He was an agnostic, but he must have been a great lawyer, or else he wouldn't have become such a famous man."

"He was, Shan, he was great."

Shanley drank from his can and was stung by regrets that he had not been more ambitious and persevering in his youth. He had had the mind and the talent. But after he had lost out when Father Geraghty had drunk too

much and been taken out of the directorship of the
Society, something had happened to him. If he had persisted in journalism, who knows, he might be a star
reporter covering the Fitzsimmons trial.

"My work is knocking the hell out of my golf game—
ou never wanted to take up golf, Shan?"

"No, I wouldn't have been any good at it."

"Bull. You can still learn."

"Poker gives me enough relaxation—I'm too old for
handball—I used to play a lot of it, and I wasn't a bad
andball player back in my high school days."

"Well, I'll be getting in some golf before the summer's
ended. I feel better and I think better."

"Of course, law is harder than the insurance business."

"I don't know—you get your tough problems and cases,
but it's fascinating. No, Shan, I wouldn't want to be anything else than what I am, a lawyer."

Shanley nodded, took a drink from his glass of beer and
felt wistful. He didn't envy Walt, or rather, he didn't
feel jealous of his friend. But he wished that he had made
more of himself. And he could have, because he knew that
he'd had it in him.

"You don't think of going into politics, Walt? You've
never thought of it?"

"Oh, I have—but never too seriously. I guess I know too
much—I'd rather keep my hands free and clean of politics."

"Yes?" Shanley asked with quickened interest.

"I'd hate like hell to be a State's Attorney—I don't have
the character for it; not that I dislike John. But I couldn't
demand the electric chair for a man. It's not in me, here
in my heart."

"It's the gentle quality of mercy in you, Walt," Shanley
told him.

And Shanley thought how Walt could call the State's
Attorney by his first name. He could do the same with
the Mayor. But this added to his respect for Walt, and to
the pleasure he derived from sitting in Walt's home in his
shirtsleeves and drinking beer. Damn, but he was impressed because Walt put on no dog.

"No, Hell, it's not in my nature."

"I understand, Walt."

"John's a good fellow—and a damned tough man to

have against you. But it's a matter of disposition, temperament, I guess."

"Yes, I know. But a fellow like you—you could be a Congressman. Heck, if a professor from the University can be a Senator. . . ."

"No, I wouldn't want any part of Washington, Shan."

Shanley's respect for Walt vaulted in quick emotion, enthusiasm. That Walt could say this proved that he could actually be a big shot if he wanted to. Walt was a big shot in a way, but he could be one in politics, too, almost for the asking. Yes, he could become a much bigger man than he already was.

"I was approached, and it was suggested to me. I could have been Sheriff when Dick Murphy died. No. I thought about it. But I'd rather do what I'm doing and as my mother used to say, be beholden to nobody."

"It's the best idea, Walt," Shanley said philosophically.

Walt spoke of his mother. She had died twelve years ago, and his Dad a year afterwards. But they had gone knowing that he and his brother, Harry, were well settled and fixed for life. It had hurt, like a knife cutting the heart, yes, it had been hard, seeing his mother go. He'd never imagined it was going to be hard in the way it had been and when she had been laid away he had felt lost, as lost as his Dad.

Shanley drank, but too fast, and felt a pain in his chest. He made a face, somewhat disturbed, but then quickly grinned in order to mask his pain. The pressure of the pain was on both sides. For a moment he was frightened even though this had happened to him before, when he had foolishly drunk something too fast. He felt proud for concealing the evidence of his pain. Then, the pain began to subside. He felt reassured.

They finished their beer and Shanley decided to go back home. He was sleepy and he'd toss into bed and be dead to the world in no time.

V

"Jenny asked me: 'Daddy, you didn't commit any sins, did you?' " Shanley said, laughing.

"She's our cutie, dear," Grace smiled.

"And Jenny is smart, a smart little kid. But wasn't that amusing, Grace?"

He laughed with pride and rather heartily, and then took a sip of milk. He and Grace were sitting alone in the kitchen; the house was quiet. They had always liked it in the kitchen, talking there at the end of a day. And now they had a big, modern kitchen. It was a pleasure, a real pleasure, being here, now, in this kitchen. He knew how proud Grace was to have it. And he had earned enough to give this to her. That was an achievement, even though he wasn't in Walt Costello's class. Yes, every time he looked at the big refrigerator, and every time he opened it for a can of beer or for a midnight snack, he was proud.

"I should have gone with you, perhaps."

"Maybe you should have. Maybe it should have been you, and not Daddy, because Daddy, he doesn't sin," Shanley said with humor and affection.

Grace smiled appreciatively. Then she said:

"I lose my head—I did with Jenny the other day. She dragged so much dirt into the house and was so out of sorts that I became furious."

"Happens to the best of us—I give the girls a slap now and then."

"What did you tell Jenny, dear?"

"I told her—'Oh, your Daddy is a terrible sinner.' "

"What did she say to that?"

"She told me I wasn't. I was too nice to her to be a sinner. . . . That Jenny, dear. . . ."

"Then what did you say, darling?"

"I told her that she wasn't the priest."

"And?"

Grace's eyes were very soft. She was relaxed, and there seemed to be a depth of quiet in her. Suddenly, she looked so pretty to Shanley. He filled up, near to tears with worship. He looked at the gray in her hair and the network of small wrinkles around her eyes, and felt the sadness of the living years, because they were no longer young. But the years and what they did to you, all this was beyond your control, beyond all men's control. It was ordained. . . .

"And then?" Grace interrupted his thoughts.

"She said—'But Daddy, I'd like to be the priest.' "

They both laughed in their joy of parenthood. Shanley's mood of the sadness of the years was gone. Like the wind. Like puffs of smoke. Like forgotten and forgiven sins.

Shanley thought of how many times he and Grace had sat like this, in their kitchen, and had talked so fondly of the girls.

Shanley sipped some milk. As he put down the half-empty glass on the table, there was a sharp pain shooting down his left arm. He strove not to reveal this onslaught of pitilessly excruciating pain.

"Darling!" Grace cried at him in alarm.

For a moment, he couldn't talk. It was like unannounced lightning, like the unexpected stroke of death.

"Darling, what's the matter?" she burst out, in a terror of alarm, rising out of her chair.

"You. . . ."

Shanley was helpless with clamps of pain pressing on his chest, like cruel, the cruelty of murder. His face was inhumanly pale. Hopelessly, he tried to talk. The massive pain was robbing him of speech. Grace rushed around the table to him.

The words. The words were in his head, while he was sagging, while his lungs were being crushed as though by a closing steel vise. He tried to speak through his gulping efforts to breathe, through his moans and groans. He tried to say something, to beg Grace to telephone her mother.

But Shanley was beyond words. He was ripped by one last tumult of pain. Then he crumpled forward. And he would have gone to the floor had not his bulky, flabby body been stopped by the kitchen table.

Grace thrust herself toward her husband, to help him and save him. It was a movement of clumsy desperation.

Shanley's lifeless, heavy body was slumped in a position of grotesque rigidity. Grace sobbed inwardly, but she was too shocked to scream. Hers was a shock which created the illusionment of utter calmness. It was a calmness of a grief that was so great that instantaneously it became like ice.

—He's dead, she told herself, as she precariously held his inert body.

She spoke to herself as though without feeling. She could have been telling herself the most banal fact in the world.

Then she told herself that God only called him, her darling husband. But God had called her dearest only after he had gone to confession. God had called him and saved him, forever.

And then, such sobs came from the depths of her self that her grip on his still-warm corpse was relaxed in weakness and helplessness. All that had been her dearest, darling loving husband fell to the floor, leadenly, and hit with a sick, thudding sound.

"Oh!" Grace cried out, the victim of a grief such as she had never before known of or felt during her entire life.

HUSBAND AND WIFE

Jack Simmons had suggested a vacation trip to New York State because he wanted to see the Baseball Hall of Fame and Museum at Cooperstown, New York. Ethel detested baseball, and because of her nagging, he almost never went to see ball games at Comiskey Park in Chicago. She would become impossible if he turned on the radio or the television to catch a game. It was mighty unfair of her, he thought. And he envied other men with wives who either liked baseball or at least tolerated it. He thought of how they could sit in the parlor at home on a Sunday, with a can of cold beer before them, and watch a game. There was no harm in baseball, and he just couldn't understand why Ethel was so dead set against it. If he drank too much, lost money on horses, blew his dough in poker games with friends, or if he had chased women when he was younger, he could have understood why Ethel should get sore. But he had never done any of these things. Why, the way she acted, you might have thought that baseball was to be classed the same as these vices. Ethel's attitude hurt Jack. No, it wasn't fair of her.

Again and again he would ask himself—what harm could there be in baseball?

Jack was settled in his ways. He didn't go out much. Once a week, he and Ethel would take in a movie. Sometimes, they went to friends' homes, just as they had friends come to visit them. Now and then, there would be a harmless poker game, but with a two cent limit. Sometimes, he would play bridge. Or they would go for a little drive in the Chevy. For years, Jack had been following baseball, and he guessed he just loved it. Like most American kids,

182

unless they had been sissies, he'd wanted to be a big league
ball player himself, and sometimes, he would even have
foolish and harmless daydreams, imagining that he had
been one and had played against Ty Cobb, and Walter
Johnson. Yes, over the years, he had been watching and
reading about the comings and goings of the stars. Baseball
just went on with his own life, and each winter, he looked
forward to the next season. Every morning and night for
years, he had always turned first to the sports pages to read
the baseball news. It was something he could understand,
but he couldn't always understand the political news and
the troubles in Europe and the rest of the world. Baseball
gave him an interest to follow. It was, perhaps, in a way
like having a hobby. He could read the accounts of the
games and imagine how it happened and, well, he just
enjoyed all of this.

Jack and Ethel were well enough fixed. He had a good
job in charge of the warehouse for a drugstore chain
corporation. His salary permitted them to live comfortably,
and they owned a nice home out at 87th Street in the
Beverly Hills section of Chicago. He had a few investments,
and carried a liberal insurance, so that if anything were to
happen to him, Ethel would be well provided for. His son
and daughter were happily married and getting along, and
he guessed that he had no complaints in life except that
Ethel just didn't want him to be interested in baseball. He
had a hell of a time managing to see two or three games a
year, and he couldn't have a peaceful week end if he
turned on the television and watched a game of a Saturday
or a Sunday afternoon. Whenever he tried to watch one,
Ethel would find something for him to do around the
house, or she would think of something that they had to
talk about, or else she would complain of a headache and
say that the blaring noise made her feel worse, or she'd
have another reason, and so he would have to turn the T.V.
off, or else he would feel like a louse.

Jack had often read about the Museum in Cooperstown
and had been pleased when favorite players of his, like
Cobb, Speaker, Ruth, Gehrig, Ed Walsh, Grover Cleveland
Alexander and Eddie Collins had been elected to the Hall
of Fame. He wanted to see the Museum before he died. He
had always believed that a Hall of Fame for great baseball players was a damned swell idea. In his younger days,

he had seen many ball games, and had read of thousands
of others which he hadn't witnessed. He remembered
many facts and achievements on the diamond and thought
that these should not remain unrewarded and unhonored
down the years. Those who had been great as ball players
should be remembered: they deserved fame and immortality. And now, with the Hall of Fame, they had been
given their due. And he just wanted to see the Museum.

Every summer, the question of how he and Ethel would
spend their vacation became a big problem. She usually
found reasons and arguments against whatever he proposed. Then, when he would ask her what she wanted to
do or where she might wish to go, she would usually
answer that she would do whatever he wanted to do and
she would go wherever he wished. During two different
years, they went nowhere because they couldn't decide on
what to do and where to go. In 1951, when the White Sox
were going good, he managed to convince her that they
should stay in Chicago on his vacation so that he could
see some games. Foolishly, he tried to induce her to go with
him, but she refused and this had roused her suspicion.
When he sneaked off and saw two White Sox games, she
suspected what he had done and nagged and criticized him
so much he lost all enjoyment from his vacation. His
memories of that year were still sour in him, like a sour
stomach.

Ethel's opposition to his interest in baseball really hurt
him. He considered her to be both unreasonable and unfair. He thought of this often and would keep reasoning
the situation out, complaining to himself, and even talking
to himself. He held imaginary conversations with Ethel
in which he argued, explained, complained, upbraided her
and even revolted. Because of her attitude, he grew to
love baseball the more. A ball game became forbidden
fruit: it was almost something sinful. And because of all
this, he determined that no matter what Ethel said or did,
he would see the Hall of Fame.

Jack proposed that they take a motor trip to the East.
New York was a beautiful state, he had heard, the Empire
State. When he dropped this suggestion on a cold night in
February, she made a face, but for once, he beat her to
the draw. He quickly added that maybe the drive east
would be a bit too hard on him because after all, he was

getting along in years. Perhaps it wasn't such a good idea. Ethel fell for his trap and said that if he drove carefully and did not do too much each day, they might be able to take the trip next summer. She had often thought that it would be nice to see something of the East, and also she didn't think that they ought to live a stick-in-the-mud existence. He had been working so long with the company that he was certain that he could get one or two extra weeks' vacation if he wanted to, and they could take their time and not hurry, or rush or kill themselves. Jack told her that he'd have to take up the question of extra time on his vacation with Mr. Weeks. But then, he was thinking that they might have a better time of it if they should take a trip to Denver. They could see the mountains and Pike's Peak.

"Climbing mountains," she said critically.

"Well, honey, mountains are beautiful."

"But you were just worrying about the driving being too hard on you at your age, and then you think of going to Denver, Colorado, and driving up and down mountains. Men are not reasonable and don't know how to take care of themselves."

"Well, I don't know," Jack said.

"You never could make up your mind about anything, Jack. I swear I don't know what you would have done in life without me."

"You've been just real wonderful, darling."

"I'm glad you know it. Mrs. Edison's husband across the street doesn't know how much Clara has done for him."

Jack did not comment. He couldn't stand his neighbor, Clara Edison, and as far as he was concerned, she was just an old gab. But Ethel and Clara were as thick as thieves.

"How about a movie tonight, darling?" he asked a few minutes later.

They saw a movie.

But Jack knew that he had planted the seed, and was both hopeful and proud of the way that he had managed to do this. Ethel thought that she always managed him and it tickled him pink to know that he was going to be able to swing her around to doing what he wanted to do without her being aware of it. Of course, he knew that he would have to play his cards pretty carefully and close to the chest, but at least he had dealt her the hand he wanted to and all of the aces were up his sleeve.

About a week later after supper, he casually remarked

"I was talking to a fellow the other day, dear, and he said he and his missus went to Colorado on their vacation last summer and he said it's beautiful."

"And it will take you two months to recover from th exertion."

"Well, I don't know about that. I'm in pretty goo shape, all things considered, knock on wood and thank to the way you take care of me, darling."

"What's there to see in mountains?"

"Well, mountains are mighty pretty with snow on top 'em."

After a few moments of silence, Ethel suddenly ex claimed:

"Oh."

"What is it, honey?"

"I don't want to miss Paladin on television tonight.

"No, we don't want to miss Paladin," he said.

A few nights later, Jack talked about Grand Canyon i Arizona, and said that it was one of the natural wonder of the world and that he had been kind of thinking that i might be a good idea for them to go to Grand Canyo on their vacation.

"What will we see there?"

"I read somewhere, you go down into the Canyon o a mule and stay overnight at the bottom. I was thinking it might be an interesting thing to try, dear, an advenure.

Ethel stared at him as thought he might have gone mad

As the days passed, Jack sometimes was hopeful bu then again, he would grow anxious, or would even decid that it was hopeless for him to try to inveigle Ethel int taking a vacation trip that would permit him to get t Cooperstown, New York. More than once, he was ready to give up. But regularly, he would bring up the subject o their vacation and would make suggestions which he knew Ethel would consider wild-eyed. One Sunday mornin when they were driving home from church, he even sug gested that it might be a good idea if they went to Mexico

"Are you insane, Jack?" she asked, more puzzled tha angry.

"I sometimes think it might be interesting to be in a foreign country."

"I wish I knew what's come over you, Jack."

"Dear, what's come over me? Nothing at all. I was just thinking of places to go on our vacation."

"I never heard you talk the way you do. Why now, I wouldn't think I'd be surprised if you woke up one morning and told me that you wanted to take me on a vacation trip to the moon. I swear I wouldn't."

Feigning injury, he turned from the wheel and stared at her.

"Watch the way you're driving or we'll both be killed," she said frantically.

A car had almost bumped them.

"It was the other fellow's fault, one of these damned fool drivers," he complained.

"His fault or your fault, we were almost killed."

"Honey, I've been driving a car for over twenty-five years and I never had an accident, knock on wood."

"If I didn't watch when you drive, you might have had an accident."

This episode worried him because it led him to fear that she might decide that he was a careless or a bad driver and could not be trusted to drive on their vacation. He did not mention the subject of their vacation all during the following week.

"I don't know why you don't take my idea for our vacation trip," she said on Sunday evening, just after they had watched Walter Winchell on television.

Jack sat up straight, surprised and somewhat alarmed. Now, his hopes were going down the drain.

"Yes, you know I want to make that trip East and see Niagara Falls and New York State, but I guess what I want doesn't count."

Her face became instantly glum. But he was silent. It was too good to be true, but he had won.

"Let me think about it, honey."

"Just like a man," she complained.

Triumph was sweet, so sweet that he sat, looking at the television, smiling inwardly, and thinking that he had a well-earned right to enjoy and relish it. But if he had only known all of these years that triumph was so easy. The joy of his victory almost collapsed and he thought of the many

times he had allowed her to sidetrack him when all that
he had wanted were harmless pleasures.

"If I didn't want to go East on our vacation, you'd be
just about dying to do it. You're just like Mr. Edison,
you're just like all men."

"I didn't say I wouldn't take the trip, darling."

"You didn't say you would."

After a pause, he told her:

"Well, all right, honey, we'll go to the East next
summer."

She went to him, bent down and kissed his forehead.

"We'll enjoy it Jack."

Nodding his head, he smiled up at her.

"Yes, honey."

II

Late in July, Jack and Ethel left, driving at moderate
speed. They went to Detroit, crossed over to Windsor,
drove to Hamilton, Ontario, and then on to the American
border and Niagara Falls. Jack said nothing of the Baseball Hall of Fame, but he had gotten maps and had planned
the journey so as to go through Cooperstown. From a
folder, he had read about the Farmers Museum and had
casually mentioned that it would be something to see and
talk about when they got back to Chicago. Leaving Chicago, he had expected to be bored until he got to Cooperstown and he also anticipated trouble from Ethel when he
did spring the Hall of Fame on her, but he was determined
that come hell, high water or Ethel, he was going to see
that museum at Cooperstown.

The trip turned out to be more interesting than he had
anticipated. He and Ethel didn't seem to have much to
talk about any more except little things and he had
imagined them being together almost every minute of the
time with nothing to say, and with Ethel not liking what
he liked, or wanting to see the things he didn't want to see.
But it did not turn out that way. Getting away from home,
driving along the wide concrete highways, smelling the
country air, stopping when they wanted to, staying at motels
and feeling no responsibility, all this was fun. They found
themselves talking a lot and enjoying their trip. On the

reets of small towns, when they would go to a restaurant, or just walk and gape, he would take her hand and squeeze it tenderly. He would chat with gas station attendants for a few moments when he gassed up, and they would talk with waitresses, people in stores, and chance travellers they met at the motels at night. They went through towns and villages they had never heard of, and hamlets that were not even on the map. They liked it, taking their time, stopping very frequently, rolling through the country, seeing greenness, trees, farms, and then suddenly stepping on the gas, because the impulse for speed gripped them both, and Jack would go faster than the moderate speed at which they had started out and had planned to maintain.

It was exhilarating and an adventure to be out of the United States, to buy souvenirs with Canadian money, and to talk to Canadians who lived under a different government. They racked their brains in order to think of more people to whom to send post cards.

"Makes us feel ten years younger, dear. Honey, it's like a second honeymoon," he told her across a restaurant table in Hamilton, Ontario.

He had said this to her six or seven times before during this journey.

And as they approached Niagara Falls, they became very excited. The Falls, now, that was something to see, and they could talk about them back in Chicago. Hearing the thud and roar, Ethel exclaimed:

"It's raining."

"It can't be, look at the sun shining. By golly, it is."

They were surprised but then realized that they had been hit by the spray from the Falls. At first sight of the tons of water dropping, Jack exclaimed:

"Golly."

"So much water."

As they watched, they grew more fascinated. They were seeing Niagara Falls. The roaring water, dropping down with merciless force, appeared to change every moment. Gazing down at the swirling foam, Jack thought of how a man could be killed falling over the falls, and of how much force there was in the water and how beautiful it was.

"Just think, for centuries that water has been going over

just like that. It was the same when only the Indians wer
here, before the white man came."

"I guess so."

Jack was trying to say more, but he did not know
exactly what he wanted to say. It was a wonderful sigh
seeing that water dropping, tons of it, falling, white wate
just dropping, never stopping, falling every second, it wa
a wonderful sight. It made him think how this was her
before he was born and would be here, with the wat
falling, tons of it, falling, and this would go on the sam
way after he was dead. But no use thinking about tha
Baseball would be here too after he was dead. He guesse
it would. It would go on as long as America did. Couldn
think of America not going on forever.

"What's the matter, Jack?" Ethel asked, noticing h
frown.

"Nothing—why did you ask? I was just looking at th
water falling down there and thinking about it. You kno
Ethel, it was here like this before there was any America

"I know it," she said, impatiently. "Jack, let's sen
some more post cards. We ought to send a lot of po
cards from Niagara Falls."

"All right."

"If you don't want to, of course."

"But honey, I do."

He turned from the railing, and walked off to a stan
where they could buy cards. He'd have to cater to her a
much as he could, because he was pulling the wool over he
eyes about the Hall of Fame. And from now on, he kne
he was going to be getting impatient to get on to Cooper
town, New York, and he'd have to be careful not to giv
himself away.

III

Driving across New York State, Jack had to make a
effort to control his impatience. It had all been interestin
and enjoyable and he was mighty glad that he had se
Niagara Falls. Everyone ought to see the Falls once befor
their time came because this was one of the wonders o
the world and one of the greatest pieces of the handiwor
of God. The Falls were beautiful and seeing them, yo

hought of all sorts of things, and of yourself, too. You
elt how nature and God were so much more powerful
han you were and than man was, and this made you
umble. And nature and the country were beautiful. Trees
nd grass, and the sky over the country. The sky looked
o much bigger when you saw it in the country than it
did in the city. You didn't take as much notice of the sky
nd the moon and the stars in the city. All this he had
njoyed, and he and Ethel were having one of their best
acations ever. But they were getting a bit tired and fuzzed
up. They ought to shack up for a day or two at Coopers-
own. There was a lake there, and it was a historical place,
ot only because General Abner Doubleday was said to
ave invented baseball at Cooperstown, but they had other
museums. They had been on the go so much and neither
-f them were spring chickens any more. Yes, the rest
hey would get at Cooperstown would do them good.

And so, driving on through the richness of New York
State with the weather not too hot, he would think of this,
of Cooperstown, of baseball, and suddenly he would realize
hat he hadn't said a word to Ethel for maybe twenty or
hirty minutes, and that perhaps he ought to talk a little
o her. Sometimes he could think of something to say to
er and at other times, he couldn't. She was sitting there,
ooking ahead, silent, too, and he wondered what was on
er mind. He didn't know why, but sometimes he would
el sorry for her. She would get tired on these long jumps,
d he could see it on her face. And he would notice the
inkles about her eyes. Ethel wasn't a young woman any
ore, and she must feel it. Heck, he did. He didn't often
hink that Ethel must be feeling the years coming on,
ust as he did.

And at times, he would think that maybe he shouldn't
ave played the trick he was playing on her so that he
ould see that museum. It had been kind of deceitful,
adn't it? And maybe it wouldn't be so interesting, and
t might not be worth all that it was taking and costing.
And Ethel might get burned up at him for this and then he
would never hear the end of it. She did nag him a little more
han he thought she ought to, but he guessed that all wives
agged. Maybe, he ought to forget about the Museum,
ecause sure as Hell's blazes, he would pay for it. Ethel
would see through all his scheming. But his heart was set

on seeing the Hall of Fame, and if he got so near to it a,
now, and then didn't go to see it, he'd always regret it
and he would kick himself for this all of the rest of his
life.

Why didn't Ethel like baseball, and even more im
portant, why did she get so boiled up about his liking
the game? He couldn't get it, and heck, it just wasn't fai
to him, no, it wasn't. He just wished that Ethel wer
different about this one thing, baseball.

And he was nervous, driving along with trees on hi
left, the air cooling him as he shot the car along at sixty
miles an hour, because they were approaching Coopers
town, New York.

IV

Annoyed and bewildered, Ethel sat in a corner of thi
Museum room. People passed her, and the man at the
desk near her was the director and he was talking to a
newspaper man. When they had arrived in Cooperstown
and driven along the Main Street here, he had spotted thi
building, parked the car and here they were.

There were cases in the room with pictures, and letters
baseballs, gloves, bats, and what in the name of God
could be so interesting about all that. There was Jack
looking at those plaques.

He had done this to her, plotted it all to come here, fo
that she was, and she had fallen for it, hook, line a
sinker. Well, he had said that he would only spend abou
fifteen or twenty minutes here, and she would hold him to
his word. He hadn't even taken time for them to check
into a hotel and get washed up. She must look a holy
fright, and it was his fault. But he didn't care, not at all i
baseball was concerned. He loved baseball more than he
did her. Well, why didn't he marry baseball instead of a
woman?

Look at him, gawking at those plaques, reading every
word on every one of them. And he had only said fifteen o
twenty minutes.

Ethel frowned and fidgeted nervously in her chair. A
group of boy scouts passed her, and spread around the
exhibition room. Couldn't that scout master, whoever he

as, think of something better for those boys to do and see
an baseballs? There was her own husband, still staring
d gawking at those plaques.

She shuffled her feet. She didn't know what to do with
erself and imagined that she looked foolish and that Jack
as making a fool of her, making her sit here this way.
nce years ago, he had taken her to a ball game and she
idn't believe that she had ever been so bored in all her
fe. It made no sense to her. Grown men playing a game
ke boys, and more grown men including her own husband
elling and getting hepped up the way they did when
mebody hit a ball or caught it. And those awful-looking
niforms they wore.

Ethel angrily shook her head from side to side and
cked. How long would it take? Why had Jack done this
o her, made her come all the way to New York State to sit
ere while he looked at baseballs and glass cases? She
new that she was going to become furious, simply furious.

Her mother used to complain about her father talking
aseball with her brothers at the dinner table. It left
er mother out of the picture, and when she talked, she
as ignored and her father and the boys went on talking
s if she wasn't there and didn't even exist. Men must
ave thought up this game of baseball so that women
ould be ignored.

She sighed with relief. Jack was coming towards her. He
ust have had his fill and now they could go. Well, thank
God for that.

"Honey, how are you?"

She glowered but said nothing. Her dark look sufficed
or an answer.

"Just wait a few more minutes, honey, and I'll be
inished."

"That's what you already told me. You said fifteen
minutes."

"Darling, I said fifteen or twenty minutes."

"It's more than fifteen minutes already. I'm not going to
wait here all day for you."

"I know it, dear. I didn't say I was going to be in here
ll day. There's just a few more things here, interesting
xhibits, I'd like to see. I'll never get here again."

As she frowned, Jack walked back towards the plaques
f the players who had been elected to the Hall of Fame.

V

Jack moved from plaque to plaque. They hung on the walls in partitioned-off rows at one end of the room. He stopped before that of Lou Gehrig, and gazed at the sculptured face of the dead ball player. He guessed it looked like Gehrig, judging from his memory of the pictures of Gehrig that he'd used to see in the newspapers. Behind the framed face on the bronze tablet, there were parts of baseball bats and floral leaves as though these lay crosswise in back of the image of the player. And he read from the tablet:

HENRY LOUIS GEHRIG
NEW YORK YANKEES 1923-1939
HOLDER OF MORE THAN A SCORE OF
MAJOR AND AMERICAN LEAGUE RECORDS,
INCLUDING THAT OF PLAYING 2130
CONSECUTIVE GAMES WHEN HE RETIRED
IN 1939, HE HAD A LIFE TIME BATTING
AVERAGE OF 340

He shook his head sadly and stood for a moment. Looking here at these plaques was almost like standing before a grave. A lot of the others honored here were dead just like Gehrig was, and what was written almost could be put on their tombstones. He felt a little like he might in a graveyard. And think of it, all of the players who were honored here once had been young and strong and full of beans. He'd seen most of them play, Cobb, Speaker, Eddie Collins, Mathewson, Alexander, Walter Johnson. He hadn't thought how sad an experience it would be coming here to the Hall of Fame.

Ethel was waiting for him and she was getting mad as a hatter. He knew that he ought to hurry up, but he wanted to stay a little while longer. These great baseball players and their records represented so many years, years gone by. Gehrig. He had played in the big leagues from 1923 to 1939. Now it was 1954. All those years were gone. Where had they gone to? Where do the years go? When Gehrig had broken in, he himself had been a young fellow, in 1923. Let's see, it was 1924, no 1925, the year that he and Ethel had been married. He moved on. He should

urry because she was sitting there, waiting and ready to
give him the good Lord Harry for keeping her waiting.

Honus Wagner. Another one of them, only he wasn't
dead. All these years gone, and the games that had been
played, the crowds, the cheers, the base hits and home runs
and these were all gone with the years.

He looked at the bust of Christy Mathewson, and out
of the corner of his eye, he saw Ethel fidgeting on the chair.
All of this and all of the exhibits didn't mean anything to
her. Matty had been a great pitcher, young and strong and
healthy, and he was gone.

Jack shook his head, sadly.

A gray-haired man in suspenders and shirtsleeves and
with a white handkerchief tied around his neck, was also
staring at the bust of Mathewson.

"Saw him pitch," the man said.

"I did, too."

"Never was anyone better than him in the pitcher's
box."

"Nope, I guess there wasn't," Jack said, thoughtfully.

"They'll never have 'em again as some of these fellows."

"I guess not."

"I'd give anything," the old fellow said, "to see old Ty
Cobb playing once again."

Jack nodded. He cast a swift glance at Ethel. He ought
to leave now. She wanted him to, he was sure of that, and
it made him kind of nervous, but he wanted to stay here
a while. There was lots to see and somehow it was
beginning to mean so much to him.

"They used to call his best pitch the fadeaway," the old
fellow said.

"Yeh."

Other visitors passed him. They went as he had, from
plaque to plaque and from case to case. They must be
remembering as he was, other days, games long since
played, and maybe wishing to have back again and to live
over the time that was gone, gone, past, and was the time
of yesterday.

He didn't want to leave. But Ethel?

He went slowly towards her. The small gray-haired man
at the desk, the Director, smiled at Jack. Jack returned
the smile.

Ethel made a move to rise as he came to her chair.

"Honey, I just want to take a quick look at a few more
of the exhibits and then we'll go."

"You've seen it all already."

"There are a couple of floors. I don't expect to see it all
I wouldn't have time, but there are a few things I'd like
to see."

He knew that this didn't sit well with her, and was
tempted to chuck it and leave. But he would never see
this place again, and the past was hanging all over it
giving him a feeling, a feeling he didn't even get listening
to old time songs on the radio.

"It won't be long, dear," he said, speaking more loudly
so that the director, poring over a book at his desk, could
hear him.

That might kind of shame Ethel, and she might not want
to object to waiting for him. She wouldn't want to quarrel
or have a spat in front of a stranger.

"Honey, I'll just take a quick look at a few of the other
exhibits."

He turned and walked off. He stared in a case at the
first contract Eddie Collins had signed with the Philadel-
phia Athletics. That had been signed in 1906. He shook
his head and stared. 1906. It was such a long time ago, and
think of it, Collins had been a young fellow, a kid, and
now he was dead.

He turned and looked at other cases. There was a murmur of voices, people talking low, almost as they might
be in a church instead of a museum like this. And he
guessed a kind of almost reverent feeling did grow upon
you in here. You thought of how all your life baseball had
been going on, and it seemed like it was only yesterday that
you were young and seeing Honus Wagner and Napoleon
Lajoie playing, and now they were old men and so were
you and you kind of wondered where did all the time go
and where had all of the years gone to? A silver cup won
by the New York Giants in 1889. And Christy Mathewson's glove. Gloves were smaller in those days. And the
pictures and the prints.

But Ethel must be getting mighty nervous and he ought
to be leaving. He didn't want to. He'd never imagined
that he would be impressed this way when he came here
remembering old games and other days, and feeling the
kind of sadness he felt. A picture of Babe Ruth and you

ooked at it and saw how young and strong Ruth had been,
nd now he was gone.

With his features softened up with sadness, dreamily he
ooked at the gloves, the balls, the pictures, the cups and
rophies. He kept thinking that he shouldn't keep Ethel
aiting like this, but how could he tear himself away? If
he was going to get sore about it, why, let her. She didn't
nderstand what this meant to him. The little gloves, how
ifferent they were from modern gloves. And Lou Gehrig's
ocker.

People moved by him and he heard the continuing mur-
nur of voices. People were talking just above a whisper.

Out of the corner of his eye he again saw Ethel, still
itting in the chair. She was mighty nervous. He went
ver to her, intending to leave. She started to rise as he
approached. He was surprised to hear himself saying:

"Honey, just a few more minutes. I want to take a
quick look-see at the other rooms."

"You already kept me here over an hour."

"But just a few more minutes, darling."

"Are you out of your mind, Jack?"

"I'll never see this place again and some of the things
are mighty interesting."

"What, bats and balls? They all look the same to me."

"It won't be long, honey."

Just as she opened her mouth to reply, he turned and
went off.

"He's mad," she said loudly.

But Jack wandered about looking at more exhibits, the
pictures, gloves, bats, uniforms. His mind remained in a
og of sadness and sentiment. Games he had seen, dreams
he had had, the old yearnings and ambitions of his boyhood when he had wanted to be a ball player himself, all
his was in the Museum. And this was what Ethel didn't
understand. He wandered about for over an hour, feeling
or his past, and he just let her wait.

Finally he was ready to leave. She looked at him coldly
and angrily, and said bitingly:

"Jack, you're mad, you're looney."

All the way home to Chicago, she kept telling him that
he was mad. And once back at home, it was more difficult
than ever for him to see a ball game. Ethel remained convinced that he was mad.

BLISTERS

Blisters was his nickname and whenever he heard it used, he smouldered within. He was Carl Newton, a broad and husky man with square jaws, a dense face, and brown hair which he had clipped in convict style. He wore collegiate clothes which he selected carefully; he shook hands limply and spoke softly to his equals and sometimes to the filling station attendants of Nation Oil who were his inferiors.

The other bosses of the Nation Oil Company Service Station Department were different from Blisters, and he felt inferior and resentful toward them. Some had gone to college. Others, who had not, did have a college manner, and had been members of high school fraternities. Blisters saw them as inhabiting a social world which was inaccessible to him and in which he never could truly feel that he was at home or belonged. He believed that they looked down their noses at him and did not consider him to be their equal. A number of them had begun in the service stations and had been promoted into the supervision; Blisters had started in as a repairman. He was only thirty-three and with his ambition, he hoped to climb much higher up the ladder of success. The oil industry was a new one, rich and still growing. Nation Oil was a big corporation, one of the largest and richest in America. It offered plenty of opportunities for men like himself, and some evenings when he drove home to the house he was buying near Wilson Avenue, he would imagine a day in the future when he had risen to become a leading executive of Nation Oil Company.

He was always preparing himself for his future. Daily,

e read the news about business conditions and the stock
market, and also he read articles about successful men in
magazines, especially *The American Magazine*. He often
aid or thought that the world of the 1920's was a bright,
new modern world, a world of progress in which men with
new ideas would climb right up there, high. One of the
new sources of ideas of this new and modern world of
progress was psychology. A man had to practice psychol-
gy to be a success, and after Blisters had been made an
Assistant Superintendent of the Service Station Department at a salary of $225 per month, he had subscribed to
correspondence course in psychology, sold by an institute in Wichita, Kansas. He believed that his study had
lped him in learning how to handle men, and this was
e of his tasks.

He always treated an employee under him according to
he man. He blistered some and was soft on others. He
regarded himself as both eminently fair and very clever
handling the service station attendants. And they all
ad to be handled. His success in handling them, getting
hem to increase sales and avoiding trouble, was important
o his future, but he had also begun to regard himself as
part of Nation Oil. The corporation was bigger then
nyone and if you worked for Nation, you owed it every-
hing you could give. The attendants were, in his opinion,
obliged to think of Nation Oil as he did.

One of the attendants who didn't seem to have the
right slant was a college kid named Danny O'Neill. Blisters
ad gotten reports that this O'Neill didn't keep his station
lean, and that he read and studied on the job. And
Blisters had gone out at night, as he frequently did, and
riven by O'Neill's station to find out for himself. He
ften called in many attendants to see him at his office,
high and overlooking the lake in the company's big
ite building on South Michigan Avenue. He called them
or serious infractions, cheating the customers, or pull-
he pumps, as the attendants themselves described it.
rs he called in for minor infractions or even so that
could give a man a good pep talk and inspire him to
t going full steam ahead on the right and only track.
his was one of the most pleasant features of his work.
He enjoyed his power and he was able to practice the
psychology he had learned from the correspondence course.

He was serving Nation Oil and, sometimes, he was in-
spiring a man.

Blisters applied his psychological skill in various ways.
He would have a clerk telephone a man at home, prefer-
ably on an off day, to order him down to the office. Or
he would have the instructions given at night, shortly before an attendant closed up his station. This was unusual
and would sometimes worry the attendant. To worry a
man was a principle of applied psychology. Likewise, it
was doing the unexpected, and this motivated his decisions
regarding the time an attendant should be notified that he
was being called on the carpet.

He had Danny O'Neill notified at his station at eight
o'clock closing time at that station. Danny was told to be
in Blisters' office at ten the next morning, and in order to
do this, he had to cut his nine and ten o'clock classes at
the University.

Attendants knew that Blisters would be hard on them
if they reported late when he had ordered them to see him
at the main office. Danny was five minutes ahead of time.

The office boy informed Blisters that O'Neill was outside.

"Tell him to wait," Blisters ordered.

He worked hard himself, and did not countenance
laziness or the wasting of company time on the part of
any attendant. But he knew that psychology must be applied, especially on someone like this O'Neill kid. After
Blisters had been informed of O'Neill's arrival, he lit a
cigar and tilted back in his chair, puffing and blowing
smoke rings. He would stare out at the lake, a muddy
gray with white caps breaking over the surface. The sky
was dark and heavy. It was a gloomy October day. But
Blisters was not gloomy. He opposed gloom as he did
laziness. Gloom was not good for business nor for the
digestion.

Blisters continued to practice psychology on this attendant, Danny O'Neill, who was waiting on a bench in
the outer office. Blisters sat. He looked at a few papers in
the basket on the right side of his desk. These were fire
notices. Finally deciding that he had practiced enough
psychology on O'Neill, Blisters pressed a buzzer. A thin,
homely office girl opened the door and Blisters said:

"Send in O'Neill."

Danny entered quickly. Blisters gave him a limp hand-shake and asked him to sit down on the chair on the right side of his desk. Danny looked around while Blisters fumbled with papers in a basket on the left side of his desk.

"All right," Blisters said importantly as he returned the papers to the basket.

Then, Blisters paused dramatically.

"I have a report," he said gravely, quite gravely, "that you have been seen reading in your station while on duty, and a customer waited five minutes on the drive for service."

Blisters paused again to allow his words to sink in and gain their full psychological effect.

Danny feigned surprise. He opened his mouth as though to speak, gazed about, hesitated and then said:

"Well, I can't remember it, and, you see, Mr. Newton, I'm taking a pre-legal course at the University of Chicago in order to study law and get into the legal department here at Nation and . . ."

"Now Dan," Blisters interrupted, lowering his voice, "I'm going to talk man-to-man with you. Don't think of me as Mr. Newton or even as Blisters." He grinned. "As Blisters who called you down here to the main office to put you on the carpet and bawl you out. Think of me as your friend and advisor talking to you, man-to-man as I am, I ask you—is that right?"

"No sir, it isn't," Danny said, hoping to create an impression of frankness.

"Is it fair to the company, to Nation Oil? The company treats all you men squarely. It pays you good money, and it rewards you with promotions as soon as it sees that you are worthy, that you are right thinking, and the right man to hold down a position of responsibility with it. But in return for treating you fair and square, it expects you to play fair and square with it. All it asks is that you repay it in service and honesty for what it gives you in wages or salary. Now . . ." Blisters paused and slapped a hand on his desk. "Now, we pay you to work out there in the station, and that pay is for your time. When you're on duty at that station, you belong to us. You work for us and our interests are what counts. When you're off duty, your time is your own. But as I said, and I say it again to be crystal clear—when you're on duty, your time is ours.

Our interest comes first. And Dan, the kind of man we
want is one who believes this—the kind of man we want
is a man who sees Nation Oil on the horizon line of a
rising sun."

"Yes sir," Danny said, parrot-like.

Blisters went on:

"Now take me! I never got where I am today by reading
books when I was assigned to do some work. When you
do what you were doing, Dan, you fail to, you cannot
possibly give good service. You cannot give the kind of
service Nation Oil expects and demands of its employees.
And if you can't give good service, you're not the kind of
man we want, you haven't got the stuff we want in our
men, the guts, the character, the inspiration that puts a
man in the front rank with Nation Oil . . . Many of us
are called, but few are chosen, Dan, and to be chosen by
us, you have gotta have the stuff. Now take me!" He
tapped his chest. "I got where I am, first of all, because I
had the right attitude, because I got my inspiration from
Nation Oil, and because I saw Nation Oil on my horizon
like a rising sun."

Blisters paused again. He fixed his eyes on Danny, who
glanced away. Blisters sat up straight.

"I worked to get where I am, O'Neill, by hard work,
and if you'll permit me the expression, by goddamned
hard work. Yes, I plugged at my job. I stuck to it. I did
my job in rainy weather as well as in sunshine, and when
I was feeling in the dumps or sick, as well as when I was
sittin' on top of the world, happy and healthy."

"Yes sir," Danny said.

"Now, Dan, you know we don't plan or expect to have
to keep a man of your ability in a service station for long.
We've got faith in you, and if you jack yourself up, you'll
be just the kind of man we want. You know our policy,
Dan. We count on every man we hire as a future super-
visor, or a salesman, and yes, as a future executive. If we
didn't count on a man to make something out of himself,
we wouldn't hire him. But, well, you know, many are
called . . . but few are chosen. And if you want to be one
of those who will be chosen . . . well, you've got to change
your attitude. Dan, you have a fine sales record, but
you've marred it by demerits like this one I'm forced to
put against your record with a red pencil. Yes, you have

he ability, but you will have to match it with a better
attitude and ambition. You ought to be what I like to
describe as . . . future-minded. Take myself. I had a vision
of the future. When I was only a common, ordinary repairman, I was future-minded. I looked ahead. I saw a
future, a goal, and I worked for it. So, I got there. I say
this to you, Dan, only because I want to try and help set
you on the right path. That's why I take myself as an example. But do you think I'm satisfied here at this desk?
Not on your life! I haven't stopped climbing that ladder
of success, not if I can help it, or can do anything about it.
I expect to keep going right on up. And if Mr. Prevost
here thought for one minute that I had given up in the
struggle, and was satisfied to remain in my present position, do you think he'd keep me here? Not on your life.
He wouldn't, because in that case, I wouldn't be the right
kind of a man, the right kind of an example for my job.
And Dan, that's the kind of attitude you ought to have.
You don't want to be the kind of a fellow who just sits
on his ass."

"Yes sir," Danny said.

"Now, tell me frankly, man-to-man, in the spirit I've
talked to you, Dan—don't you think I'm right?"

"Yes sir. However, I was reading when business was
dull because I desire, I want to get an education. If I do,
I'll be better prepared to work for Nation; I'll be a better
in the Nation Oil machine. And I was studying because
I had a quiz in a history course the next day. I was trying
to brush up. But I promise you, Mr. Newton, this shall not
happen again."

"That's all fine. An education is a fine thing, and we're
always ready to help you get one but you have to remember, Dan, if you want to grow with us, then, Nation Oil
comes first. Make that your motto and you can't go wrong
—Nation Oil, first, last and always. Right now, Dan, your
biggest job is out there at your service station, 708. If you
realize this, make it your job, succeed at it, you'll be re-
paid, just as I have been, and just like every man who
has given Nation Oil his best has been rewarded."

"Yes sir, Mr. Newton."

"Now Dan, I do want you to get this, take it to heart
so that the next time I drive by 708 or stop in, it will be
to compliment you. You think over what I've said, mull it

over, and you'll get along with all of us in this department.
And if you do, why we'll go along with you, one hundred
percent. Now, you go back to 708, and let us see you show
your stuff."

"Yes sir, Mr. Newton. You watch me speed," Danny
said with a straight face.

"That's the spirit, old man."

"And thank you, Mr. Newton, for being so kind to me,
for talking to me in this frank and friendly and intelligent
manner about my infringement."

"That's perfectly all right. This is what I'm here for.
My time is always at your disposal. I didn't want to bawl
you out. Bawling out, that's old-fashioned—it's not the
new business psychology. We're one big family here, with
one aim—to sell Nation Oil."

Blisters walked to the door with Danny, shook his hand
more firmly than before and looked him in the eyes, sin-
cerely.

"I know you can make it, old man."

"Yes sir, Mr. Newton, and thank you."

Danny left. Blisters returned to his desk, and glanced
out of the window at the gray choppy waters of Lake
Michigan.

He made a note to have the spotters watch Station 708
carefully and to send him in regular reports on O'Neill.

He applied about ten minutes of psychology to the
next filling station attendant who was sitting outside
nervously waiting to learn his fate.

THE MAYOR'S COMMITTEE

I was speaking with a friend of mine about politics, the trade union movement, the pressures which are exerted in our society, leading to conformity, and related subjects. My friend, a radical, knew a great deal about the labor movement, and he is a very witty man. We got to talking about what happens to so many trade union leaders.

"Money?" he said, with a expression of contempt, "No, nobody has to give them money. They don't sell out. Don't think of it. You couldn't buy them. They're honest bureaucrats."

He paused for a moment, and chuckled.

"Honest bureaucrats. Jesus Christ—they're honest bureaucrats. They have an office." He walked around and came close to me, bent down and waved a finger in front of me, and asked with a broad inflexion of his voice: "And you know what? I'll tell you. They have their own desk and they sit at it, and they can press a button and she comes in, and do you know what?—She's a secretary. There he is. He sits at a desk, and his belly has almost learned to rub up against the desk, almost—but not quite. That takes time." He made some expressive gestures with his hands. "That, my friend, takes a little more time. But here he is, sitting at his desk, and he presses a button and the girl comes in. She might even be a cutie. He thinks. I don't know how it goes on in his mind, but here's the idea—'Look at me. Here I am,' and maybe, he taps himself on the chest. 'I got a desk, and I got a secretary, and I got a button on my desk. I can press buttons just like J. P. Morgan. I'm getting there. Why, Jesus Christ—me, Joe Doakes, me, I was once a factory worker in the shops,

205

and now look at me. I smoke cigars. I sit across the table with the bosses, and I tell them a thing or two. They know me. I'm honest. I'll never sell out to them . . . .But I'm sane . . . Sane. Not an agitator. A socialist? Never heard of the word. I get my hair cut once a week.' He pointed his finger like a man rapping a desk decisively. 'I don't agitate, I negotiate. I get the best I can for my working stiffs. And my manners—I don't eat with a knife, but neither do I read poetry. When I sit in a dining car on the Super Chief—the Super Chief . . . .' "

My friend bent forward, paused, pointed his finger at me.

" 'The Super Chief, I always take it to California. I save time. Time, I got to save time for the rank-and-file. I got to look fresh, and my mind—it can't be tired when I get off a train. So, I take the Super Chief. It's a good train. When I sit down—in the diner on the Super Chief—do you think I eat with a knife?' "

My friend burst out laughing.

"Jesus Christ . . . You know, if you have a little education you can talk, you know how to read a contract, write an editorial or two, have a few ideas—you can get a desk like that, and you can press a button, and you can ride on the Super Chief."

I thought of my interview with Sam Neurath, but my friend was warmed up and he went on talking.

"Well, there's a telephone call. He answers it and g who's telephoning? Can you guess?"

I shook my head and waited.

"The Mayor. His honor—the Mayor. 'He's calling Me . . . Joe Doakes, and he doesn't call me Joe, he me Mister. The Mayor wants to speak to me. Mr. Do Why ten years ago in the strike, the Mayor's cops beat me up and flung me into jail, but now . . . the Mayor calls me *Mister*.' "

Again my friend chuckled, a warm, good-natured and friendly chuckle.

"So—it's the Mayor. 'Mr. Doakes, this is the Mayor. I wanted to know if you'd serve on my committee.' Now that's something . . . the Mayor's Committee . . . 'Yes, Mr. Doakes, I have Mr. J. P. Morgan on my committee, and' . . . well, after all, you don't have to give him the other ames, a liberal, a professor, a clergyman, a representative ommittee . . . The Mayor's Committee."

My friend paused, chuckled again, and then exclaimed with good natured contempt:

"Jesus Christ . . . the Mayor's Committee. Well, Mr. Doakes, nee Joe, goes home to the old lady. Jesus, he comes home full of enthusiasm, piss and vinegar. Why he's as happy as a boy. You'd think he led the workers in a big strike victory. He comes in bubbling and stuttering. You know how he feels? He feels overjoyed . . . comrades, he is overjoyed."

" 'Mommy, Mommy, Myrtle, Myrtle,' he yells . . . and she comes out of the kitchen where she's frying his steak, a dollar fifteen a pound . . . So, the old lady comes rushing in, and there he is in the door way . . . he's speechless with joy . . . comrade, he's overjoyed."

My friend patted his cheeks, chuckled with warm and genial contempt, and went on:

"His jowls are wreathed in smiles . . . They fold up in smiles . . . And so, the old lady rushes in . . .' Myrtle, Myrtle,' he yells . . . 'Myrtle, guess what happened? . . . I'm on the Mayor's Committee . . . And do you know who else is on it? . . . Guess . . . Myrtle, lovey dovey . . . Guess! . . .' And then there is a pause, and then he tells r . . . 'J. P. Morgan . . . Myrtle, I'm on the Mayor's mmittee with J. P. Morgan . . ."

omrade, that's the story."

lit cigarettes and sat thinking for a moment.

s a long, long road ahead," I said.

sus, is it!" he exclaimed.

ut that's part of the story . . . Now, you take our nary Mr. Doakes, but I assure you, he isn't imaginary . he's many of these leaders and secondary leaders in e labor movement . . . You couldn't buy him with money. his way, he's loyal, loyal to the workers. He's loyal to union. But that's the way it is. He's on the Mayor's ommittee, and he goes out and hires a tuxedo, because ow could the Mayor have a committee without having a dinner. And the old lady buys a new dress. He goes to the dinner with the Mayor . . . and Mr. Morgan . . . and it's all very nice. He tries to remember how the Babbitts ate in the dining car of the Super Chief . . . well, you know, someday he might even be invited to visit the White House and use the side entrance."

My friend chuckled.

"Did you ever hear the story about Jim Larkin, the Irish labor leader?"

"What story?" I asked.

"During the big transport strike in 1913, when Jim was fighting his enemy, Martin Murphy . . . Larkin made Murphy and the Irish bosses tremble. They shivered in their boots . . . Larkinism . . . Jim said he was going to speak on Sunday, and he was forbidden. Tell Jim Larkin he can't speak . . . Tell him he can't agitate . . . Do you know what a fish in the ocean would do, if you told him he couldn't swim? . . . He'd swim. Jim said . . . 'I'll speak' . . . In those days, the peeler wasn't born who could tell Jim Larkin he couldn't speak in Dublin in a strike, in a general strike. Sunday comes. The workers, the strikers, their kids, the slums of Dublin . . . they're all out. The street's jammed. The Countess Markiewiz, she was quite a gal herself, you should see her picture, a beautiful gal, with a belt slung over her shoulder and a gun in a holster . . . she hired a room in the best hotel in Dublin, for her country cousin who's a parson. Jim rigged himself out as a parson, and got through the lines of the peelers unnoticed, and got his room. But it wasn't good enough, so he borrowed somebody else's room, and dramatically appears at a window. It's Larkin. Who said he can't speak Martin Murphy? . . . The peelers? . . . The British Crown . . . they tell Jim Larkin he's not going to speak . . . spoke . . . Old timers told me that as a speaker, he terrific . . . terrific . . . And Jim spoke."

My friend cleared his throat, and imitated an or He stood in the center of the room, and said:

"It is my divine mission to preach subversion and discontent to the working classes."

My friend sat down. His mood changed. His face became gloomy.

"That was bloody Sunday in Dublin. Jesus Christ, they clubbed the people, broke heads. That strike was lost . . . It was a terrific defeat for Dublin, for the Irish workers. It was after that strike was broken that the Irish Citizens Army was organized . . . a workers army. That reminds me of a story about Connolly."

"I never heard of it. I told him I would try and find out.
I did, I might add, think of telling him that he could perhaps find out for himself if he merely read, or even
skimmed through the pamphlet himself. But I didn't say
that."

My friend chuckled.

"Anyway, we talked meaninglessly for a moment or so.
He told me twice in less than three minutes that he was
very busy. He talked about how he wished he had the time
to read books but didn't. You know I don't know why, and
I don't know him well enough to interpret it, but I did
observe that he didn't look at me. He was with his face
to the side wall of his office, looking at it, talking as much
to the wall as to me, his thumbs stuck in his gray vest, so
I saw him in profile. He's a little ruddy."

"That's because he eats beefsteaks instead of pork
chops."

"So, I made talk about nothing and then I spoke about
our committee. I told him that we had hundreds of names
of anti-fascists, trade unionists, needing food and medical
aid in Europe, and that many of them were in desperate
circumstances. I told him stories."

"Dirty stories?"

"Stories from what I've seen in the files of our little
committee. A Spanish trade unionist, a rank-and-filer.
He'd fought Franco, and he got consumption, he was just
run down. He had to be hospitalized. We had to get
streptomycin to him, and it involved three hundred and
fifty dollars." I paused. "Do you know, in a country as
rich as this, it is sometimes goddamn hard to raise three
hundred and fifty dollars to save the life of an anti-fascist
worker of a loyal and fighting worker who wore his health
out, gave up everything in the fight?"

"Do I know it?"

"I didn't talk too much. As I said, Sam was busy. I
call him Sam because, you know, trade union democracy
exists, and you don't call people Mister. People are Mister
on the Mayor's Committee. I assumed that Sam knew
something of conditions in Europe. He did. Everybody
does. He sat, looking at the wall, putting his thumbs in
his vest, taking them out, listening to me, remarking on
how much there was to do. I did try to suggest that there
were many cases, that the anti-Stalinists were the ones who

suffered so much, and received the least care and aid in so many instances, and so on. You know the story. And I told him how the Commies had gotten a lot of doctors because nobody else had even thought of this, and that we were trying to interest doctors on a non-factional basis, and that even such a thing as collecting the medical samples that doctors got would be of value. Every aspirin tablet, even, counts."

We sat for a few moments, both of us becoming gloomy, silently thinking. Bitter feelings, feelings of hopelessness, were rising in me.

"The real heroes of Europe," I remarked. "Men who have not given up, who have faced Franco's terror, Mussolini's terror, Hitler's terror, Stalin's terror . . . herded at times into camps by the so-called Third Republic . . ." I stopped. Then I said, "Hell, let's not agitate ourselves."

"Uh huh!"

"I was talking about Sam. He was friendly. He's a nice guy. 'I'm so busy,' he said, looking at the wall, not at me. 'There's so many things a man doesn't think of. Take what you say about medical samples. That's a good idea. My wife knows a lot of doctors and she got together samples and sent them to relatives in England. She got a big box of stuff. Some of it, of course, couldn't be sent because it's got to be taken with a doctor's prescription.' I remarked that we had doctors who could send such drugs. But he didn't bite. I didn't ask him for anything, and he didn't volunteer any help."

"Yes, Sam is a nice fellow. I hear he's a little tight but a nice guy . . . nice guy."

AUNT LOUISE

I think that her death marked off a chronological boundary between my early childhood and my boyhood. She died in May, 1911 when I was only seven. Even in boyhood, much of this period was forgotten, repressed. My grandfather, her father, had died of cancer late in 1910. Then, she died of galloping consumption. She passed on, shortly after we had moved to the flat on Calumet Avenue, near Fifteenth, from the one in the 4800 block on Indiana. She was unable to walk, and was moved in a car, and carried upstairs. She was put in the bright, blue papered bedroom off of the parlor. She knew that she was dying. I don't think that she wanted to die. She cried and complained. She didn't like the noise that I made. I didn't like to go into her room. I didn't like the smell in her room, and I didn't wish to see her. I was resentful, resentful and bewildered. Something was being torn away from me. I had already confronted death. For a couple of years, now, I had as a young boy lived in a household of death. There was my grandfather. I called him Father. He had retired. His cancer had developed. On Indiana Avenue, he had lain in bed all day. Then, he had been taken to the hospital. Aunt Louise began to get worse. She had galloping consumption. She had gone to Denver with Aunt Margaret who was her older sister. There had been excitement in the house. But this trip had done Aunt Louise no good. That was back in 1909, I believe, and I was only five. Aunt Louise grew thin. She was no longer able to work, and was almost bedridden when my grandfather died. From then on, she faded fast.

She was a beautiful girl of twenty, dying of galloping consumption.

I was "a bad boy" during her last days. I didn't want to see her, and I didn't want to go out of the house. I played alone in the parlor, and I made a lot of noise. I stomped my feet and raised my voice to a shout. I also whined and complained about little things. Uncle Al was on the road. Aunt Margaret was working in a hotel, but she was home a great deal of her spare time. She and my grandmother took care of Louise. Something was being taken away from me, and I was resentful. And I was not getting as much attention as I might otherwise have gotten. Louise asked that I be quiet. But I wouldn't be quiet. I was mad. I was mad at my beautiful Aunt Louise. She had no right to do what she was doing. She had no right to leave me. She had no right to die. And I knew that she was dying.

I had met death, face-to-face. My grandfather's corpse had been brought home. During his last days, they were different at home. There were more telephone calls. Uncle Ned came in from Madison. Father loved his son, Ned. They were all afraid that Ned wouldn't get to Chicago in time, but he did. He got to see us around Christmas, 1910. He had seen Father. He was coming out to see us. I was glad. There was a change in the spirit of the house. Ned's coming had done Father good. My grandmother spoke of him—her husband—as "that poor man". I knew that Father was in pain. I understood pain. Pain was terrible. Pain hurt. Father died. I liked the wake. I could stay late. At eleven, twelve o'clock at night, I could sit at table with grownups and eat cake, have sandwiches, even drink coffee. The house was crowded. People stayed all night. I was fussed over and I liked it. But I bewildered and afraid. There was not only excitement and a change of all routine, there was quarreling, with loud voices, curses, bad words. Aunt Margaret had a big row with Uncle Ned. She was all nerves and upset. She cried and sobbed and screamed. My mother came and stayed all night. Mom cried, too. And there in the house was Aunt Louise, cold, as Father was months before. Aunt Louise was his baby, the baby of the whole O'Flaherty household, until I came to live with them. And she knew she was going to die very soon.

My grandfather's corpse was in the parlor. He was

dressed in a dark blue suit. His face was grayish. It was not like the face of a live person. The grownups were in the back of the house. At the moment, they were not fighting. They were talking. There was a murmur of talk. The parlor smelled of flowers. It smelled too sweet. The shades were drawn. Outside, there was sunshine. The sun colored the drawn shades.

I looked at the corpse. I wanted to touch it. I feared that I would do something wrong if I touched the corpse. You should not touch the dead, I thought. I was afraid. I looked at Father's face. It was like ashes, formed and pressed into a face. I thought it moved. I wanted it to move. It didn't move. I was alone with Father, and he was dead. The dead got buried, and you couldn't ever see them again in this world. Father's hands were folded in front of him. His eyes were closed tight. I touched his face. The skin was soft and cold. I touched the hands. Soft and cold. I touched the leg, covered with the trousers. I was afraid. I was almost ill. I had done something I shouldn't do.

Aunt Peg begged me not to make so much noise. They were grownups. They didn't understand. I didn't care. They begged me to be a good little boy. I would not be a good little boy. They didn't understand, didn't know that I did not care. I did not like Aunt Louise anymore. I was mad at her. She was mad at me, and I was mad at her. I was mad. I was mad, and I didn't care at all, I was mad. I would make noises. I would shout. I would scream. I would raise the devil if they didn't take care of me. I would stamp my feet, run up and down the hall, raise my voice, I would keep on doing that for a long time. Everything was all over between myself and Aunt Louise. I used to think that when I grew up, I would marry her. But it was all over. I didn't even want to see her.

One night, there was great excitement. I heard it in bed. When I got up early in the morning, Aunt Peg told me.

"Brother, Aunt Louise is dead."

My grandmother cried. My aunt cried. She called Uncle Al by long distance. I was glad he was coming home. Also that day—I think it was that day—my Aunt Peg told me:

"Aunt Louise died cursing you. She died hating you because you were a bad boy."

I had been a bad boy. I knew I had been a bad boy. But I would not admit it. I was sullen. My defiance remained.

I was all alone, and nobody understood me. They were grownups, and they whispered about their grownup secrets. They could punish me. They were grownup. I was not. I was all alone. I didn't care And I needed kindness. I had been a very bad boy. I wouldn't admit it, but I knew it.

And I knew something else.

I was glad she died.

II

Aunt Louise was more beautiful than Aunt Peg. Aunt Peg was handsome. Aunt Louise was slender, nice and slender, and kind of tall, and she had the most wonderful hair. It was long auburn hair. I used to watch her combing it and washing it. I loved her hair, and she would let me touch it and smell it. I knew she loved me. She was good to me. I was her favorite. Sometimes, she called me "My little Sweetheart". I used to say at home that I loved her. I was a kind of doll for her. She used to pet me, kiss me, and give me things. Many times when she went out, I screamed and kicked and cried, demanding that she take me with her. She often did, even with her beaux.

One night, my brother Bill and I were playing with some kids in front of the apartment building. Aunt Peg and Aunt Louise came up with two gentlemen in a hired car. I ran to the car and demanded to go with them. My aunts did not want me to go. I insisted. One of the men said that he would like to take me along. So Bill and I went with them in the big automobile. One of the men was very nice to me. I sat on Aunt Louise's lap. I liked to stay on her lap. She was warm. We went to an amusement at the Midway and Cottage Grove, Sans Souci. and given everything I wanted. I rode on all the rides, had corn and candy, and I saw the lights and the people. I took her hand, and one of the men took my hand and said I was a fine little fellow. I was the center of attention. But I knew that I had done something I shouldn't have done. I knew that I shouldn't have gone. I knew that Aunt Peg and Aunt Louise didn't really want us along. But I was there, and I was up late. It was night. I couldn't be punished because they had let me go, and the gentlemen had liked me, too. I had a wonderful time.

Aunt Louise was really very good to me. But she didn't

ike my childish tyranny over her. I never screamed or
ried when anyone else went out. It was only when she
id. Sometimes she would have to sneak out on me and
un away from me. I would scream and pull at her dress,
nd kick her. I would have scratched her, too, if I could
ave done it. I would get very mad at her. But whenever
hey said she was so beautiful, I was very pleased, in
Heaven, almost. When they said that I looked like her,
I was proud as all the peacocks anybody ever saw.

She was my beautiful aunt.

I was her little sweetheart.

When I grew up I was going to take care of her and
marry her.

III

Aunt Louise was often sad. I remember her sadness
more than I do her laughter, her joy, her fun. And I
remember her sadness especially at the time when she
was operated on for a fistula. This was but one of the many
bewildering excitements in the house, one of the many
things that were happening that I didn't understand, that
they whispered about and shut up talking about when I
listened.

"Isn't he the nosey little one?" my grandmother would
say.

"Ah, but he's a wise little one," she would also say.

The doctor came to the house. Something happened
ind a closed door. She was in bed. Mother and took care of
I didn't go into the room very much was was hurt.
afternoon, I was playing. I played a say y myself.
ssed down the hall where she was sleeping. She lay on
her face, and her naked buttocks were in the air. They
med awfully big. I shouldn't have looked knew I
doing something bad, a sin, that hurt God's feelings!
e boogey man came and got little boys for doing things
ke that. I was very sad. I was sad for my Aunt Louise.
I wished she was not sick, not hurt. I didn't like the sight
I saw. She was sick, and it was so quiet in the house, so
quiet that, as Mother said, you couldn't hear a pin drop.
But I continued looking. I was fascinated, and the sight
made me so unhappy. And then, I went off, fearful, for if

they caught me, if my grandmother caught me, I would get a walloping, you bet. I had done something bad.

I have other memories of Aunt Louise, memories of pain and child-like sadness. Once, I remember her sittin, me on her lap. She was so sad. I was sorry for her. wished that I could do something to make her not so sad, but I was powerless. There had been some fighting in the house. I was frightened by the loud voices and the cursing. They had spoken loudly, and Aunt Louise was sad about it, and everything. It had something to do with her, and she wore a light dress. It was on a Sunday, and we sat in the parlor. I knew she was very sad, and that made me sad. I saw a tear in her eye. I wanted to cry, too, but I didn't cry, only inside myself. I could not do anything for her. I was a little fellow, and what could a little fellow do in the world of the grownups? When I grew up, I would take care of her, and I wouldn't let them do anything to my beautiful Aunt Louise. I was on her side of the quarrel, any quarrel. I wasn't on the side of Aunt Peg when Aunt Peg quarreled with her.

Yes, she was not only my beautiful aunt. She was, also, my sad aunt. But why was she so sad? I didn't know. That made me more sad, twice as sad.

IV

I sometimes had tantrums. I had tantrums when I w three and four years old. I would scream, and I would sick, sick with a kind of helplessness, because I d know what to do. I could only clench my fists, and sc

There would be lots going on, then. They would about me, and my grandmother would hold me, and m Aunt Peg would hold me, and Aunt Louise would hol me. They would talk excitedly, with fear, about the b They would give me the bottle. But if I didn't want bottle, I would scream. I remember screaming, and two aunts bared their breasts. They seemed shy, hesitant, and their shyness and hesitancy toward me was only the more disturbing. They bared their breasts and put me to suck, but no milk came out. I didn't like the feel of their nipples from which milk didn't flow. I cried furiously. I screamed and screamed, and they were very worried. They

alked and tried to fool me and told me to suck their
breasts. I tried to, and nothing came out. I was blind in
my anger. I didn't like their breasts. I didn't think or tell
myself that I didn't like them, but I just knew it. I didn't
want them to hold me or do this to me. I felt sick.

It was sometime after this period that I used to notice
Aunt Peg and Aunt Margaret when they didn't have their
dresses on. They wore long black silk stockings which
made their legs, and the flesh above, look wonderful. They
also wore corsets and fluffy lacy underwear. Sometimes
Aunt Louise wore underwear with blue ribbons on it.
Once she was in the kitchen that way, half-dressed. Mother
was cooking oysters, and Mother or Aunt Margaret took
an oyster out of the pot. I suddenly became so nauseated
that I wanted to, and almost did, vomit. I got very weak.
I wished I hadn't seen the oyster, that slimy awful thing
that made me sick in my stomach. I turned away into the
dining room. I wouldn't eat oysters. I couldn't, they made
me sick. I had been looking at Aunt Louise. She didn't
have all her clothes on, and I liked to look at her when she
didn't have all her clothes on. And then I saw the oysters.
They were milky but you couldn't swallow them, and you
were weak and afraid you were going to fall down when
you looked at them, but the grownups could eat them.
It was awful. I sat alone. I was ill. I felt badly. I was
afraid, afraid something was going to happen to me. I had
no one to tell how I felt. I couldn't tell them. I didn't know
but I couldn't tell them. There were bad things. Bad
happened. You looked at bad things. And you
not tell the grownups of bad things, and you dared
Aunt Louise be ashamed of you, either, and she
grownup.

She was learning to be a stenographer. I was proud of
r. She practiced in the dining room, and I listened to
Uncle Al dictated his letters to her, and it made
Al very important and somehow made me glad. I
also jealous of him. He liked her. He made her do
things. I watched him. I was glad. I was not glad. I didn't
like it. I liked her writing with a typewriter, and the
machine made noise. It was very important that she could
write on a typewriter, and Uncle Al sat, smoking a cigar,
telling her what to do. I watched her a lot. I felt she loved
me. I liked her to hold me because she loved me. I liked

her to take me up and hold me. I liked her to tell me things.
I liked her to kiss me. I liked her to kiss me more than I
liked anybody to kiss me. She was my aunt. My beautiful
Aunt Louise.

V

After she died, I didn't like to think of her. I remembered being bad when she was dying. When Aunt Margaret
would tell me about her, I would not say anything, but I
did not like to hear it.

"Little Brother, Aunt Louise loved you. Oh, she loved
you so much."

I wouldn't answer. It wasn't true. But I wanted them
to think it was true. Did Aunt Margaret think it was true?
Didn't she remember that she told me that Aunt Louise
died cursing me for being a bad boy and making noise?
She told me, also, that Aunt Louise couldn't forgive me.
And so, Aunt Louise didn't die loving me. I didn't like
to think of her. If she was in Heaven, and she was, because they said she was, and said she was a beautiful girl
and she was a virgin, why then, what did she think of me?
She maybe still didn't like me? I was very sorry. When I
made my first Communion, I confessed to the priest that
I had been a bad boy and made noise when my aunt was
dying.

One night in the summer of 1912, after we had moved
to a place on Prairie Avenue, south of Fifty First St.,
I went to the nickel show with my Aunt Peg and my
mother. I had not thought much of Aunt Louise. She
dead over a year.

I was enchanted with one of the movie actresses,
was watching closely. Suddenly, my Aunt Peg remarked
in a whisper to my grandmother:

"That actress looks like Louise."

I heard.

"Oh yes, she's beautiful and she looks like my
Louise and my Aunt Louise looked just like me," I said
aloud.

It seemed as though everyone in the small theatre—and it
was almost full, burst into laughter. My Aunt Peg laughed,
but also she seemed embarrassed. I didn't like it nor did I
understand why they laughed. I had only said something

hat was true because they had always told me that I
looked like Aunt Louise, and I believed them. I wanted
to look like her, and they had all said that she had been
beautiful, and I was convinced that she was very beautiful. And now, when I told what was only the truth as I
saw it, they laughed and thought I was saying something
funny. It was not funny. It was true. I was saying what
was true. They laughed when they had no right to laugh,
laughed at me when I said something that was the truth.

I repeated what I had said, repeated it with a certain
earnestness and stubbornness. I wanted them to understand, and not to laugh.

And there was more laughter. Aunt Peg laughed again,
too, and then she leaned towards me and in whispers, she
tried to shush me up.

"But it's true. She looks like Aunt Louise and Aunt
Louise was beautiful and I look just like her," I asserted
loudly, only to be greeted by more laughter.

I sat, watching, thinking of Aunt Louise, and I could
not understand why they laughed. It was not funny. I had
said something that was true and I had been laughed at.
I didn't like Aunt Peg laughing, either, nor did I like her
telling me not to say what I was convinced was true. I
didn't understand this.

This was one of the last times in my boyhood when I
said anything about her. But sometimes I thought of her.
I wished she had lived. I wondered what she would have
been like if she had lived. I wanted her to be alive, why,
sometimes wished this, but more and more she faded
from my memories.

VI

Was Aunt Louise a virgin? How unimportant the ques
tion is, now that she has long since rotted away, now that
perhaps nothing remains of her but bones and ashes. These
bones lay in a sunken grave in Calvary Cemetery along
with the bones of her parents and those of her brother,
Ned, and her sister, Lizz O'Neill. At times my Aunt Peg
had made remarks to the effect that Aunt Louise was not
all the family thought her to be. This would focus the
question in my mind, and I would want to think that she
was a virgin, that she had died a virgin. The family

thought of her as such, as a beautiful girl who had died
pure. And now I can see what this question means, and
how it relates to that impression of sadness which I gained
from her, gained without understanding when I was a
small boy and she was my big and beautiful aunt. For
she died without having had any life. She grew up to illness and death in a possessive ingrown family. That pattern of possessiveness was absorbed by myself as a boy,
and I, too, was possessive of her. She would run away
from me, or try to sneak out of the house, but I would be
so often on guard. She would sometimes complain. Her
little nephew, who came and took her place as the baby
of the family, clutched onto her, held her, fought with all
that was in his power, with his tears and screams and tantrums, to keep her. It was life and freedom she wanted, and
she was born never to have it. A few years of girlhood
looming into womanhood, and illness, illness and her
early death. I know how she grew up. There was fighting
in the house, fighting and cruelty and violence, physical
beatings, cursing and drinking. She was physically frail,
and her disposition was sweet, sweet and loving. On me
this love was poured. To me it was given, given until it
found another need. How could it have found an object
for such need? She had dates, but there was no talk at
home concerning her having a regular fellow. Aunt Peg
had a man friend, Mr. Robinson. But there was no talk
of Aunt Louise having any such friend. She began to
decline by the time she was nineteen. Uncle Al, her older
brother, did not like her to go out, and that was one of
the reasons why he had her learn typing, and had her
stay home practicing, learning, and doing secretarial work
for him. She was young and filled with life, wanting to fly,
to fly away into some kind of freedom. She didn't know
how. And then, illness came on her. She did not want to
die. She cried a lot during her last days. She cried when
I annoyed her and screamed and shouted and stamped my
feet, cried that even her little nephew whom she loved,
should betray her. She died, withering away, losing weight
so that she was skinny, very skinny. She died, spitting
blood, coughing, racked with her illness, weak, betrayed.
And none of this was comprehensible to me. I could only
know that I wanted her affection, wanted it more than I
wanted the affection of any human being in the world.

Often, passing thoughts of her come into my mind, thoughts shrouded with sadness, sadness and a tormented sense of death, and colored with a personal sense of uneasiness. I thought that her early death was tragic. I wonder —was it? Would she, could she have escaped from the effects of violence at home, violence and aggression and possessiveness? To me, she was a lady. Now, I think of her as a girl, beautiful, wistful, the flush of beauty on her cheeks false, a false flush of illness. She remains only as a memory in a few lives. She remains in my life. She had been there all of my life, unseen, transmuted and unknown to me. After I went to grammar school, I became devoted to the Blessed Virgin Mary. I prayed to Mary. I said rosaries to her, pleaded for intercession, looked at Mary's statue in many churches in Chicago. Mary, the Virgin Mother, who was forever young, forever beautiful, forever innocent. Mary, the Mother of God who was Deathless to me as a boy, Deathless and filled with compassion and understanding. And now I know that when I prayed to Mary, there was, lost in the recesses of my mind, the images, the memories of my beautiful, sad Aunt Louise, who had died so young, died a virgin. I would kneel before the altar of Mary as a boy, praying, and She would seem so sad. Mary, the Mother of God, was always an image of sadness to me. Her beauty was a sad beauty. And her blue robe—I always remembered my Aunt Louise in connection with the color of blue. And May was the month of Mary, and May was the month when she died, the month of fine days when I, a boy who wanted to play, would not go out but would stay home and have tantrums in the parlor right by the door behind which she lay dying. For years, I never could write anything about Aunt Louise. I carried her with me, and yet my memories of her became distorted. I thought of her as black haired. My mother had black hair. When I thought of her, I did so with no freedom in my associations. She would appear in my thoughts, tall, sad, motionless, dressed in dark velvet, an image set against a background of formless darkness, a darkness of forgotten memories and fears, a darkness that seemed womb-like and that seemed like death. I could never visualize her clearly, and again and again I recalled her in this way, tall, silent and sad, emerging to stand in front of some impenetrable and mysterious darkness.